NO DUTY TO RESCUE

THE LOST APPRENTICE

TARA O'TOOLE

This book is a work of fiction. All characters, events and places in this publication, other than those clearly in the public domain, are fictitious and any resemblance to real persons, living or dead, is purely coincidental.

www.taraotoole.com

PRONUNCIATION GUIDE

The Irish language, also known as Gaeilge, has different dialects. While the author has provided a general pronunciation guide below, please keep in mind that words can sound different depending on the dialect used and the parish, town or village where the Irish language is spoken.

An Taoiseach	On Tea-shuck
Buach	Boo-uck
Buachaill	Boo-kull
Croagh	Croak
Fáil	Fall
Fáilte	Fall-ta
Fiadh	Fee-a
Peadar	Pa-der
Phelim	Fay-lim
Tuath Dé	Too-a Day

This book is dedicated to the Marys:

Mary Dorothea Heron – the first woman to be admitted to the roll of solicitors in Ireland;

Helena Mary Early – the first woman to obtain a practising certificate in the then newly formed Saorstát Éireann; and

My mother, Mary – for encouraging me to shoot for the stars.

CONTENTS

1

SHE WHO SEEKS EQUITY MUST COME WITH CLEAN HANDS

"Muriel, where are you?"

I let the chill October wind pull the whispered words from my lips as I stare up at Blackhall College, a limestone building silhouetted against a cotton-bud sky that towers over me. Oak trees with lashes of burnt-orange leaves line its entrance. Blackhall, the site where the academic portion of my apprenticeship will take place and the eye of my personal storm.

But, annoyingly, I can't quite summon the courage to pass the delicately tapered iron bars and walk up the cow's lick of a driveway to find what was taken from me. So instead, I just stand on the side of the road.

Lost and alone.

"What happened to you?"

I dare to utter the question that has plagued me these past few months and, too late, I hear someone come to a halt nearby.

"Talking to yourself on the first day of Michaelmas term is not a good sign," a baritone voice rumbles behind me.

I whirl around and my battered, brown leather satchel whacks the unexpected interloper, leaving a scuff on the arm of his pristine, wax jacket. The man, who looks to be in his mid-twenties, takes a step back, in suede loafers so new they've never seen a speck of dirt.

He raises his hands to ward off any further attacks.

"No offence intended."

He's mocking me. The slight tilt of his lips gives it away.

The stranger tugs the cuff of his starched white shirt back into place.

"Have you ever heard of the swan effect?" He asks, his gaze lingering on my hands, white-knuckled from gripping my recalcitrant satchel.

What the hell is happening?

I purse my lips and attempt to brush off my newly acquired shadow with a curt response.

"Can't say I have."

The stranger carries on with an explanation I didn't ask for.

"On the surface, swans glide gracefully through water but underneath, where no one can see, they're paddling for all they're worth."

"So?" I ask, letting an edge of annoyance creep into my voice.

His dark gaze wanders over my head to the imposing eighteenth century building behind me.

"My point is, you should never let them see you sweat and that is the best piece of advice you'll ever receive."

His lips part to reveal a wide, toothy grin and it takes far longer than it should to rebut his erroneous presumption that I am somehow in need of his advice.

"Wow, thanks for that," I say, but my lacklustre response bounces off his broad-shouldered back as the swan man glides up the path to Blackhall and disappears inside.

I'm still nursing my bruised ego when a fat droplet of rain hits me square in the face, forcing me to forgo any immediate retribution. I break into a light jog before the icy water can ruin the sleek style I'd strong-armed my unruly hair into this afternoon. But the heavens do not care and they deliver a deluge that scatters the seagulls sitting atop the copper cupola skyward with vengeful cries.

I pass through the front entrance and make a beeline for the notice board. My eyes wander down the paper tacked to the red felt until I find the words 'Heron Early LLP Apprentices'.

Nausea wells in my gut but I ignore it. I make a mental note of the classroom number and tramp up a grand mahogany staircase. Guided by the iridescent light that streams through a stained-glass window. The jewel tones depict the blind lady of justice supported by two Irish wolfhounds. A Latin motto written beneath.

'VERITAS VINCET' – the truth will win.

I clutch those words close to my heart. Because that's why I'm here. To discover what caused my cousin, Muriel, to go missing six months ago. And expose everyone responsible for her disappearance.

I hurry down an empty corridor. Indistinct voices murmur within the walls of closed classrooms. My damp coat drips water in my wake but, eventually, I locate a white-panelled door with a round brass knob. My sweat-slicked hand makes it difficult to turn. After a few false starts, I manage to wrench the door open and walk inside the classroom before I lose my resolve.

"Fiadh Whelan, nice of you to join us," Joyce, a thin, sour-looking woman chimes.

She points a perfectly manicured nail at an empty chair.

I nod and try to calm my racing heart while her heavily lined eyes track me to my seat. Thirty or so other apprentices, the majority in their mid to late twenties, sit around old-fashioned, teak tables. Their heads turned towards Joyce who stands at the front of the room in nude heels half-sunk into the plush carpet.

"Now that you're all here," she says with a pointed look in my direction that has me fight the flush that rises to my pale, freckled cheeks. "We can begin. For those of you who don't already know me, my name is Joyce Larkin and I am the apprentice mentor at the pre-eminent Irish law firm, Heron Early LLP."

A restrained bout of applause greets Joyce's words, led by an auburn-haired woman in an elegant, cream cashmere jumper who sits across from me, straight-backed in her chair.

"Tomorrow, each of you will be assigned to a partner who will mentor and provide you with hands-on experience of the work we do at our law firm. While, every Friday, you will be permitted to attend lectures here at Blackhall. This will fulfil both the practical and academic requirements of your apprenticeship."

Joyce pauses to flick a strand of raven hair over a shoulder covered in a silken fuchsia blouse. It matches her painted lips perfectly.

"You are all incredibly lucky to be here. We receive thousands of applications for thirty places on our annual apprentice programme. And thanks to your college graduation results and extracurricular activities, you are the lucky candidates to be offered this once-in-a-life-time opportunity. That being said, our clients expect excellence. To work for a firm like Heron Early is to commit yourself to exceed their expectations in every regard. To go above and beyond for your clients, colleagues, and the firm."

While Joyce drones on, I remove my sodden coat. With its tall walls and floor-to-ceiling windows, the classroom feels too haughty for its own good. Goose bumps break out across my arms and, covertly, I scan the room for any kindred souls who are not wholeheartedly buying everything Joyce is selling.

And that's when I spot him. Arms folded, wax jacket strewn over his chair, the swan man sports an expression bordering dangerously on petulant. His dark eyebrows disappear behind his fringe when our eyes meet. Then, he lifts his elbows into the air and makes a flying motion I assume to be an imitation of a swan. I scowl, turn away, and focus my attention back on Joyce. But his little display has caught the unwanted attention of the other apprentices. The auburn-haired woman in particular seems a little too intrigued by the swan man's mortifying display.

"Your first rotation begins tomorrow. Arrive at the office of Heron Early no later than nine a.m. to meet the head of your practice. Though heed my words of advice. First impressions matter, so make it a good one. Be known around the firm for the right reasons. Present a professional appearance. Develop a reputation for being prompt and responsive."

I swear Joyce's red-rimmed eyes slide to me when she says this.

"An apprentice's role is to assist their team in whatever way they require. Do not sit back and wait to be asked to do something. Anticipate what they'll need and stay one step ahead at all times."

With each sentence Joyce utters, more goose bumps break out on my arms. Any more of this and my skin will crawl away from my bones to hide under the table. The polished surface so smooth it reflects the raw mixture of hungry and hopeful expressions on my fellow apprentices' faces.

"There are thirty apprentices in this year's Heron Early intake. And unlike those who apprentice at smaller law firms, each of you have the added advantage of being able to rely on the other members of your intake. Heed my words when I tell you that no one will understand the next two years of your life like the people seated beside you. So, I encourage you to take this opportunity to get to know one another. Introduce yourselves, where you're from, and what prompted you to apply to Heron Early to become an apprentice solicitor."

Oh, no.

The handful of apprentices seated nearby cast nervous glances at one another. After a pregnant pause, a tall, gangly-limbed man wearing wire-framed glasses is the first to speak.

"Brigid Hughes," he says rather awkwardly to the auburn-haired woman in a thick Cork accent that carries through the room. "I heard you went to Harvard. What are you doing back in Dublin? Did you not want to become a hot shot lawyer in New York?"

This elicits a few laughs from some of the other apprentices, but Brigid doesn't rise to the bait. Instead, she sits back and inspects her nails. "Nope, never applied. Didn't need to when I was offered an apprenticeship with Heron Early two years into my undergraduate degree." Brigid pauses and tilts her auburn hair to the side. A pearl earring dangles daintily above her shoulder and, of all the people in the room, she looks at me.

I stop breathing.

"You, the quiet girl who arrived late. Save me from having to answer any more mundane questions and tell us about yourself?"

This is it. Don't say too much. Try not to attract their curiosity. Keep it together for Muriel's sake and breathe, God damn it.

"My name's Fiadh. I studied law at Oxford Uni and I'm originally from Waterford. A fun fact you might not know is that County Waterford has around fifty beaches. It's the prettiest place in the world if you ask me. But I may be biased."

If I could pat myself on the back, I would. My response was simple, to the point, and perfectly boring. Nothing that should arouse suspicion or attract any further unwanted attention. I fold my arms. Ready for someone else to introduce themselves, only for the swan man to make waves and stick his beak where it's not wanted. He leans forward in his chair and asks, "What part of Waterford are you from?"

God damn it.

"Ardmore."

The truth comes out before I can think of a better lie and, in an attempt to steer the conversation away from my home or my connection to Muriel, my mouth runs away with itself. "And am... the reason I became an apprentice solicitor is because of something that happened when I was a child."

I have to pause and block out an image of my cousin's smiling face on the day she graduated from Trinity College Dublin with her law degree.

All of the apprentices are staring now, waiting for me to continue.

"A district court judge was stepping down. At the retirement party, his colleagues arranged for a special guest appearance. One of the locals came dressed like a movie style felon in an old-fashioned prison uniform complete with a ball and chain tied to his ankle. The felon and the judge were well acquainted. Over the years, the felon had been hauled before the court on numerous occasions. And when the felon arrived at the party, he walked right up to the judge, clapped him on the back, and said he'd miss their time together."

Brigid raises a tentative hand into the air. "Why on earth would that make you want to become an apprentice solicitor?"

I smile, genuinely this time.

"No one made the felon come to the judge's retirement party. He came entirely of his own volition. Because at some of the lowest points in his life, that judge could have thrown the book at him. But instead, he'd listened. Heard what he had to say and, when the felon needed psychiatric treatment, the judge ordered it be given."

I try to centre my thoughts and bring this discussion to a close. "It's not the only reason I decided to put myself through years of study to become an apprentice solicitor. But it's one of them. Because when you become an officer of the court, you have the ability to do some good, in whatever form it may take."

The swan man chooses this moment to speak up. His elbows mercifully at his sides and not flapping about the place.

"But if you have ambitions to become a judge someday, you should devil with a barrister or work at a firm that specialises in criminal law. Why did you accept an apprenticeship with a corporate law firm like Heron Early?"

Because of Muriel, I think to myself as heat rises to my cheeks but I remain silent. I've already said too much. My eyes flick to the fading afternoon light that streams in through the white sash windows.

Was I mad to think I could pull this off?

It's Brigid who takes pity on me. Perhaps she sees my discomfort or, more likely, she's sick of sitting around in this ice box of a classroom. Brigid waves her hand at the swan man.

"Leave her be, Keefe. The Michaelmas Mixer is starting and I'm in dire need of a drink. We can finish our introductions over at the members' bar."

The other apprentices agree readily. They follow Brigid, chatting amicably amongst themselves, while I dash for the door. My hand all but touches the handle when Joyce's voice rings out too loudly to ignore.

"Fiadh, may I speak with you a moment?"

Feck.

2

EQUITY FOLLOWS THE LAW

Joyce leans against a battered teak desk that has seen better days.

"Is everything alright?" Her melodic voice makes the question sound so innocuous. Almost friendly. Yet still, it strikes a chord of disquiet deep within the marrow of my bones.

We're alone in the classroom. Through the sash window I can see the other apprentices stroll across the courtyard. Without a worry in the world, they kick rust-coloured leaves in the fading sunlight of the brisk October afternoon.

I clench my fists to stop them from shaking and plaster a sanguine smile on my face.

"I was late to the induction because my landlady's cat tried to follow me. All attempts to dissuade it failed and this is how the little terror thanked me."

I hold up my right hand to show the angry red claw marks running from my little finger to the tarnished bracelet that sits on my wrist. Then, remembering Muriel's name is scrawled across the claddagh pendant hanging daintily from the silver link chain, I tug down the sleeve of my maroon turtleneck to cover it.

Joyce's polished nails tap a steady beat against the desk.

"That's a nasty scratch, Fiadh. Please don't be late to the office tomorrow."

"Absolutely," I reply and dash for the door but, before I can make a grab for the handle, she asks the very question I've been dreading.

"I overheard you're from Ardmore village?"

It takes every ounce of willpower I possess not to bolt for the door.

"Yep. Have you ever been?"

I have to bite my tongue from adding, *I know you have.*

She glances away. "Once. I imagine it's stunning in the summertime."

Joyce gives me one last searching look that I weather like a passing storm.

"I've delayed you long enough. Go and meet the rest of your intake at the Michaelmas Mixer. All of the other apprentices will be there." A faint smile graces her lips. "Some of my fondest memories are from Blackhall. The friends I made within these four walls danced at my wedding." And then as if she hadn't meant to voice that thought aloud, her nude heels sink into the carpet and she's all business once again. "Turn up late for work tomorrow and you'll find the partners are less forgiving than I am."

I winch and close the door behind me.

Back in the hallway, I block out the world and breathe. The weight of all the unspoken words nearly suffocated me and I draw deep lungfuls of air into my chest. But the moment I close my eyes, she appears. As she always does. An image of Muriel lost at sea. Her body bloated. Skin discoloured from the corroding effects of the salt. Eyes unseeing. Dark hair flowing to the current's call.

But it's not real, I remind myself and dig the heels of my hands into my forehead. She's alive. She has to be. I just have to find her.

"Are you ok?"

My eyes fly open. For the second time today, a stranger has snuck up on me. Tall and gangly, I recall his earnest face, if not his name, from our induction. He frowns down at me. Probably worried I'm unwell. Maybe I am.

"I'm grand. A bit of a headache coming on, that's all."

I offer him a brittle smile and walk away. Hoping I'll lose him somewhere along the corridor but, with his long-legged stride, he catches up to me in moments.

"You're from Waterford, right?"

What is it with these apprentices' unquenchable thirst for answers? How many more unwanted questions am I to suffer through today?

"Is that why you hung around after class, to confirm my origin story?"

I'm only half-joking but watching this lad nearly trip over his own feet when I call him out is the most fun I've had in... six months.

"I did not," he blusters but the flush that rises from the base of his neck all the way up to his cheeks says differently. "Well, I mean, yes I obviously did. But not in a creepy way or anything." At this point his hands are raised in front of his chest, palms facing outwards in surrender. "It's just you mentioned you were from Waterford and, well, I'm from Cork."

He says it with the confidence of someone who thinks this should mean something to me.

"Congratulations?" I hedge.

"What I'm trying and apparently failing to say," he continues, and I have to begrudgingly give him credit for his persistence, "Is that I'm like you."

He's completely lost me.

"Come again?" I ask as we approach the main staircase that offers an escape from this torturous conversation.

"Neither of us comes from or attended college in Dublin," he says as though this is a normal thing to remark upon. Like a casual comment about the crisp autumn weather we're experiencing.

"What are you talking about? Didn't you hear Brigid say she went to Harvard? Last I heard, that's a long way from Dublin."

The gangly man lumbers after me down the stairs. "Sure, but her grandmother was a partner at Heron Early before she retired a couple of years ago."

I stop. Rest my hand on the smooth mahogany bannister and ponder this interesting piece of information. This lad with the slicked-back hair of a nineties heartthrob may have more to him than I'd initially thought. And so, I hold my hand out to him.

"Well, my fellow culchie from the country. What should I call you?"

He beams. "Peadar," and noticing my trajectory towards the exit he adds, "Are you not coming to the Michaelmas Mixer?"

His question stalls my ill-fated attempt to slip away unseen. I'm awfully tempted to leave. The plan had been to attend Blackhall for the mandatory induction, skulk back to my flat, and prep for my first day in the office. But perhaps that plan was short-sighted. I'm here to learn everything about the firm and the people in it. What am I going to achieve sitting alone in my flat?

I give one last longing look at the door. It's now or never. And so, I turn back to Peadar, give him a devilish grin, and say, "Lead the way."

We descend the stairs to what I assume will either be a private members' bar or a secret dungeon. I glance sideways at Peadar. With his navy trench coat and cream chinos, he doesn't look like the murdering type. But since my cousin Muriel disappeared, I've developed some trust issues. So, I put a little more distance between myself and my newfound friend.

At the end of the stairs, the steady thrum of beats along the hallway becomes louder the closer we come to a set of wooden doors. Peadar pushes them open and music washes over me, fighting to be heard above the chatter of a hundred or so apprentices crammed into Blackhall Bar.

We squeeze past countless young men and women wearing Blackhall's unspoken uniform of turtlenecks, piles of plaid, countless cardigans, and shirts dyed every colour under the sun. I basically have to pry my boots from the sticky wooden floor as I make my way to the bar. Stained by the thousands of apprentices who have spilled their overflowing drinks upon its varnished surface throughout the years.

With a great deal of effort, we make it to the counter and Peadar manages to flag down the bartender. The man is grey in the face, attempting and failing to satiate the thirst of countless twenty-something-year-olds whose money is burning a hole in their pockets. I ask for a light lager and admire how the frosted mirrors reflect the sparse light emitted by the low-hanging fluorescent lamps. The bar is electric. Practically vibrating from the combined expectations, hopes, and dreams of the gathered apprentices from every law firm in Ireland.

The future of the Irish legal profession sat around chatting on high stools or making moves on the makeshift dance floor.

Peadar hands me my drink. We decide to make a beeline for a quieter spot in the corner of the room. Somewhere we can hear ourselves speak. We shoulder past countless cliques in the process of clicking into place and shimmy by dancers swaying to the rock anthem crackling out of the battered old sound system. Cream paint peels from the wall, not helped by the waterfall of condensation that shimmers under the yellowy light.

The swan man gives me a nod of recognition from where he leans against a pillar, sipping a pint of stout. I'm inclined to ignore him and shuffle away, still mortified by our earlier exchange. But I'm foiled by Peadar who sticks out his hand and introduces himself.

"Peadar Ahern, good to meet you."

"Keefe O'Kelly," the swan man replies, and I watch his grin morph into a grimace the second Peadar asks, "Where are you from?"

I'm so mortified I actually consider joining the dancers. That is how much I don't want to be here when all warmth leaks from the swan man's face. His proud nose twitches like he's smelled something foul, and his response is sharp enough to cut glass.

"Ranelagh," he says with a distinctly south Dublin accent. "But my mother is originally from Hong Kong, if that's what you're getting at?"

"Nice," Peadar says and takes a sip of his whiskey, either completely unaware of the tension radiating from Keefe or simply unconcerned by it.

"And let me guess," Keefe says and looks Peadar up and down. Which ends up being a rather exaggerated gesture considering Peadar is the taller of the two men. "You're from Cork."

"How did you know?" Peadar replies with a wide-toothed grin, delighted by the recognition.

Thankfully, I'm spared from partaking in this train wreck of a conversation when Brigid wanders over, balancing what looks like an Irish cream liqueur in one hand and her camel jacket in the other. I offer to hold her glass while she hangs up her things. The drink smells so sugary it reminds me of chocolate chip cookies fresh from the oven.

"I have a wicked sweet tooth," she says and takes back her drink. "We each have our vices, right?"

I shrug in a noncommittal way and take a sip of my beer.

"Why did Joyce want to talk to you alone?" Brigid asks casually.

I keep my expression neutral. Watching the throng of apprentices gyrating on the dance floor become more boisterous by the bottle.

"To warn me not to be late to work tomorrow. Apparently, the partners don't take kindly to tardiness."

"Ah." She toys with her necklace, a golden sheep dangling from the chain. "Don't mind Joyce, she's all bark and no bite. Although I've heard she's gunning for partnership this year."

"Oh ya?"

She nods. Her pearl droplet earrings jingle to the beat of the music. "She's a senior associate as well as our apprentice mentor. They say she's a workaholic. Last home every evening and first through the door the next morning. That is, if she ever left the office in the first place."

I take a sip of my room temperature beer. "Must be tough on her family."

Brigid shakes her head and leans closer so that Peadar and Keefe won't overhear. But she needn't worry. Keefe is staring open-mouthed at Peadar as he asks, "Have you heard the joke where a Cork man, a Dublin man, and a man from Hong Kong walk into a bar..."

I block out the rest of their conversation, suddenly feeling sorry for the swan man as Brigid whispers into my ear, "Joyce and her husband divorced years ago."

Maybe that's why Joyce had seemed so on edge when she'd mentioned her wedding. I try to think of an appropriately sympathetic response but I needn't have worried. Brigid is no longer paying me any heed. Her attention is focused on the sun that has risen in the form of a young man with slicked-back flaxen hair.

"Dawson."

Brigid utters the name like it's both a prayer and a curse. And as if invoking his name casts a spell, the man in question is suddenly stood before us. Piercing blue eyes bounce from Brigid to me. One side of his mouth tilts upwards. I'm instantly reminded of the comic book villain with two faces.

"Brigid." He has the straight-toothed smile of a man who has graced the orthodontist's chair in his youth. "I heard a rumour you were back in town." He purses his lips like a sullen schoolboy. "I'm hurt you didn't reach out."

I glance around. This little rendezvous is attracting more attention than I would prefer. Inquisitive looks through lowered lashes are being thrown our way by male and female apprentices alike. But Brigid ignores them. Her lip curls. The expression on her face could sour milk. Unfortunately, it's Brigid's hand that gives her away. She's clutching the glass so tight her knuckles are as white as the cream liqueur. Brigid notices my pointed look and places her drink on the counter with a discernible thud.

"Must have slipped my mind."

"Hey," Keefe places his hand on Dawson's elbow. "Is he bothering you?"

Dawson makes a point of peeling Keefe's fingers from his arm. He glances over at the group of lads watching from the bar as if to say, the cheek of him! But even more surprising is Brigid's reaction. Eyes ablaze, she hisses, "You can both take a long walk off a short bridge." And to Keefe specifically, she says, "I don't need your help."

Good old swan man. Flies in to save the day wherever he's least wanted.

Something like hurt flashes over the swan man's face and Dawson doesn't miss it.

"Keefe, it's been too long. Last I heard you'd moved to the back arse of nowhere. Where was it again," he twirls his fingers through the air. "Ah yes, Galway." He flashes a smile that's all teeth. "And yet, here you are, having flown back to Dublin, which means," he says in an over-the-top fashion, his hands raised to encircle both Brigid and Keefe, "we're all in Blackhall together. And I don't know about you two but I think we're going to have a lot of fun. Just like the good old days."

The words seem light-hearted, but goose bumps rise on the skin of my arms. The kind that makes a superstitious person throw salt over their shoulder. And with a graceful twist of his hips, Dawson shimmies back onto the dance floor where the other apprentices are drawn to him like moths to a flame. But I don't have the luxury of time to mull over Dawson's words because a newcomer has walked into the bar. An eclipse of a man that blocks all light and laughter from the room. And my heart stutters to see that he still looks the same as he did six months ago. Back when I first laid eyes on him. The apprentice who changed the course of my life. Because he is the reason I applied to Heron Early. He is the reason I'm here.

His name is Oscar Pierce, and I believe he's responsible for my cousin's disappearance.

3

— · —

EQUITY ACTS PERSONALLY

Growing up, my cousin was my best friend.

We were inseparable. Where Muriel Hunt went, Fiadh Whelan was never far behind. She was my constant companion. My North Star. A beacon of light in the darkest days of our childhood.

I sought refuge with her from the nightly fights, name-calling, and door-slamming at my house. Because, in Muriel's home, the radiators were always warm in winter. And to my younger self, like two halves of a soul, it felt like I became whole only when we were together.

Earlier, in that musty old classroom at Blackhall, I'd recounted the story of the felon and the judge. Had grandly proclaimed it to be the reason I chose to pursue a career in law. But as with most stories, the part I'd shared was merely an abridged version of a larger tale. Stripped down to its barest components. A skeleton outline with the names, places, and people redacted. Because I'd omitted a vital piece of information from the story of the felon and the judge.

The fact that the felon was my father.

Absent most of my life due to a string of poor decisions, my dad was rarely around. And when he was, rows ensued that were so heated

20

they could burn the house down. My parents had me young. Mam was still in secondary school. She'd relied on help from family to finish her studies. But when my grandmother passed away some years later, my aunt, that is Muriel's mother, had stepped in. She helped raise me while my dad dealt with his declining mental health.

Barely one year younger, I followed my cousin wherever she went. And when Muriel chose to pursue a law degree at Trinity College Dublin, it had seemed a natural choice for me to apply to study law as well. Armed with a bookish nature and an argumentative disposition, I happily set about following in Muriel's footsteps.

But when I was offered a place at Oxford, the twin rivers of our lives that had flowed smoothly together throughout our youth diverged into tributaries of our own ambitions.

Over the years that followed, we made passing efforts to see each other.

Christmas dinner at Muriel's house, followed by a lazy St. Stephen's Day stroll along Ardmore beach. As the pressures of our studies, exams, and internships demanded what little of our time we had to give, we came to be like ships passing in the night. Caught in the currents of our new lives and the opportunities our mothers could only have dreamed of.

Muriel accepted an apprenticeship at Heron Early, one of the prominent Irish law firms who routinely fished from Trinity's pool of highly motivated candidates. She jumped at the offer of a decent salary and was reeled in by the promise of mentorship from the firm's partners. Muriel signed her indentures of apprenticeship and was ensnared.

Our mothers were so proud.

Six months after Muriel began her apprenticeship, my aunt called me. It was an April afternoon. The air heavy with the scent of daffodils while I trudged to the Bodleian library. A lengthy reading list held in my hand, and hoping that, if I were quick, I'd manage to snag a book before the rest of my class barged in.

My aunt asked if I'd heard from Muriel. Her shrill voice made more than one curious student peer over their stack of books. I tiptoed out of earshot to a quieter spot and, in the tax section of the library, I faced the terrible truth that I hadn't spoken to Muriel in weeks. So focused was I on my mounting course work, I'd barely had time for my family.

I hadn't for a while.

I remember how my gut had churned with guilt. Because Muriel had texted me. She'd reached out a couple of days before. Asked if we could talk. But I was busy. The end of Lent term was fast approaching. Essays were due and final year exams were coming up. In truth, I'd completely forgotten about her message. So engrossed was I in the rat race that is a final year law student's life, I'd never even responded.

I told my aunt not to worry. That she was overreacting. Muriel's a grown woman with a hectic work schedule. I'd call her and let my aunt know when I received a response.

But, to my never ending shame, I didn't.

Instead, it took me an hour to track down the textbook I needed. Only to be accosted by another student who wanted it. So rather than come to blows, we agreed to photocopy the relevant chapters. This led to another couple of hours faffing about the library. And it wasn't until later that night, while I lay in bed, that I finally texted Muriel. My mind focused on the tasks I needed to complete the next day, and I promptly fell asleep. Exhausted.

I woke the next morning to a phone call. It was my mam. She was beside herself with worry. A representative from Heron Early's Human Resources department had reached out. They said Muriel hadn't shown up for work in a week.

No one knew where she was.

When we first learned my cousin had gone missing, my family held out hope she'd simply had enough. Had taken some time off from her stressful job. Gone on a holiday without telling anyone. That was what Heron Early's HR department suggested. They told us Muriel had been struggling at work. Her partner at the law firm complained of performance issues. Apparently, my brilliant cousin had dropped the ball on an important project and simply ran away.

But as the weeks went by and she didn't reappear, Muriel's mother asked the parish priest to hold a vigil at their family home. Have the community come together to pray for her daughter's safe return.

Grief is a river that carried me in its cold embrace. All-consuming, it overwhelmed and left me gasping for breath. It rendered me speechless. But, eventually, I faced a choice. To give myself wholly to the tide of despair and sink into deeper, darker waters, or swim for the shore, in search of what was lost.

One month later, on a mild May evening, in a room that isn't really mine, sat on a bed more familiar to me than my own, I waited for them to appear at Muriel's vigil. I watched, unseen from the upstairs bedroom where a cold draught sang through the single-glazed window.

My fingers gripped the rough wooden sill for support. Warped from years of condensation that pooled in the shallow drain. The square top cracked open to let the fresh sea breeze into the house.

They came with the clouds.

Rolled in on a hired bus and blotted out the sun's blazing plunge from the sky. All twenty-nine Heron Early apprentices disembarked onto the salt-stained street outside of my cousin's home. They were accompanied by Joyce Larkin, Muriel's apprentice mentor. Dressed head to toe in black, her thin frame combined with her naturally mournful, raven-black hair meant Joyce looked like she was attending a funeral rather than a vigil. And I hated her for it. For making me imagine the worst.

From the upstairs window I watched my mam join her grieving sister on the wilting daffodil-lined driveway. Together, they warmly ushered the Heron Early procession into the house. Touched they'd made the three-hour long journey all the way down to Ardmore for Muriel's vigil.

I didn't go out to greet them. In fact, I may have stood at that window for more than an hour and watched the waves lap against the distant shore. Because, deep in the recesses of my mind, I wondered if that's where we'd find her. Lost at sea. The current having dragged Muriel from the safety of the shallows. If she was waiting for us to rescue her. For anyone to hear her call.

It was the creak of rusty hinges that alerted me to his presence.

At first, I'd assumed it was my mam. Come to chastise me for neglecting our guests. Likely with a request to arrange a platter of sandwiches for the poor priest to take home. But the bedroom I stood in remained empty and silent. The dark, having settled down for the night, disturbed only by the rare beam of headlights from a passing car.

I took a step towards the closed door of the bedroom I'd hidden in. My shoes silent on the old carpet. The swish of my nylon green dress the only sound until I heard the same hinges creak once more.

But I knew every sound this house made. The groans of the cantankerous planks of wood. Each crack in the wall when the temperature plummets. The hum of the boiler in winter. The sigh of the sea breeze when it sings through the open windows in summer. The creak of rusty hinges distinct to each door.

The little girl who sought refuge in this house remembered them all.

I walked past the unmade bed and pressed down on the handle. The door opened a crack on silent hinges. Slowly, I peered through the narrow gap. One of the Heron Early apprentices stood in the hallway. Outside of Muriel's bedroom. His head bowed as if in prayer. Slender fingers still pressed against the white doorknob. He had the air of an animal waiting for a trap to be sprung. Ready to bolt before the cage closes.

And without warning, he turned. Intense, chestnut eyes bounced around the hallway as though he felt my eyes upon him. I jerked back before he could see me. Heart racing. The man paused and listened. On the other side of the door, I could hear how he breathed. Slow, steady, and self-assured while my own lungs cried out for the oxygen I denied them.

"Oscar?" A woman's voice called from down below.

Eventually the stairs groaned in displeasure. Informing me the man had re-joined the vigil taking place in the sitting room. Blood pumped loudly through my veins. Only Muriel's door screeched like a hungry seagull chasing a fishing boat.

I walked across the hall and into Muriel's bedroom. The scent of vanilla clung to the sea-blue bedspread beneath a painting of Ardmore's round tower. I flicked on the light switch and fought against the wave of grief that threatened to drown me.

Nothing appeared amiss.

Still, I searched for signs of anything having been taken. Riffled through the shelves and hurled open her dresser. It was there that I found my half of our friendship bracelet. The claddagh pendant tarnished from years of disuse. I had to stifle a sob when I realised Muriel must have kept it. Must still be wearing her half of the claddagh pendant with my name engraved upon it. I slipped the bracelet on my wrist and pressed my forehead against the old wooden wardrobe.

Click.

I stood back as the door swung open. Someone had gone through this closet. The clothes that had been neatly folded before lay in heaps as though the apprentice, Oscar, had been searching for something. But try as I might, I couldn't figure out what, if anything, had been taken.

My legs gave way to despair, and I knelt on the floor. The thin carpet did little to soften the feel of the hard-wood beneath. Hot tears singed my eyelashes. Burnt trails down my cheeks. I looked at myself in the dusty mirror on the inside of the wardrobe. My eyes puffy. Red raw from lack of sleep, but then I saw it. Another object out of place in Muriel's bedroom.

A picture lay face down on the dresser. The man must have knocked it over in his haste.

I picked it up.

Two little girls grinned back at me with gap-toothed smiles. Blustery wind from the beach blew strands of hair loose from our tight ponytails and Muriel held the frayed edges of my grey school sweater. I ran my finger over their faces, wondering when the joy in our eyes had faded and found something unexpected.

My fingers grazed against an uneven edge at the back of the frame. I pulled. An old-fashioned piece of parchment came loose. A strange, stiff, granular quality to its texture. I unwrapped it carefully. Terrified of tearing it and read the three letters scrawled across it in splotchy, coal-coloured ink.

'SOS'.

I scrambled to my feet. This was Muriel's cry for help, her SOS in the night. This is the clue I'd been searching for. The proof something was wrong. That not everything was as it seemed at Heron Early.

I rushed out the door and into the hallway. Eager to confront Oscar and demand an explanation. But all was silent. The vigil was over.

I ran over to the window to see the man who'd trespassed in Muriel's bedroom board the bus. He took one last lingering look at the house before the glass doors swung shut and the vehicle rumbled forwards. Bringing the man and my unanswered questions back to Dublin. My opportunity to discover the truth, lost.

Until now.

4

—·—

BLACKHALL

The stereo music fades away and Blackhall bar falls silent.

The man I last saw five months ago looks around. Searching for something. His intense gaze wanders to the apprentices huddled in the darkest corners of the room, enthusiastically participating in the social side of Blackhall's professional practice course. But when his eyes land on our little group, the man's expression morphs into a devilish grin. I have to stop myself from recoiling.

To my horror, the swan man waves him over.

He approaches us confidently, his stride light, almost weightless. His right arm outstretched, he embraces Keefe.

"How's tricks?"

Keefe reciprocates with a friendly clap on the back.

"Better now you're here. Everyone, this is Oscar Pierce, a second-year apprentice at Heron Early."

I can already tell Brigid is intrigued. She drinks in his burgundy gilet, the silver-embossed buttons gleaming under the fluorescent light. A brown woollen jumper underneath that's so tight it shows off his toned arms. Brigid winks, actually winks at me. And between

Dawson and this trespasser, it appears Brigid has an unfortunate proclivity for psychopaths.

Keefe coughs uncomfortably in her direction and continues, "Oscar is on secondment at Hades Partners, one of the firm's biggest clients."

"Is that so?" Brigid says with a quirk of her lips. "Then why has a second-year apprentice come all the way down here to mix with us first-years?"

Oscar's smile is so wide he could gobble Brigid with one great gulp.

"As this year's apprentice representative, it's my duty to welcome you to the firm." He shoots his hand into the air and waves down the bartender. "Shots for my friends, please. The most expensive bottle you have. None of that cheap shite you served me the last year."

The bartender gives him a long-suffering look. The kind that indicates he's toying with the idea of kicking Oscar out of his bar. But, having decided it would be more hassle than it's worth, the bartender hands out a round of shots containing, I kid you not, actual gold leaf flakes. And without even considering asking first, Oscar passes round the shimmering shots. Peadar happily takes the drink and downs it in one go.

Oscar tries to hand me one but I decline. I can barely stand to be in the same room as the man who rifled through my missing cousin's private possessions. Not a chance am I going to get inebriated in front of him. His sharp gaze drops to the beer I've been cradling since the beginning of the night. And, suddenly, he's raised the shot glass and is holding it against my lips. Brigid and Peadar watch with wry grins on their faces. They think this is all fun and games. A bit of harmless banter. It takes the entirety of my self-restraint not to gag on the liqueur's pervasive cinnamon smell and smack the glass right out of his entitled hand.

Oscar raises his eyebrows. Light dances in his eyes. He's daring me. Testing my resolve. And, like the fool that I am, I take the shot and down it with a grimace to a chorus of cheers from my fellow apprentices. The alcohol blazes a trail down my throat. But, before I can even blink, another shot has been shoved into my hand and Oscar raises his glass to give a grand toast.

"Here's to your first big night out as apprentice solicitors!"

Oscar drinks like a fish. He's all false smiles and fake platitudes.

"Did you know that Heron Early is the best law firm in Ireland, if not one of the best firms in the entire world?" He pauses for dramatic effect.

Peadar nods solemnly as if to say that yes, he is aware of this outrageous claim and believes it to be true.

"No seriously, though. I'm not bullshitting you," Oscar continues, even though none of us had bothered to refute his statement. "No one is making me say this. Heron Early is a great place to work. I mean, it has the best legal minds this country has to offer, all under one roof. Can you even imagine?"

Keefe rolls his eyes, clearly not taken in by Oscar's little speech. "Take a break from the firm propaganda for a minute, would you?" He places a hand on the other man's shoulder. "Just enjoy a rare night away from the office."

I look at Oscar more closely and, for the first time, I note the stress lines that mar his forehead and the bruised purple smudges under his eyes. They tell a very different story to the utopia of an apprenticeship he described.

Oscar shakes his head at Keefe. "You don't have to take my word for it. You'll see for yourself what kind of a place it is when you rock up tomorrow. Like, the partners are unreal. They're next level intelligent, incredibly nice and some of you will even get to share an office with them."

Peadar opens his mouth, a pile of questions pouring from his lips. But Oscar stops the torrent with a wave of his hand. "Let's kick this party up a notch. Some of the other second-year apprentices are drinking over at a different place. Come on, I'll introduce you."

Brigid gestures to our own bustling bar. "Can't the others meet us here at Blackhall?"

Oscar hands Brigid her camel coat. "They've already gotten a table at a pub that's opened up nearby. They say it's unbelievable. Now drink up and move out."

Peadar covers his ears with a woollen hat greener than the Irish flag. "Shall we invite some of the other apprentices to come too?"

Oscar places an arm around him. "Nah, it's a small pub. Best keep the numbers down," and leads Peadar out through the side door.

Brigid buttons up her coat with a huff. "Doesn't sound like we have much of a choice in the matter. What do you think, Fiadh?"

I pick up my still damp coat and ignore the twinge of guilt in my gut.

"Let's go, it'll be fun."

I'm here to investigate my cousin's former colleagues. And Oscar Pierce was the apprentice I saw leave Muriel's bedroom on the night of her vigil. Where he goes, I go. He's already two shots to the wind. Maybe I'll find a way to pull some honest answers from him while he's too drunk to censor what he says. Who knows if I'll get another opportunity like this.

Keefe throws on his wax jacket and gives a world-weary sigh. "After you."

Dawson casts a curious look in our direction as we leave through the side door. The earlier downpour having faded to a forlorn mist that blankets Dublin. The brisk night air slaps me hard in the face. The sun having set an hour ago.

We wander down the driveway, past the iron gates and I follow the other apprentices across the quiet street. My attention trained on the back of Oscar's tightly shorn head. Opting to sacrifice my well-loved boots to drown in countless waterlogged potholes as I follow in his footsteps.

Brigid expertly sidesteps the yellow husks of dead leaves. Her hair set afire under the streetlights. "Where did you say this bar was again?"

Oscar turns from his position at the front of our procession and shoots her a winning smile. "It's right down the road. I've heard people say it's almost like a spiritual experience to drink in this speakeasy."

"Oh great," Keefe responds, sarcasm dripping from his voice. His hands shoved deep into the pockets of his seaweed-green jacket. "If it's a speakeasy, then that means it's going to be a cramped, uncomfortable space which was never designed to be a pub in the first place."

Keefe stops in the middle of the street and looks down at his watch. Like he's seriously considering turning around and heading home.

Smart lad.

Oscar must notice this too because he comes to a stop at a crossroad and says, "The other second-years were looking forward to meeting you, but we can pull the plug on this and call it a night if you'd prefer?"

Peadar's eyes widen and bounce between the two men. "No, wait, come on. This is our first big night out in Dublin. We can't stop now." He says this last part to Keefe, who still looks unconvinced.

Unfortunately for the swan man, I can't afford to have Oscar pull the plug on this big night out. I have questions that need answering.

"I've never been to a speakeasy before. Seems like a shame to turn back now. Might as well pop our heads in and take a look?"

Oscar beams brighter than the nearby streetlamp. It's all show and no warmth. "That's the spirit," he says and waits up ahead with Peadar for the traffic lights to turn green.

Keefe stares at me. A puff of air leaves his lips, and the steam rises in the frigid air. After a couple of minutes of his appraisal, I turn to him and say, "Something on your mind?"

Keefe smiles. "You made it through the first day of your apprenticeship, congrats."

"I did. No, thanks to you or your unsolicited advice."

"Keep telling yourself that," he says with a shake of his head. "When I saw you standing by the gates, you looked ready to run for the hills. What had you so spooked?"

He's goading me. I grit my teeth and say nothing.

"Do you find me intimidating?"

I give him my unfriendliest scowl. "Whatever you think you saw, you didn't. I was simply enjoying a breath of fresh air before I was rudely accosted by a man offering me his unwanted opinion." I probably should have left it at that but something about how he said it has me riled up. "And for that matter, what were you doing loitering around outside?"

My question appears to have taken him by surprise. Startled ebony eyes stare down at me as we cross the road and turn onto another, quieter side street. "What do you mean?"

"Both of us were late for the induction. Everyone else had gone inside by the time you met me at the front gates of Blackhall. Then, for the duration of Joyce's induction, you were half-slumped in your chair, completely checked out. I'm surprised she didn't give out to you for being late too."

His mouth hangs open and I flick a blonde strand of hair from my face. It is entirely his fault if he mistook me for a wallflower. I'm an apprentice solicitor. If I have an opinion, I speak it.

Keefe scowls right back at me. "Big words from the woman with ambitions to become a judge. Why are you bothering to complete a two-year long apprenticeship at a corporate law firm like Heron Early? Why not apprentice with a barrister? Plenty of them specialise in criminal law."

I look up at the bloated gibbous moon, barely visible through the mist and back at the insufferable swan man. "Money. Large corporate law firms like Heron Early pay Blackhall's tuition fees. While the barrister-at-law degree over at King's Inns costs thousands of euros those poor devils have to somehow pay out of their own pocket. And many of them don't see a cent for years while they build up their client list over at the Four Courts. To try and become a barrister is to attempt to break into a profession with insanely high barriers to entry. At least the big corporate law firms pay a liveable salary to the graduates they accept onto their training schemes."

Keefe fiddles self-consciously with the brass zipper of his jacket. "Don't worry, they're not doing it out of the kindness of their hearts. They'll get their pound of flesh."

I'm about to ask what he means by that when a group of teenage boys on bicycles appear ahead of us. Four of them ride down the street in perfect formation. Not a single one older than sixteen. The boy leading their charge sits on his saddle. Hands casually stuck inside his grey hoody while he expertly directs his bike with the minutest shift of his weight. Then, just as he passes Peadar, his hand darts out and like a wolf, he strikes. The boy plucks the green hat right off of Peadar's head in a single, graceful movement and rides away.

"Hey!" Peadar shouts and runs after the boy. But it's too late. They've already disappeared into the labyrinth of Dublin's foggy side streets.

After a laughably short period of time, Peadar gives up. "They were too fast," he gasps, winded.

"You look like a man who could use a drink and a good thing too, because we're here," Oscar says and comes to a stop in front of a mottled wooden door set within a high stone wall. Moss grows between the crumbling, grey bricks. The mortar holding the stones together long since turned black by the dirt that's embedded itself between the cracks.

"You're going to love this," Oscar says and turns the weather-worn handle. The door swings open. I peer over Brigid's shoulder into a garden, lit by a lone light from an old church. Gravestones are littered throughout the abandoned green space. The limestone worn down by decades worth of rain.

I pause on the perimeter, suddenly unsure. It smells of freshly dug earth and rotting plants. But Oscar strides past the door and takes the pebble stone footpath that snakes through the graveyard. "Didn't I tell you it'd be great?" He shouts, his head tilted towards us, while he gestures at the majestic, old church. "Come on, the others are waiting inside."

"This is a rather random spot to have a speakeasy," Brigid says uncertainly.

Peadar tilts his head in contemplation. "I guess it kind of makes sense though. Monks are known for their brewing skills. If that church is no longer in use, then it would make perfect sense to lease it out and apply for a liquor licence."

I'm not convinced. "Seems a bit dead though, doesn't it?"

"Good one," Keefe says and steps into the graveyard. "It's creepy as hell, is what it is." But he doesn't hesitate to follow Oscar up the path and into the church. Brigid turns to Peadar and, with a daring grin she says, "after you," and together they walk through the door.

I find myself alone on the silent street. Cars honk in the distance over by Inns Quay. I reach into my pocket to take out my phone. The battery's at fifty percent. One lonely bar of coverage left to me in this eerie place. But it's better than nothing. And I'm not about to turn back. I changed my entire life to get here. To investigate Oscar and his connection to my cousin. To do whatever it takes to find Muriel and bring her home. So, I stroll into the enclosed graveyard and let the door to the outside world swing shut behind me.

5

—・—

KNOWLEDGE IS FOR THE WORTHY

The church is chilly. It's colder in here than it was outside. And the smell. It's a heady mixture of dust and disuse. A lethal combination that wreaks havoc on my sinuses. Thrown together with what I suspect may be mouse droppings, judging by the trap at the base of the priest's pulpit. Altogether it makes for a pungent stench.

By the time I arrive at the altar, Brigid has already helped herself to a glass of some exceedingly expensive champagne, judging by the uncorked bottles. A handful of glasses, filled to the brim with bubbly are stacked atop a vibrant vermillion cloth embroidered with golden leaves that frame the edges of the altar.

"Where is everyone?" I ask.

Peadar merrily accepts a glass of fizz from Brigid and replies, "I bet it's one of those speakeasys where you have to enter a random room first and wait around for a bit. It's a test to root out the people who don't really want to be here. Any second now, someone dressed like a priest will walk in and ask us for a secret password. I assume that's where Oscar's gone. The actual entrance to the bar area is probably hidden in plain sight."

I look around the deserted church, shrouded in shadows save for the light cast by a handful of ornate, bronze candelabras. Something feels off.

"But what if this is all some elaborate prank and a real life priest is about to burst out of his chambers and threaten to call the Gardaí on us for trespassing?"

Looking altogether bored of the antics and less than impressed with the venue, Keefe picks up a glass and makes his way over to the front pew.

"Oscar is many things, but a prankster, he is not."

"How do you know?"

The swan man slumps down a velvet cushioned bench. "Because I've known him since we were kids. We grew up down the road from each other in Ranelagh and now he's my flatmate. Oscar works so hard, he has no time for fun and games. A good night for him these days comprises a solid seven hours of sleep."

In front of Keefe, Peadar feels along the walls for a hidden door or secret panel. After a minute, he gives up and asks, "If you're from Ranelagh, why not live at home and save yourself a bomb in rent?"

Keefe shifts uncomfortably on the hard-wood and pointedly ignores the question. But Peadar persists. "Oscar said his surname is Pierce. Any chance he's related to Sandra Pierce, the politician?"

Keefe takes a swig from his drink. "Sure, she's Oscar's mother. But tell me, Peadar, what do your people do down in Cork?" He asks, abruptly changing the subject.

Peadar who had made his way to the side of the altar stops in front of a side door. I can already tell by the sure set of his shoulders, he plans on investigating it. "They're mostly engaged in the legal profession in some way or another. My parents have a law firm down in Cork." And, without a backward glance, Peadar disappears into the side room as though he fully expects to find a rave in the priest's vestry.

The swan man places his shoes on the pew and takes a sip of his drink.

"Show a little respect," Brigid snaps at him and swats his foot with a flick of her hand. "It's still a church. This is hallowed ground."

"Says the one drinking champagne," I snort and take a nervous gulp. I scrunch my nose at the acidic, almost salty taste of it.

"If priests can drink wine in here, I don't see why I can't put my feet up and imbibe in a bit of bubbly," Keefe retorts.

Brigid almost keels over, her eyes positively bulging. "Good God, you heathen. You're talking about the body and blood of Christ."

Keefe grins. "Now, Brigid you shouldn't take the Lord's name in vain."

She sighs and turns away. "I don't know why I bother with you. I get burned every time."

"You're not much of a believer then?" I ask Keefe, while I take the opportunity to inspect the forlorn organ at the back of the church, so large its pipes almost touch the ceiling. Displeased, gold-plated angels stare down judgmentally at us.

"I would say I'm a man of fact rather than faith," Keefe replies dropping his glass onto the wooden pew with a thud. "What is taking Oscar so long? I know for a fact his mother taught him not to keep guests waiting."

Peadar strolls back from the vestry. He's donned the white-and-red robes of an altar boy. Far too short, the robes float awkwardly about his body. "I expect he's gone to find the others. They're probably drinking down in a cellar, which would explain why we can't hear the music. Pretty smart really. They don't have to worry about any noise complaints from the neighbours." He plucks another glass of bubbly from the altar and ascends the priest's pulpit.

Brigid looks like she might drop dead of a heart attack while Keefe sniggers behind her. "What are you wearing?" Even I can't keep a smile from my face at how ridiculous he looks. Peadar's gangly legs are so long the white robes barely touch his knees. The airy sleeves finish just after his elbows.

"These?" He says looking down at himself with his arms strewn wide, "Found them in the vestry. And considering the venue, I thought I'd get dressed up for the occasion."

"Take them off right now!" Brigid shouts, finger pointed at Peadar.

"Are you mad? I will not. The owners of the speakeasy obviously left them for the more adventurous customers to get dressed up in. It's a bit of harmless fun. Plus, if you haven't noticed, this venue is freezing and tonight was a less than ideal night to have my favourite hat stolen." He runs a self-conscious hand through his light brown locks. Peadar's premium strength gel has failed him in his time of need and stray strands of hair impede his vision.

"What can you do, Peadar. The Lord giveth and the Lord taketh away," Keefe says, his voice slightly slurred and arms outstretched sacrilegiously from where he preaches from his pew.

But Brigid has fallen silent and still. Eyes wide, she takes an unseemly step back for one so generally well composed. Something has spooked the unflappable Brigid Hughes.

And then they appear.

A wave of dark-robed figures flow through the front door. Their faces concealed under masks of burnished brass. A dozen or so men and women, all wearing matching gloves and boots. Every inch of them covered in long flowing robes that whisper across the carpet. Hoods pulled up high to shield their heads.

Peadar looks positively giddy. A million-watt smile on his face.

"How are ya, boys. Do you know how to get into this speakeasy?" He gets down from the pulpit and gestures to Brigid. "There, I told you other people would come in fancy dress and would you look at these lads." He walks down the green-leaf aisle, altar boy robes billowing behind him. "What did you come dressed as?"

It's a fair question. Under the flickering flame of the candlelight, the polished brass texture of the interlopers' masks appears unique in their own way. Delicate animalistic patterns carved into the soft metal. Each mask serves to completely obscure the features of the face underneath. The high-necked collars, black robes, and leather gloves as dark as the midnight sky hide the skin beneath. Though I can still hazard a guess there's more men than women among the group.

Still, the newcomers say nothing. They stare at us through narrow slits. Silent as the dead in the graveyard outside. And Peadar, smarter than he sounds, stops just shy of the group. Out of reaching distance. His fists balled by his sides as though suddenly unsure of himself.

"Could someone please tell me what's going on?" Brigid shouts, the slightest warble of worry in her voice.

Keefe, who had been watching the proceedings from the comfort of his pew, sighs. "I need another drink if I'm going to get through this night." He slaps his knees, walks over to the altar and pours himself another glass of champagne.

Bubbles fizz and pop while one of the masked figures steps forward. Long, grotesque brass ears protrude from the mask's forehead. A button nose carved into the metal with the barest hint of whiskers cut through the burnished face. It looks like a rabbit but the ears are too long.

The man wearing a hare mask takes a black-booted step closer to Peadar who is looking rather less assured by the second.

The hare stops, tilts his head, and draws a silver knife from behind the folds of his robes. The sharp edge glints under the flickering candlelight. Maroon drops of liquid drip from the tip of the blade, down the burled elm handle to dry upon the hare's dark gloved hand.

"Jesus Christ, is that blood?" Peadar stumbles back up the aisle. His elbow shoved out like the world's most ineffective shield.

As one, the masks creep past empty pews with short, purposeful strides. While the hare angles his blade as though ready to strike.

Brigid screams. The piercing cry shatters the stupor we'd fallen under and Peadar gallops for the vestry. Altar boy robes flapping in the breeze of his speedy departure. Brigid drops her glass and it smashes into tiny shards on the ground before the altar. She rushes after him.

Blood rushes to my ears but I reach into my pocket. With sweat-slicked hands, I pull out my phone. But I forget the carpeted steps that lead to the altar. One moment, my finger is poised over the call sign; and the next, the air leaves my lungs in a great gush. Pain shoots from my backside where I land bottom first on the step. My phone flies forwards and hits the worn carpet with a thud. I'm up and reaching for my phone, ignoring the pain that lances its way up my spine, only for Keefe to catch me by the crook of my elbow. "It's not worth your life," he shouts and pulls me into the vestry, past the vestments hanging mournfully from the rails and out a side door.

The cold air hits me like an icy wave. The light October drizzle provides short, sharp relief. It revives my befuddled senses. I shake Keefe off and fling the door closed. Utterly ineffective given I have no way to lock it but, before the door slams shut, I catch a glimpse of the hare bounding through the vestry.

"They're hunting us."

Keefe tugs at my jacket. Peadar holds open a hatch door that Brigid disappears inside of. "Get in," he roars, finger pointed at the masks tearing up the graveyard. Our way back through the wall and into civilisation blocked.

I panic and dive into the dark cellar. Peadar slams the hatch shut.

Plunged into darkness, my hands grope blindly along the uneven stone wall. My fingers come away caked in sticky spiderwebs. I miss a step and stumble down the stairs, knocking into someone ahead of me.

"Watch it!" Brigid shouts and catches hold of my jacket before she takes a tumble with no end in sight.

Brigid, thankfully, has the good sense to turn on her phone. A light flares to life and the bleakness of our surroundings is laid bare. Thick, uneven stone walls press down on us. Forcing Peadar to crouch while we descend the last of the steps and find ourselves facing a long, narrow tunnel. Barely wide enough to fit more than two grown adults side by side.

With a half-sob, Brigid whispers, "there's no signal down here."

My breath comes out in heavy pants and I turn to the person who led us down into this hellhole. "What's the plan, Peadar?"

To my horror, the glow of Brigid's phone illuminates his clueless face with stark clarity. "I don't know. Search for another exit out of this cellar?"

"And what if there isn't another way out?" My voice comes out as little more than a croak but in the silence of the tunnel, I might as well have shouted. The tone belies my fear.

I feel Brigid stiffen beside me. "There has to be another way out. Monks in these kinds of holy places always had secret escape routes. We just need to find one." I trail my fingers along the crumbling wall and try not to cough at the overpowering smell of mould and mildew. "You're confusing this church with old monasteries that stored priceless artefacts worth hiding from Viking raids."

Keefe squeezes past me. There isn't much space down here. The thick, dirt-streaked walls that hem us in don't leave a lot of room to manoeuvre.

"This is St. Michan's Church. These grounds date back to the eleventh century. We could find anything down here."

Keefe takes the lead. The rest of us scurry after him in single file. Kicking up loose pebbles and dirt with our shoes. Keefe curses when he walks through a thick spiderweb and I have to stifle a shudder every time I think the shadows are watching us while dust coats the inside of my lungs.

"Look, there are gates up ahead," Brigid points, the light from her phone bouncing off tarnished steel in the distance. "Hurry, it must be a way out of here."

We race through the steel bars, a bud of hope blossoming in the pit of my stomach. But the stone chamber we find ourselves in is empty except for some long wooden boxes that look suspiciously like coffins in the corner. Deeper into the room we walk and search the walls for any sign of a doorway. But we find nothing. It's a dead end.

With a clang, the bars of our cage swing shut. The unmistakeable click of a key in the lock reverberates in the barren space.

"No!" I scramble for the gates. Realising our fatal mistake far too late. I can barely hear Keefe over the rush of blood to my ears as he whispers, "They weren't hunting us. They were herding us."

Three masks watch us through rusted bars. The hare stands in the middle, flanked by two others. A bulkier individual with an intricately scaled mask holds a bronze candelabra taken from the church. The candlelight flickers over the shorter individual with pig-like ears. They place the candelabra gently on the stone floor.

The hare, the salmon, and the sow step closer to our cage.

Brigid sees her opportunity and soars. Arm stretched through the bars, she makes a grab for the hare's mask, but he's too quick and hops backwards. Not one to be deterred, Brigid makes use of the weapon that is her voice instead.

"Let us out," she hisses at them. Practically spitting with rage. "Bridewell Garda Station is one block away and I'm willing to bet that, if I scream loudly enough, someone will hear. And all it'll take is one look at you masked freaks and this place will be crawling with Gardaí."

Peadar attempts to shush her. "Perhaps don't insult our jailers, Brigid. Remember, they're the ones with the key to our cell."

This only serves to enrage her all the more. "If you don't let us out of here right now, I promise that, if it's the last thing I do, I'll figure out who each of you cowards are and I will make you pay for this."

Peadar groans and places his hands over his forehead. "Ignore my friend. She doesn't know what she's saying and, for the love of God, do not take off your masks." Out of the side of his mouth, he hisses at Brigid, "If they keep their masks on, then we don't know who they are. And if we don't know who they are, then we can't testify against them in court so they should have no reason not to let us go."

Peadar's quick thinking lends me courage.

"What do you want from us?" I'm relieved to hear my voice come out steadier than I feel. But then again, I've been readying myself for months to face the monsters who took Muriel from me.

The hare cocks his head in my direction.

"Knowledge is for the worthy. And four apprentices have stumbled into a trap from which only three may walk free. Choose who amongst you will not leave here tonight, or we shall do it for you. Decide, who is worthy and who is weak?"

The hare tosses a bloody knife into our cage and walks away.

6

NECESSITY IS NO DEFENCE TO MURDER

Their footsteps fade and we're left alone in silence once more.

"This isn't happening. None of this is real," Brigid says and slaps herself with the palm of her hand to prove a point. The smack rebounds against the dank cell walls followed by a soft "ow" as Brigid sucks in a breath and cradles her hurt hand to her dirt-stained cashmere jumper.

It's going to be a nightmare to wash if we ever get out of here.

I turn my attention away from her to the bloody knife lying on the floor at the centre of our cell. The candelabra's flames dance enticingly across the blade only to disappear where dried blood mottles the reflective surface.

"What did they mean by only three of us can walk free?" My cautious voice comes out as little more than a croak.

Brigid shakes her head while Keefe inspects the bars of our cage for any weak points.

"And what was all that nonsense about knowledge is for the worthy? If we've been herded into an underground fight club by a satanic cult with a fetish for terrible animal disguises, the least they could do is let us know."

Keefe's voice doesn't waver. He seems so calm. But underneath the candlelight's soft glow, the tense set of his shoulders combined with his white-knuckled grip on the bars tells me the swan man is more worried than he appears on the surface. And just like the rest of us, Keefe keeps the dagger within his line of sight.

Peadar hasn't looked away from the blade once. As though it's a puzzle he's struggling to solve. Eventually, with a strangled voice, he asks the question we've all been wondering.

"The blood on the blade. Do you think it's Oscar's?"

Keefe's face pales. He steps closer to the dagger.

"No. Surely not."

Given the predicament we find ourselves in, I cut right to the chase.

"Well, if it's not Oscar's blood on the blade, then he's probably the one who wielded it."

"What!?" Keefe's surprise seems genuine. But I remember the expression on Oscar Pierce's face when I spied him leaving Muriel's bedroom. He looked like a man with dark secrets.

Brigid regains her composure and stands a little straighter. "Fiadh's right. Think about it, Keefe. Oscar led us to the church, but disappeared the moment we entered. He was nowhere to be found when the masks showed up. So, logically, either the masks did something to Oscar or he's one of them."

And I followed him right into his trap.

I lean the back of my head against the cold, damp wall. Out of the corner of my eye, I see a spider scamper away while dirt trickles onto my meticulously styled hair. And I can't help but smile at the mundanity of the things I cared about only a few short hours ago. How quickly my priorities have changed.

Keefe pinches the bridge of his angular nose. "I know this looks bad, but none of you know Oscar like I do. He's not a cruel person. He wouldn't do this to me." He looks down at the bloodied knife. "I hope he's ok."

I place my hand on his shoulder in solidarity. Not that I'm overly concerned about Oscar's wellbeing. But I know how it feels to wonder and worry about a missing person. How the unknown can drive a person over the edge. I give his arm a squeeze of reassurance, but Keefe's eyes are focused on the floor and I doubt he even notices me.

"Right," I say and take my hand away. "We need to find a way out of this hellhole. Search the cell for anything useful. I'll take another look at the gate. Maybe there's a rusty hinge we can pry open."

Adrenaline flows through my veins and I lean into the urgency of the situation. With the entirety of my strength, I pull at the corners. Testing the bars' weak points. But they hold. And I succeed in doing nothing other than rubbing my skin raw. Eventually, I give up and walk over to the others only to nearly trip over a round object lying on the floor. I'd overlooked it before in the shadowy corners of the cell.

"What is that?" Brigid turns on her phone's flashlight and my fingers graze over the thing's bulbous surface. Dust and dirt fall away to reveal a vegetable.

"A turnip?" Brigid asks, incredulity lining her voice and I don't blame her.

My fingers rove over the root vegetable, expecting it to be a dried, rotten husk. Abandoned here long ago, but it's not. "It's fresh."

"You found one too?" Keefe holds up another turnip by the leaves sprouting from its head. The bruised purple flesh peers out from underneath a thick layer of mud. As though it were pulled from earth not long ago.

"They're turnips," Peadar whispers and stumbles back against the wall. As far away from the things as he can get.

This does not endear him to Brigid. "Well done, Sherlock. Now if you could only turn that first-rate mind of yours to solving the problem of how we can get out of this cellar alive?"

"No," Peadar hisses and brings his hands to his head. "Don't you understand? Four of us are stranded with nothing but a knife and two turnips."

Keefe looks from Peadar to Brigid with a raised eyebrow. "Did he hit his head on the way down here?"

"Beats me," Brigid says.

But something about the way Peadar stares wide-eyed from the turnip to the knife makes me pause. Because I once heard a story about four people stranded at sea. With nothing to eat except for some turnips. It was an old criminal law case I half-remember from my first year of college. Although the name or facts of the case currently elude me.

But Peadar remembers and he won't let it drop. He grabs Keefe by the arm and forces him to turn around. "Don't you understand what's happening here? What this means?"

Brigid raises her hands into the air. "Of course we don't. None of this makes any sense."

Peadar grips the edge of his glasses and in little more than a whisper he says, "They're re-enacting *R v Dudley & Stephens*."

My stomach drops all the way down to the dirt-caked floor.

"Come again?" Keefe says and tosses the turnip at Peadar. It hits his chest, falls to the ground with a dull thump, and rolls to a stop by his shoe.

Peadar refuses to touch the thing. "It's a case from the Victorian era. Four people by the names of Dudley, Stephens, Brooks, and Parker were cast adrift in a lifeboat off the Cape of Good Hope. Shipwrecked and stranded at sea, they had nothing to eat save for some turnips."

I turn away from the baffled expression on Keefe's face and look down at the turnip still held in my hand. Suddenly I want to drop it too. "You're talking about the old criminal law case where the crew chose to eat one of their shipmates rather than starve to death."

Peadar nods his head solemnly. "Yes, that's the one. After two weeks marooned at sea, Parker was so thirsty he drank seawater and fell ill. He slipped into a coma. The other crew members claimed he would have died in a matter of days. And with no reasonable hope of rescue, three of the malnourished crew members decided to eat Parker rather than die too. They decided to sacrifice one life to save the rest."

Keefe unfolds his arms and comes to stand beside me. "And you think a case concerning cannibalism is somehow related to our current predicament because..."

"Isn't it obvious?" Peadar says with a wave of his hand at the locked gate.

"It really isn't," Brigid says with a grimace. "Please elaborate."

"We may not be marooned out at sea," Peadar starts and is interrupted by Keefe who adds, "or starving."

"But," Peadar persists, "first, we are essentially stranded down here with no way out. Second, our jailers said only three out of the four of us would leave. And third, they left us alone down here with the only food source the shipwrecked men had available to them." He plucks the turnip from the floor and holds it up to the candlelight. The turnip rotates menacingly in the air. Round and round in a circle, much like Peadar and Keefe's debate.

"So let's say you're right." I raise my hand to halt Keefe's rebuttal before he can utter a word and he stares stonily at me in retaliation but remains blessedly silent. "That, in some fantastical turn of events, we have been locked in a cellar by a bunch of fanatical legal enthusiasts re-enacting the facts of a case concerning cannibalism from the late nineteenth century. I am not saying that is the correct interpretation of the facts at hand but, if it were, what's your point, Peadar? That three of us are supposed to kill and eat the fourth member of our group?"

Keefe presses his hand to his forehead. "Exactly, it's absurd for so many reasons. We are not marooned at sea with no rescue in sight. We are locked in a cellar with a Garda station less than a mile away."

"Incorrect."

Our heads swivel to where Brigid shines a light at the boxes abandoned in the corner of the cell. She falls to her knees and I rush over to place a steadying hand on her back. She turns to me. Tears mark a path down her dirt-smeared face. I lean over her shoulder and peer into the closest open container. The skeletal remains of a human being lie lost and forgotten in the coffin.

"This isn't a cellar," Brigid breathes. "It's a crypt."

"I knew it!" Peadar shouts as the light from Brigid's shaking hand makes the deformed head of the skeleton seem like it's laughing at us.

I stand frozen in place. Unable to look away. Muriel's name echoes through my head. Drowning all other rational thoughts. I knew something bad had happened to her. Had imagined what her dead body would look like ever since the vigil. The masks killed her, left her body down here to rot, and now they're going to do the same to me. Bitter tears burn a trail down my cheeks.

It wasn't supposed to end this way.

Keefe tells Peadar to be quiet and inspects the remains. "Look at the decomposition and colouring of these bones. They have to be hundreds of years old."

Slowly I come to my senses. It's not Muriel. Like Keefe said, the skeletons are ancient. And without a body, there's still hope.

Somewhat recovered, Brigid rises to her feet and uses the cuff of her dirt-stained camel jacket to wipe away her tears. "We have to find a way out of here."

Peadar exhales loudly and shoves his mop of brown hair from his face. "I need you all to face the truth and realise the danger we're in. The masks told us to decide who is worthy and who is weak. Because if we don't, none of us may make it out of here alive."

Brigid hangs her head in shame. "I hate to say it, but Peadar has a point."

"You can't be serious," Keefe starts but Brigid has had enough.

"I don't like this any more than you do but, if those freaks are willing to let some of us go, that means there are three chances for one of us to get to the Garda station and sound the alarm. Because if those crazies are following the facts of Dudley & Stephens, we're all as good as dead if we don't select a sacrificial lamb."

"Aren't you forgetting the entire point of the ruling in Dudley & Stephens?" Frustration lines Keefe's voice as he wipes his hands over his clammy face. "It established a precedent that necessity is not a valid defence to murder. The defendants in that case were found guilty because you cannot justify the killing of one individual in order to save the life of another. Necessity, no matter the circumstances, should never be a defence to murder."

Brigid sighs. "Peadar isn't suggesting we kill someone."

Peadar looks as though this is news to him, but smartly stays silent.

"Then what are you suggesting?" I ask her.

"That one of us stays behind while the other three escape and get help."

Keefe tries to reason with Brigid. "The masks will notice if the person left behind is still alive."

Brigid shakes her head. "We can make it look like they were murdered. Leave a pool of blood, have the person lie down in it, and pretend to be dead."

Keefe laughs. A mad, hacking kind of sound that makes me wonder if the swan man is losing it. "You are trying to justify murder, Brigid, because, if we leave someone behind, they're as good as dead. The masks will realise they're still alive and kill the poor sod we abandoned."

Peadar sighs. "It's a risk, yes. But we find ourselves in an impossible situation and faced with no good options. They've trapped us in a crypt and, on the balance of probabilities, it's looking like they're going to kill us. And despite the decision in Dudley & Stephens, in this scenario, it really is better to save three lives rather than condemn all four of us to die."

No one says anything and, buoyed by the silence, Peadar continues. "The public was on the side of the defendants in that case. Because if Parker was going to die anyway, then why not sacrifice one to save the many? And do you know what their punishment was for taking the life of another human being? They were only sentenced to six months' imprisonment."

I shake my head. None of this is sitting well with me. "But that's not quite true, is it? None of the defendants could say with absolute certainty that Parker would have died before they were rescued by a passing ship a couple of days later. They might all have survived if they'd simply had faith and trusted one another."

Keefe smiles at me, followed by a flash of something so brief I question whether my eyes are playing tricks on me. "Exactly," he says. "And let's not forget a rather important fact you're choosing to omit. That Parker was only seventeen. He was murdered by two older and stronger men who held him down and slid a knife into his neck before they ate his flesh and drank his blood in order to save their own lives."

Brigid gags and looks away which only seems to add fuel to the fire of Keefe's conviction. "Don't like what you hear? Tough. Those were the ugly details of his supposed sacrifice."

Peadar opens his mouth, ready to argue some more, but Keefe's done. "If you're so certain one of us should be sacrificed to save the rest, then you'll have no problem being the one to stay behind, Peadar."

Peadar points a finger at Keefe and says, "That won't work and shall I tell you why?"

Keefe narrows his eyes and motions for Peadar to explain. "This should be good."

"Because if I were a cannibal, I'd want to eat the rich. So clearly, Keefe should be the one to stay behind. He's the obvious choice."

Keefe huffs out a laugh. "Weren't you the one banging on earlier about how you come from a southern dynasty of solicitors?"

"Excuse me. I am Cork comfortable, whereas you are Ranelagh rich. In the eyes of a cannibalistic court, a reasonable person would view me as nothing more than a mere starter to the juicy sirloin steak of a main course that is Keefe O'Kelly."

"Says the one wearing altar robes. You've all but dressed yourself up as a sacrificial lamb to be gutted on the altar."

"I have not!" Peadar shouts and makes a grab for the knife.

Keefe must have been waiting for him to strike because, in a second, he's on Peadar and the two men roll over the dirt-encrusted floor. Tussling for the dagger.

"Stop it!" Brigid shouts and tries to pull the two men apart. Failing at that, she picks up the turnip and literally tries to whack some sense into them. "You are solicitors. Use your words and not your fists!"

"Whoever gets the knife, get's to live," Peadar shouts and lifts the blade out of Keefe's reach.

"Fine by me," Keefe says breathily and hooks his elbow around Peadar's throat. A choked noise escapes Peadar's mouth but still he holds onto the knife.

I close my eyes, unable to witness their descent into depravity and a wave of nausea hits me as Muriel's floating body flashes before my mind's eye.

"We're not killing anyone."

Not a single one of them listens to me. So, I walk behind Peadar and press down on the sensitive part of his hand with my thumb. The knife clatters to the ground and I pick it up.

"Do you really think you can live with someone's blood on your hands? Because I can't. I already have enough guilt to last a lifetime weighing me down. I think we should call our captor's bluff and see what happens."

Now I have their attention.

"If push comes to shove," I say with a pointed look at the two lads sprawled on the floor. "I'd rather go down with this sinking ship than take another person's life just to save my own."

Peadar scrambles to his feet.

"Think about what you're saying. If it's sink or swim, for the love of God, swim, Fiadh. How can forcing us all to go down with the ship be the rational choice in this scenario?"

Brigid leans against the wall and, with a sigh, she sinks to the floor.

"Fiadh's probably right, Peadar. There's a chance they weren't going to let any of us leave anyway. Maybe it's better to try and save our souls before we meet our untimely end."

Peadar looks at each of us and, realising the debate has been lost, he wipes the dirt from his face, and plonks himself down beside Brigid with a weary sigh.

"Then may God have mercy on us all."

I turn to Keefe who looks at me with something akin to admiration and, not allowing myself to dwell on how that makes me feel, I throw the blood-stained dagger through the bars, and it clatters to the ground out of arm's reach of our cell.

"Only time will tell," comes the disembodied voice of the hare who steps from the shadows into the candlelight. The salmon and the sow, close behind. "Either way, your time is up and now we shall be the ones to decide who proved themselves worthy or weak."

The hare blows out the candle and my world goes dark.

58

7

DUE DILIGENCE

The wail of my alarm pulls me from sleep's sweet embrace. With great effort, I wrench my eyelids open and squint at the clock on the barren wall of my pokey flat.

8.30 a.m.

Feck.

I roll out of bed, miscalculate the dimensions of the mattress, and collapse on the wooden floor. My arse hurts almost as much as my head. Having only moved in the other day, the surroundings are still relatively unfamiliar to me. Other than the messy, makeup-stained sheets, the only sign of habitation in the entire bedroom is the rickety desk piled high with books.

There's nothing to indicate Muriel once lived here. She'd rented this basement flat from the elderly woman who lives upstairs. And, considering my aunt had kept up the rental payments in the hope that Muriel would one day return, it made sense that I move in.

I reach for the alarm.

Hold on.

Why did I go to bed fully clothed? I look down at my hands. They're filthy. Dust sticks to my skin and dried dirt falls off my red jacket and onto the alabaster sheets in clumps. I must have drunk way too much. Goddamn Oscar Pierce and his bloody shots.

Oscar... and the church.

Hazy memories of the night before flicker through my memory like an old movie reel and a torrent of emotions gush out like a broken faucet. I reach for my phone. How did I get my phone back? No missed calls or messages. The wail of the alarm pierces my muddled thoughts.

I can't be late for my first day at the office.

Head pounding, I wobble to the bathroom and fall into the shower. The frigid water sharpens my senses. And when I get out, I shove a handful of dry cereal into my mouth, down a glass of bitter orange juice, and swallow some ibuprofen. Maybe it was just a nightmare. It wouldn't be the first. God knows, I've had worse dreams over the past six months. And anyway, I don't have the other apprentices' contact details. If I want to figure out whether the fight club in the crypt was real or just a liquor-fuelled fever dream, I'm going to have to track them down at Heron Early.

Fifteen minutes later, I grab my satchel and rush out of the front door.

"Meow."

Of course, my landlady's cat is blocking the only exit.

"Stay, kitty. Stay."

The stubborn, coal-coloured cat stares back at me with what can only be described as a look of lazy contempt. I stretch my leg over the feline and pray it won't shred my tights with its claws. But I needn't have worried, the door to the upstairs flat opens and my elderly landlady ushers the cat back inside with a cheery wave at me.

"Good luck on your first day, Fiadh."

I smile back at her only to curse my bad luck when I veer right out of Pearse Square and it starts to rain. Because of course it does. It's Dublin and I'm the fool who didn't bring an umbrella. I turn left onto Merrion Square and dodge the splashes from determined taxi drivers that trundle through potholes. I stuff loose strands of my hair underneath the hood of my jacket and zip it all the way to the top. Trying my best to protect as much of it from the elements as I can. But despite my best efforts, icy water trickles unpleasantly down my neck. My tights become sopping wet and my brand-new leather brogues pinch my toes.

My misery knows no bounds.

As I pass Merrion Square Park on my left, one of those giant, amphibious Viking Tour busses rolls up alongside me while it meanders slowly through traffic. Inside, the tourists wear horned helmets like they're off to pillage a parish. Eager eyes trained on the tour guide who shouts into the microphone from the wheel of the bus.

"Ladies and gentlemen, coming up on your left is a lovely, Georgian red-brick building that goes by the name of Mornington House. And a name like that would suggest a mournful tale, would it not? Well, Mornington House was once the home of Valentine Lawless. A renowned rule breaker, member of the United Irishmen and ardent supporter of a free Ireland. You see, Lawless allowed gatherings to take place at Mornington House where republican revolution was openly discussed.

"But when word of this reached the Crown, Lawless was arrested on charges of treason and imprisoned in the Tower of London. But it was his father who struck the final blow. He betrayed the cause his son had given his life to. Valentine's father voted in favour of the Act of Union. This meant Ireland would be ruled directly from London until the Irish State was founded in 1922.

"Mornington House eventually changed hands and is now home to the legal offices of Heron Early LLP. But the solicitors who work there say that Valentine Lawless's ghost still roams the halls of his former home. A troubled spirit, he likes to scatter documents and terrorise the apprentices. And when something goes awry on a deal, it's not unheard of for an apprentice to complain that Lawless is to blame."

The Viking bus veers right onto St. Stephen's Green and the tour guide's voice fades into the distance. I walk up the steps of Mornington House and the glass doors slide open the moment my black brogue lands with a squelch on the foyer of Heron Early LLP.

A welcome wave of hot air greets me. It warms my weary bones and I run a quick hand through my windswept hair as I walk through the door.

A front of house staff member glances up from behind their polished desk, gives me a quick once-over, and dials a number. I drip water onto the marble tiles as I gaze up at the magnificent artwork on prominent display over the staircase. Even I recognise this piece. It's Gustav Dore's illustration of Paradise Lost. Dark wings spread wide, the black-and-white drawing depicts Lucifer's fall from Heaven down into the pits of Hell.

"Spectacular, isn't it?" Joyce says as she descends the marble staircase.

"It's really something," I reply while nerves gnaw at my insides.

Joyce gestures for me to follow her. "Why don't I show you to your desk. You're a little late and, unfortunately, we're already behind schedule." She beams a bright smile at the reception desk. "Thank you for letting me know Fiadh was down here."

The staff member nods their head and goes back to answering the phone that doesn't seem to stop ringing.

The building is five storeys high and, as we exit the staircase onto the fourth floor, I get the distinct impression Joyce is punishing me for my tardiness. The new brogues pinch my feet painfully with each step we take along a corridor framed by floral plaster work. A holdover from Mornington House's grander days.

"Fiadh, you've been assigned to the mergers and acquisitions department, where I myself am a senior associate."

Joyce leads me into a meeting room that stinks of stale coffee and I do a double take. It turns out I won't have to track the other apprentices down. Because Brigid is seated on a brown, leather-backed chair, before a large, rectangular table. Pen and notepad at the ready.

While Keefe leans against a white-painted windowsill that looks out over Merrion Street. The sounds of traffic outside muted by the thick layer of glazing on the sash window. Keefe turns when he hears us enter. His eyes widen minutely before they bounce from Joyce to me. He pulls out a chair beside Brigid and sits down.

Neither of them says hello.

Interesting.

Brigid, I can't help but notice, looks far better put together than I do. Her navy blazer combined with a silk shirt strikes just the right balance between fitted and fashionable. The same demure pearl earrings she wore yesterday jostle against her auburn hair, blow-dried to perfection.

I'm accosted with an image of how they twinkled under the light of a candelabra in a cold crypt where no one could hear us scream.

"Now that we're finally all here," Joyce shuts the door and takes a seat. "I can brief you on the deal you've been staffed to."

I stare at Brigid and Keefe but, hard as I try, I can't seem to catch their eye. It's like they're avoiding me. Attention solely focused on Joyce and their notepads while I fiddle with the claddagh pendant hanging from my wrist.

Where's Peadar?

"Fiadh, do you have a pen and paper?" Joyce looks pointedly at my empty hands.

"Am no," I say and glance around the boardroom for one I can borrow.

She tuts like I'm a disobedient child.

"Never walk into a meeting without a pen and paper. Always be ready to take notes or you will forget something important. At a busy firm like Heron Early, we do not have time to repeat ourselves."

Keefe hands me a spare pen while Brigid rips a sheet of paper from her own notepad and passes it to me with a sympathetic smile.

"Sorry, I just arrived a moment ago and didn't have a chance to grab anything."

Joyce looks down at her wristwatch with a raised eyebrow. "Good for you. However, some of us have been working since dawn and haven't even had a spare moment for breakfast."

Keefe rolls his eyes while I suddenly feel guilty for having had the audacity to eat this morning.

"Each of you will assist me on Project Puzzle. Do you have access to the matter number?" She looks at us expectantly as if we should innately understand what she means despite a lack of explanation or context.

"No," Keefe replies saving me from having to admit I don't know what that is.

"I see," Joyce sighs, dumping her large handbag on the desk. She pulls out a laptop. Switches it on and starts typing at a speed I didn't know was humanly possible. With a final dramatic press of her forefinger, she leans back in her chair and says, "You now have access to the Project Puzzle files. When you get back to your respective desks, you'll find an email waiting in your inbox with further details."

Huh, my desk. I wonder where that is.

"You're probably wondering what Project Puzzle is. Well, one of the firm's biggest clients, a private equity fund that goes by the name of Hades Partners, wants to acquire an international publishing house whose European headquarters are based here in Ireland... ugh, what now," Joyce says causing me to jump. Her eyes dart across her laptop screen. She frowns at whatever's written there and takes a sip from the takeaway coffee cup she's pulled from her bag.

"As I was saying, this is a very competitive situation and, given the level of interest, the sellers have opened up an auction. Fiadh," she says picking up a royal-blue felt pen and points it at me. "Why would a seller engage a financial advisor to stage an auction process?"

"Because the sellers believe there is enough interest in the target company to create a competitive situation and increase the amount of consideration buyers are willing to pay to acquire the publishing house in a relatively compressed timeline?"

"Exactly," Joyce says taking another swig of coffee. "Our client, Hades Partners, have already made a preliminary bid for the asset and have been invited to the next round. And while the financial advisors are working on a purchase price palatable to both sides, we need to trawl through a legal datasite. Keefe" she says, pointing her pen in his direction. "Tell me what kind of a review we're going to carry out?"

"A red-flag legal due diligence review?"

"Yes, indeed. Fiadh and Keefe, as our two resident M&A apprentices, one of you will take charge of the due diligence report. Let's see who proves themselves to be up to the task. Any questions?"

Honestly, I have many questions but Keefe and Brigid remain silent, so I decide to follow the pack and keep my mouth shut.

"Review the legal documents and draft a report highlighting any legal issues, liabilities or risks that our client should be made aware of. Depending on the nature of the issue, we may want to bake a suite of warranties or a specific indemnity into the share purchase agreement."

"Fiadh and Keefe, you'll need to review the corporate, constitutional documents."

I'm scribbling furiously, worried I'll miss a single thing. While Keefe sits back in his chair and nods sagely at Joyce every time she glances his way.

"Brigid, I understand you're completing your rotation in the intellectual property department?"

Brigid clears her throat. "That's correct, yes."

"Then you can review all of the publishing documentation. Pay close attention to the contracts in place with authors. They are the bread and butter of this industry. Take a look at their standard IP licences and check what rights the publisher has to the work. Check the term and termination clauses. When and in what circumstances do the rights revert back to the author. Does the publisher have rights to the written work alone or audio and film rights as well? Are they limited to certain jurisdictions or does the publishing house's standard terms stipulate worldwide distribution rights?"

Brigid bobs her head as she writes on her notepad.

"Fiadh, outside of the IP licences a publisher has with its authors, what other important contracts should we review?"

"Supplier and distribution agreements?"

"Exactly. Make sure the publisher has robust agreements in place to print hardback or paper books and create audio recordings of the author's work in the appropriate format. Check that they have solid agreements in place with the each of the big commercial and independent retailers who sell the product directly to consumers."

The door swings open and in walks Peadar Ahern. His eyes widen the moment he sees me.

"Peadar, please take a seat. I'm delegating the due diligence tasks for Project Puzzle."

Peadar takes a seat and faces Joyce.

"You're the apprentice in the employment department, correct?"

Peadar looks like a man facing down the barrel of a gun. "Ah, that would be me, ya," Peadar replies, pen poised and ready to go.

"Search the data room and locate the employment contracts for each of the publishing house's top executives and summarise the terms of their employment. Pay close attention to their salary, their bonus targets, their termination clauses, and any unusual terms."

"Such as..." Peadar stammers, interrupting Joyce's flow.

Joyce leans back in her chair and frowns at him. "In Heron Early, there are no silly questions, but there certainly are lazy questions. In the future, before you waste another practitioner's time, I'd urge you to consider whether you can find the answer yourself."

Peadar goes so pale I think he might faint while Joyce drowns on and barely bats an eye at the confidence she crushed with a casual comment. "Watch out for an unusually large allotment of annual leave days or other such benefits. Pay particularly close attention to notice periods. Flag if the employment contract contains any non-compete clauses or if there are any restrictions on their operation. What kind of restrictions do you think I mean, Peadar?"

Silence. He doesn't appear to know the answer, so I raise my hand and receive a grateful look from Peadar for focusing Joyce's attention back on me.

"Non-compete clauses are typically only enforced by the courts if they are limited in their duration and extend no further than is reasonably necessary to protect the employer's legitimate business interests."

"Correct. So check such clauses don't run for longer than two years, make sure the employee will be adequately compensated, and that the relevant clause is limited by geographic scope."

"Will do," Peadar replies, having finally found his voice.

"Watch your inbox for an invite to the data room. The financial advisors have said we should receive access imminently. Which in banker talk could mean anytime within the next hour or a couple of days from now."

Joyce rises from her seat, totters to the door, and over her shoulder she says, "Welcome to your first day of big law, little apprentices."

The door slams shut and, I wonder which of us will be the first to speak up and tell the truth.

8

SoS

Silence as thick as the rain clouds over Dublin covers the boardroom. Peadar scribbles in his notepad while Brigid inspects her nails. She doesn't look up when Keefe grabs his coffee cup from the table and goes to stand by the window. There, he crosses his arms over a perfectly pressed white shirt and stares out at the grey sky.

He looks tired.

No one wants to talk about what happened. No one wants to be the one to step forward and speak up. Because to do so would leave them open to ridicule. No, these stiff-lipped apprentices would rather endure than complain. And so, I'm left to wonder how many people it will take to admit the truth and trust that someone will believe us.

I pour myself some sparkling water. The liquid fizzes pleasantly in the glass and I take a swig. Then, when I'm sure I have their attention, I place the glass back down on the table and speak.

"I woke up this morning with a rather peculiar craving for turnip."

The reaction is as instantaneous as it is hilarious.

Peadar drops his pen. "Jesus Christ, it was real."

Brigid manages to outdo Peadar by measure of hysterics. She rises from her desk, pulls at her hair and wails, "I wasn't really going to kill anyone, I swear!"

But it's Keefe's reaction that surprises me the most. He continues to gaze out at the street below and completely ignores the drama unfolding behind him.

"You seem oddly calm, Keefe. Why's that?"

He turns away from the window, a serious expression on his face. "Because it was Oscar who woke me up this morning. He banged on my door and told me not to be late for work."

Brigid's hands fall to her sides. "Oscar's alive?" She looks relieved. But then her relief quickly turns to annoyance. "What else did he say?"

Keefe shakes his head. "By the time I got out of bed, he was already gone. He hasn't responded to any of my messages."

Peadar shoves his notepad away and looks at each of us to gauge our reaction before he says what we're all thinking.

"Does that mean Oscar was there last night, hiding behind a mask? Like the rabbit, the fish... or the pig?"

"The hare, the salmon, and the sow," I correct him. He raises his eyebrows at me and I'm forced to clarify. "I mean if we're going to bother naming them, each of the masks had specific markings that identified them as a hare, a salmon, and a sow. Didn't you notice the fine lines carved into the brass surface of their masks?"

Keefe blinks at me and shakes his head. "Must have missed it while we were running for our lives."

Brigid pulls out a piece of paper and waves it in the air. "Did one of you slip a note in my pocket last night hoping I'd give it to the Gardaí if I got away?" She asks, her blue eyes roving around the table. "If so, you might want to be a little more specific the next time you need rescuing."

She lays the crumpled piece of paper flat on the table so we can see what's written on it.

'SoS.'

I spring from my chair and reach for the parchment but Peadar beats me to it.

"Brigid," Peadar breathes. "You've been tapped," he exclaims excitedly. "This is huge!"

"What do you mean?" Brigid and I ask at the same time. Energy buzzes beneath my skin. The small slip of paper is the same as the one I found in Muriel's room. This means something, it has to.

"How have you never heard of the SoS?"

Keefe strides over from the window and plucks the paper from Peadar's hand to inspect it himself.

"Because Brigid and Fiadh studied abroad. And I can't imagine anyone outside of Ireland cares about a shadowy group of legal practitioners that's not supposed to exist."

My mind whirls. "Hold on, are you saying there's a secret society of solicitors?"

Peadar nods his head enthusiastically. A broad smile on his face.

"SoS - <u>S</u>ociety <u>o</u>f <u>S</u>olicitors. Pretty cool, right?"

"Shush, keep your voice down," Brigid snaps. Her eyes dart to the boardroom's glass door and the practice assistants and paralegals who work just beyond it. "If it's supposed to be a secret, how do you know about it?"

Peadar lowers his voice. "One of my cousins told me."

Keefe snorts. "Let me guess, they're a solicitor too?"

"Naturally," Peadar says with a nod. "My cousin mentioned the SoS when he was a few too many drinks to the wind and then refused to say anything more about it when he sobered up the next morning. All I know is that it's considered a huge honour to join their ranks. The SoS are a very old, incredibly selective, and super secretive society."

"Well," Keefe replies flatly, "if those masks were a part of the SoS, then it's not the kind of organisation I want anything to do with."

Peadar actually has the gall to look surprised by that imminently sensible statement.

"But don't you understand? It was a test. The masks must have watched us from the shadows to see what we'd do. To determine who was worthy to join their ranks. And apparently they chose Brigid." He nods to the parchment, "where did you say you found it?"

"It was inside the jacket I wore last night. One of the masks must have slipped the paper inside my pocket, which is kind of creepy. And while we're on the subject, I can't actually remember how I got home last night..."

"Me neither," I reply.

Keefe rubs his hands over his eyes. "The champagne we drank in the church, they must have drugged it somehow."

And then tucked us into bed? Eww.

"Oh my god," Peadar shouts and pulls a piece of parchment out of the front pocket of his chinos. "Everyone, check every item of clothing you wore last night."

Brigid's nose twitches. "Does that mean you're wearing the same trousers you wore yesterday?"

"I woke up in them and it was that or be late." Peadar lays the piece of parchment on the table and we huddle around it.

It says, '*Más mian libh a bheith linn*' - *If ye want to join us.*

"Keefe, check your clothes," Brigid commands but he folds his arms and staunchly refuses.

Peadar sighs. "Look, we're wasting time. It is my belief that last night, the four of us were tested by the Society of Solicitors in the crypts of St. Michan's church. To test whether we're worthy to join their ranks."

Brigid mumbles, "That would explain the case law reference."

Peadar nods. "And it would appear that two of us passed their... initiation test, but unfortunately," he waves his piece of parchment in the air, "it looks like we're going to have to work together to figure out what the messages mean."

"Whoa, hold up," Keefe says and puts his hands in the air as though to try and ward off Peadar's enthusiastic energy in case idiocy is catching. "The lunatics locked us in a crypt with a bloody knife. And don't think I've forgotten how you wanted to sacrifice me for the greater good!"

Peadar has the decency to look somewhat ashamed by his behaviour but Keefe isn't finished. "Do you enjoy being mistreated? Because if that was only their first test, I'd hate to see what the second one looks like." He looks from Brigid to Peadar. "Why on earth would you want to join an organisation like that?"

Peadar makes a noise that sounds decidedly like an "urgh" and places his hands on the back of his chair. "Because it's the SoS."

Keefe shakes his head at Peadar and seems to realise he's a lost cause. He turns instead to Brigid.

She shrugs. "I mean, last night was bad... but it could have been worse. And we passed the test, didn't we? It would be a real shame to have put all that work in just to turn back now. So, maybe we should try to figure out what the SoS are trying to tell us," she says with a flick of her hand at her piece of parchment.

Keefe turns to me. I can see it in his eyes, the hope that I'll be the one to see reason. But all I see is my missing cousin's face every time I close my eyes.

"If Peadar is to be believed, then we may have been offered a once-in-a-lifetime opportunity to join an organisation so power-ful, most people have never even heard of it. And the ones who have wish they'd been given the chance you're considering walking away from. Because that's what it is; a rare opportunity that's offered to a select few. And what you call lunacy, I call gratitude. Because a lot of people would give anything to be in our position. So, I'm going to go find my desk, wherever in this building it might be, and hope that I too passed their silly little test and that there's a piece of parchment somewhere with my name on it. Peadar, Brigid, and I have made our choice and now it's your turn. Fight or flight, swan man. The choice is yours."

I walk to the door, but before I press down on the handle I face him once more. Ready to make my closing argument. "Aren't you in the least bit curious? Don't you want to find out who hid behind the mask? And if Oscar might not be the person you think he is?"

I shut the door behind me and trudge past the paralegals work-ing away in the open-plan area. My footsteps echo off the marble floor to the steady beat of my heart. Barely muffled by the maroon carpet draped over it. My thoughts focused solely on my cousin. Was Muriel a member of the SoS and are they somehow linked to her disappearance?

The only way to find out is to lower myself into the belly of the beast.

"Are you Fiadh?"

I look up to find a middle-aged woman with a neat, ear-length bob peering at me through thick rimmed glasses.

"Yes?"

She plucks a pair of headphones from her ears and plonks them on the desk.

"Good, I've been looking for you. My name is Una Bewley and I'm Buach Scannell's practice assistant."

Una motions for me to follow her down the hall to a frosted glass door with 'Buach Scannell - Partner' written across it. She shoves the door open and wanders inside.

One thing becomes abundantly clear to me. Not all offices in Heron Early are made equal. This one is far bigger and grander than the other pokey rooms along the corridor. Here, bookshelves overflowing with Irish law reports cover every available wall and an antique hardwood desk with a bottle green bankers' lamp takes pride of place in the centre of the room. Behind it, mid-morning light streams through a maroon draped window with a prominent view of Merrion Street.

Una plucks a cardboard box from beneath a robust leather armchair and throws some books into it.

"Well, don't just stand there. These aren't going to move themselves."

I linger uncertainly in the doorway because nothing about this office indicates its owner wants to share this space. Even the overpowering smell of spicy cologne lingers in the air like a warning to stay away. But Una gives me a look that suggests I have no say in the matter. So, I walk in and help her lift a stack of hefty books from a small desk. She bustles away, taking the box with her, and I'm left alone in the office. With a start, I realise the dinky desk Una cleared is where I'm supposed to sit.

I feel like an unwanted coatrack shoved into the farthest corner of the room.

But that's the least of my concerns. I close the office door and take some time to think. I'd left the dirt-stained jacket I'd worn to Blackhall at home, but I have my satchel with me. I lift it onto the desk and dip my fingers into the front pocket. I come away with nothing other than a packet of mints. With a keen eye on the door, I fish around the satchel's main compartment. Pencil case, laptop, textbook. I don't have time for this and, unceremoniously, I dump out the contents and watch a familiar piece of parchment flutter down to the dusty desk. My heart soars as I uncurl it. The delicate spidery writing unveils itself.

'*Ag sé a chlog anocht*' - *At six o'clock tonight.*

My mobile buzzes in my skirt pocket but I ignore it. I read the message a second time to make sure my translation from Irish into English was correct. My phone buzzes again and I take it out.

I almost drop it.

Peadar created the group chat 'Save Our Souls'.

Peadar has added you.

Brigid - Nice, really subtle.

Keefe - Agreed. Perhaps change it to something a smidge more on the nose like 'this is probably a bad idea, but...'

Peadar - I found another piece of parchment!

Brigid - Well, don't keep us in suspense. What does it say?

Peadar is typing.

Brigid - I found another one in my handbag. It says 'Comhghairdeachas' - *Congratulations*. So, not very insightful.

Peadar is typing.

Brigid - Keefe, there's no way in hell you didn't receive a piece of parchment. Stop acting the muppet and just tell us what it says.

Peadar is typing.

Brigid - Are you writing an autobiography there, Peadar?

Keefe - '*Tá pas faighte agaibh sa tástáil*' - *You have passed the test.*

Peadar - sorry, mine was tricky. '*Tar go dtí an Halla Dubh*' - *Come to Blackhall.*

Keefe - My six-year-old cousin could have translated that faster than you, Peadar.

Fiadh – Mine was in my satchel. So, all together the message is: *Congratulations. You have passed the first test. Come to Blackhall at six o'clock tonight, if you want to join us. SoS.*

Peadar – Well done!

Keefe - You're not still seriously considering going?

Brigid - Why not? It's not like they've asked us to meet them in some creepy old church again. It's Blackhall. What can possibly happen to us there?

Peadar - Exactly. This time we won't let them lure us to a secondary location. It will be fine.

Brigid - Agreed. We stick together. Safety in numbers. Fiadh?

Keefe - is this group chat just an echo chamber of Peadar's bad ideas?

Fiadh - I'm in.

Keefe has left the group chat.

The door slams shut and a sweaty man in a form-fitting lycra charges into my office. He lays his cycling helmet and rucksack on the brown leather chair, sits behind the desk, and logs into his computer.

I sit frozen. Nerves rattled, I'm utterly on edge. Should I say something? Maybe announce my presence so the man doesn't have a heart attack when he eventually cops me skulking in the corner. "Hi, I'm Fia..."

He touches his forefinger to his mouth for me to be quiet, presses a button on his phone, and a beep sounds.

"Buach Scannell from Heron Early on the line."

Elevator music fills the room and an automated female voice replies, "Please hold while we connect you to the meeting."

"Who or what, may I ask, are you?" He watches me with a calculating expression while perspiration glistens on his forehead curtesy of his early-morning commute.

"I'm Fiadh, your new apprentice."

It's a struggle to keep my voice steady on account of the sheer awkwardness of this interaction.

"Are you sure you're supposed to be here?"

Am what?

He leans back in his chair and stretches his back until it cracks. My eyes wander to the protein powder stacked on the bookshelves. "Una seemed to think so..." He gives me a look that seems to say, you'd better be sure, and I blurt out a more determined, "Yes."

He frowns at the wobble of uncertainty in my voice and, with a weary sigh, he says, "No one ever tells me anything. I assume Joyce has brought you up to speed on the Project Puzzle acquisition. Hades Partners are one of my most valued clients. I trust you'll prioritise them and do a better job than the last apprentice who dropped the ball and ran off into the sunset. Leaving the rest of us to clean up her mess."

The breath freezes in my lungs.

So, this is the partner Muriel was assigned to when she went missing. The man who claimed my cousin wasn't fit to work in a fast-paced corporate environment like this one.

A series of beeps indicates the virtual meeting has commenced. I look at Buach with fresh eyes, but he's already dismissed me. So, I sit back in my chair and wonder how I'll make him pay, if I discover he played a hand in her disappearance.

9

DON'T CRY BEFORE IT HURTS

"I was wrong, this place is spookier than a church."

Peadar pushes the iron gate open, his eyes fixed on Blackhall. It's six in the evening. The sun has set and the grounds are deserted. The building's beady black windows, dark and devoid of life, stare down menacingly at us.

I follow Peadar up the cow's lick of a driveway. Thankfully the rain has finally stopped. Replaced by a forceful breeze that pulls the autumn leaves from the trees to twirl through the air and dance along the lawn. Brigid catches the sleeve of my tweed blazer and I turn to face her. Light from a nearby street lamp lends an ethereal glow to her auburn hair.

"Maybe Keefe was right. Maybe we shouldn't have come."

Peadar glances back at us through his wire-framed oval glasses. "Don't chicken out on us, Brigid. Sneaking out of Heron Early without Joyce noticing was no easy feat."

We pass the main education centre and cross under the old archway. Brigid tugs at my sleeve again. "But maybe we should reconsider. I mean, look at this place. If ever there were a quintessential backdrop for a horror movie, this is it. There's even a full bloody moon tonight."

She's not wrong. I wouldn't be here if I didn't have to. But like Brigid said, there's safety in numbers, so I'm going to need her to hurry up and grow a backbone.

"Unless werewolves are actually real, I don't think you need concern yourself with the lunar cycle, Brigid."

We reach the back of the main building, but Brigid still looks unsure and I have to stamp down on the guilt that wells within me. I want to turn around. I want to tell Brigid her instincts are right. To trust her gut. Tell her that I suspect there's something rotten at the core of the SoS. But I can't. Because it's like I'm a piece of debris being pulled towards the same whirlpool that stole Muriel from me. And I have no intention of fighting it. I'm ready to drown for the truth. But like a coward, I don't want to go down with this sinking ship on my own.

So, I place a smile on my face that isn't real and muster up a dollop of bravery I don't really feel. "Don't cry before it hurts, Brigid. And anyway, what's the worst that can happen?"

She grimaces but follows along when Peadar keys the code into the back door and we duck inside. Ready for anything.

"Is that music?"

"Sounds like it's coming from the bar," Peadar says with a hopeful look on his face. "Maybe it's a party to welcome the new initiates?"

We trek downstairs. Brigid throws me an incredulous look when the distinct screech of a fiddle echoes down the corridor. We follow the sombre music and I push the door to the bar open.

The bar is closed, the shutters drawn down tight and the lights turned off. White candles burn brightly on every available surface. Casting long shadows over the entire room. But more unexpected than that is the fact that we're not alone. More than a dozen other apprentices I vaguely recognise from the Michaelmas Mixer are huddled around the room where hushed conversations are being held in small groups. Champagne glasses clasped between their clammy fingers. Judging by their clothing, it looks like they too came here straight from work.

Brigid smiles and nods to some familiar faces. But out of the side of her mouth she says, "Looks like we weren't the only ones to be tapped for membership. A selection of apprentices from each of the big five Dublin law firms have been invited. I thought you said this was supposed to be an extremely exclusive society, Peadar? Because from where I'm standing, it looks like the worst kept secret in all of Blackhall."

And just as those words leave her mouth, Dawson Garvey of all people saunters over, a wicked gleam in his eyes and a bottle of beer in his hand.

"The calibre of candidates has taken a nosedive if you lot were tapped to join the SoS."

Poor Peadar looks genuinely affronted. He puffs out his chest, ready to defend his honour, but Brigid places a light hand on his shoulder to hold him back.

"Don't bother. I wouldn't want you to give Dawson the attention he so desperately desires."

"Oof." Dawson puts a hand over his heart and bends down to Brigid's height. A distinct whiff of lemongrass cologne oozes from him. "Your harsh words wound me, Hughes. Continue to address me with such vehemence in your voice and I'll have no choice but to believe you're still in love with me."

My head whips round to Brigid, but she's already stalked off, mumbling, "I'm not paid enough to deal with this nonsense."

Dawson watches her leave with a frown on his face. Eventually, he notices Peadar and I are still there and clarifies, "She and I used to date."

"Let me guess," I reply dryly. "She dumped you."

His demeanour shifts and something akin to naked rage flashes in his eye.

"Do you actually think that's funny?" All lightness has left his voice and I'm reminded of how much bigger than me Dawson is. In both width and height, he has the build of a lad who knows his way around a rugby pitch. I bite my tongue and say nothing. I can't afford to draw too much attention to myself.

"Get lost, Dawson."

Keefe 'swan man' O'Kelly saunters over. And never have I been so happy to see his seaweed-green wax jacket.

"I thought you weren't coming?"

Keefe shrugs. "I changed my mind."

"Keefe," Dawson says far too loudly, garnering curious glances from the other apprentices. "Good of you to join us. But then again, you were never going to pass up an opportunity like this, were you?"

Keefe artfully dodges the bear hug Peadar tries to ensnare him in.

"I'm here for one reason. To figure out who locked me in a crypt and tried unsuccessfully to make us turn on one another. In no way have I decided to become a member of this electricity-hating, candle appreciation society."

Dawson tilts his head curiously at this. "Your group didn't sacrifice someone?"

Peadar's ears perk up. "Yours did?"

Dawson raises his palms into the air. "Of course. That was the brief."

Keefe rubs his hand over his eyes. "What did you do, Dawson?"

"Exactly what the masks told us to do," he grins. "They brought me and a handful of other Bebb Gwyn apprentices to Kilmainham Gaol, shoved us in the old hanging cell, and said one of us wouldn't be leaving. And that it was up to us to choose who."

He takes a drink of his beer like he's casually telling an anecdote from class. "It took a little longer than I would have liked. But after a bit of back and forth, we came to an understanding as to who the weakest Bebb Gwyn apprentice was."

I do not feel well.

"Did you hang someone?" I ask, my voice coming out as little more than a croak.

Dawson raises an eyebrow at me. "Of course, not. The masks intervened before we tied the noose around his neck."

I take a step back and Dawson notices. He levels his steely blue eyes at me.

"I wouldn't feel too sorry for that particular apprentice, if I were you. He'd have done the same in a heartbeat if you'd been unfortunate enough to have been locked in a cell with him."

Peadar, who seems oddly unfazed by the morbid turn the conversation has taken asks, "How many Bebb Gwyn apprentices were invited tonight?"

"Three," Dawson drawls and takes another swig of his beer. "The fourth apprentice got cut because he wasn't able to convince us or the SoS he was worthy enough to keep around."

Keefe shakes his head in disbelief while Dawson leans against the stained countertop and appraises him.

"Why is it you didn't arrive with the rest of your intake, Keefe?"

Keefe doesn't dignify the question with a response, but that doesn't stop Dawson from prying. "Let me guess. You kicked up a fuss about the morals of the initiation process and refused to come. But the moment you realised the rest of your intake went ahead without you, Keefe couldn't stand to be left behind. You couldn't stomach the idea of failing any test that's put in front of you."

Keefe says nothing, so Dawson turns to me and says, "I'm right though, aren't I?"

I keep quiet but Peadar, the traitor, nods.

Dawson grins at Keefe. "I know you better than you know yourself. You can fly all the way to Galway just to get away from Daddy dearest, but you can't get away from who you really are. Because you, my old friend, are a competitor who's out to win. Pure and simple."

Keefe regards Dawson coolly but a blue vein pulses faintly in his neck, just above the collar of his shirt. Underneath his calm exterior, the swan man is incensed. Dawson knew just the right buttons to push to make Keefe angry. Had done it to Brigid as well. Dawson played them both. So, I cast my eyes over Dawson anew and watch the skilful player in a game I still don't quite understand the rules of.

But before Keefe even has a chance to respond, the doors of the bar fly open and in walk the masked members of the SoS. Scores of them stride inside until the bar is flooded with an overabundance of black-robed, mask-wearing members of the SoS.

Brigid rushes to my side and whispers, "This is a worrying turn of events," while more masks stream through the emergency exit.

"I bloody well told you we shouldn't have come," Keefe shouts at Peadar.

"Don't panic, they're probably here to watch our initiation ceremony," Peadar replies, but the warble in his voice gives away how worried he actually is. Still, he grabs a pool cue from the wall as though for good measure.

The hare strolls in, followed by the salmon and the sow. He hops onto the counter and raises his gloved hands for everyone to quieten down.

"Fáilte," he says in the same distorted voice from last night. "It is my great honour to welcome you to the Society of Solicitors."

A smattering of applause breaks out around the room. Most of it comes from Dawson and the other Bebb Gwyn apprentices. The rest of the gathered apprentices look as worried as we do.

"Each of you were hand-picked to undergo the first initiation test and there, under immense pressure, you proved yourselves worthy of being invited here tonight. To take part in the second initiation test."

Brigid hisses at Peadar, "What's this about another test?"

Murmurs break out among the Costelloe, Ingram, and Nettleford apprentices.

The hare cocks his head in their direction.

"I see there is some confusion. You thought we would invite you to join the SoS tonight, didn't you? But the piece of parchment you received didn't expressly state that, did it?"

The Nettleford apprentices shake their heads.

"Let this be a valuable lesson for each of you. Read what's actually written down in front of you. Because if you really want something to be true, the mind is capable of tricking you. And words whispered on the wind don't hold up under close review."

Keefe huffs beside me. "They're messing with us."

The hare jumps down from the counter. Black leather boots land with a thump on the sticky wooden floor. "Each of you passed the first test, but it remains to be seen if you have the perseverance required to be a member of the SoS. Let's find out how committed you really are, because the secrets we keep and the knowledge we guard can only be shared with the worthy."

"Get your hands off me!" Brigid shouts as a robed figure in a badger mask makes a grab for her elbow. Peadar sees Brigid's distress and whacks the badger with his pool cue. This causes the other masks to step back and give us some space. Suddenly unsure of themselves, they eye his makeshift weapon warily.

I look around desperately, but the masks have blocked every exit route. There's nowhere to hide so we do the only thing we can and bunch together. We form a cohesive unit while other intakes split apart and make a run for it. One Ingram apprentice hops over the counter and crawls behind a keg like she thinks this is a game of hide-and-seek. While Dawson takes a different tact. He attempts to negotiate with the masks. His hand outstretched as he makes his case for freedom or, at the very least, further information concerning the next trial.

The hare hangs his head and I swear I hear him mutter, "Why is this intake so much more difficult than we were?"

He strolls over to Peadar, stays well out of reach of the pool cue and says, "There's no need to threaten anyone with physical violence. On my word, we are not trying to harm you. My associates and I are merely following procedural requirements to ensure your safety."

Keefe turns to me. "Did he just reference health and safety procedures?"

The hare raises his hands and asks us to hear him out.

"Unlike what the masks might suggest, we are not actually animals. We simply need to stand close to you, so that we can catch you when you fall. Otherwise, you could get hurt and that would require me to fill out an awful lot of paperwork. It would be quite the headache, I assure you."

The sow nods her head in agreement.

Peadar is the first to recover from this unexpected piece of information.

"What do you mean by catch us when we fall?"

Brigid hisses at him, "Don't ask them questions like what they're doing is acceptable."

The badger attempts to approach Brigid once again and misses Peadar's cue by an inch.

"Brigid, look around. We're outnumbered. So, if you wouldn't mind, I shall attempt to learn more about the situation we find ourselves in. Thank you."

The hare sighs and turns his back on us.

"Fine. You don't have to participate in the second test. No one is forcing you."

Peadar stumbles back a step. Horror etched across his face. "Wait, what!?"

The hare ignores him and asks the other masks, "Who has the deed?"

The salmon steps forward and hands a piece of parchment to the hare. Distinct, spidery writing is scrawled across its cream textured surface. But I can't see what it says from my vantage point. It looks like some sort of a list.

The hare lays the piece of parchment on the countertop. The sow and badger produce two further pieces of parchment from the folds of their robes and they each take out a cylindrical brass stamper.

An air of anticipation enters the room. The sow and the salmon bring their stamps down on the first piece of parchment and, I swear to God, a third of the apprentices fall to the floor. As though they're dead. And only a handful were caught by the masks. The rest fell flat on their faces and there they remain. Unconscious bodies strewn across the floor of Blackhall bar.

"We rehearsed this," the hare says with a shake of his head. "Try to execute this better the next time, please. No more mistakes."

The badger and the sow bring their respective stamps down on the second piece of parchment. Adrenaline shoots through me as Dawson and the other Bebb Gwyn apprentices pass out. This time, the masks manage to catch the majority of the apprentices before they hit the floor.

"Wait!" Peadar shouts and drops his pool cue. "Take me with you. I want to participate. I consent!"

The hare and the salmon bring their brass stampers down on the final piece of parchment and everything goes dark.

10

A Mountain Of Work

The cold hits me first. It seeps through my skin and burrows deep into my bones. I shiver and the motion rouses me from wherever I went. Nudges my mind back to consciousness.

I awake, resurrected.

I'm prostrate on an unforgiving cement floor. The unconscious bodies of my peers lie sprawled around me. Oil lanterns spill light over a raised altar. At its centre, an imposing statue of a man clothed in green robes takes pride of place. Plastered hand raised in a gesture of peace. A shepherd's staff held in the other. And at the foot of the stairs sits the hare. Mask pushed up over his forehead.

Oscar Pierce, the man under the mask, gazes into the distance. A mournful look on his face, like a man at a confessional, drowning in sin. I see him in that secret, contemplative moment before he realises anyone has awoken. Before he realises anyone is watching. And when the other apprentices begin to stir, I watch Oscar tug his mask back over his face, pull the hood of his robes over his head, and the hare rises in his place. His identity concealed once more. That vulnerable expression wiped from his face as though it had never existed and the hard, uncompromising brass mask takes its place.

I lean over Brigid who is slumped beside me and prod her. She wakes with a start. Eyes wild, she takes in our new surroundings.

She's spitting mad and with a hiss she shouts, "For feck sake, not again.... What the hell am I wearing?"

She holds up her arms. They're wrapped in a green woollen cloak. The sleeve of her navy blazer peaks out beneath. The woollen fibres are thick and hardy. And at her neck, the cloak is fastened by a silver broach engraved with the three interlocking circles of the Celtic Dara knot.

I look down at my own identical cloak and shrug. "To be fair to the SoS, the legal profession does have a well-known fondness for robes."

Brigid grimaces and gives Keefe, who is passed out on the other side of her, a good shake.

"That may well be the case, but it's still creepy as hell that they somehow rendered us unconscious and shoved cloaks on us while we were unconscious. We're not dolls to be dressed up for their amusement! Is it too much to ask to maintain personal boundaries and bodily integrity throughout this ridiculous initiation process?"

She's not wrong and, from a quick glance around the desolate space, each of the other apprentices dumped here alongside us have woken up wearing the same rough-spun green cloaks. And as the other apprentices rise to their feet, it's easier to see who's here. And who is not.

"Brigid, they've only brought fourteen apprentices here."

"So?" Brigid says, glancing sideways at the others as she holds out her hand to a groggy Keefe.

"So," I reply, dread pooling in the pit of my stomach. "It means five apprentices who were with us in the bar have gone missing. Peadar among them."

Keefe rubs his face and mutters, "Maybe the hare followed through on his threat and left Peadar and his pool cue behind."

"What did they do to him?" Brigid asks, frowning.

Keefe peers disapprovingly at his newfound cloak before responding.

"Not a clue. And unfortunately for us, Dawson wasn't one of apprentices not to make it to whatever dilapidated church they've dumped us in this time."

Keefe points to where Dawson is huddled with the other Bebb Gwyn apprentices. His eyes dart around the church like he's coming up with a plan. And a pang of alarm shoots through me because that's exactly what we should be doing.

The sow and the salmon walk to the altar, and Oscar, hidden behind the hare mask once more, raises his hands. A hush settles over the room. I glance at Keefe out of the side of my eye. How will the swan man react when he discovers his friend was the one who locked him in a crypt? When I uncover Oscar's secrets and unmask the man he truly is, for all to see.

Keefe fiddles with the Celtic Dara knot at his throat and surprises me by shouting, "You know, for a secret organisation with a penchant for pagan symbols, you're oddly fond of Christian churches. Couldn't come up with a spookier secondary location to drag us to, no? I guess lawyers aren't known for their imagination."

The sow sniggers while the salmon replies, "The building you're standing in is not a church, little apprentice. It's an oratory."

And before Keefe can say what we're all thinking, the sow cuts him off by stating, "Yes, there is a difference between an oratory and a church."

The hare ignores them all and raises his arms once more.

"Welcome to the next SoS initiation test. If you walk out that door," he gestures to the dilapidated exit on the opposite side of the room, "then you willingly choose to compete for a place in the Society of Solicitors. And I must warn you, the path ahead is difficult, but every SoS member that has come before you has completed this journey."

And even though I can't see his mouth under the mask, I swear I can hear Oscar smiling. That does not bode well for us.

"But first, there are some things you should know," the hare continues only for Keefe to interject, "Like where you have taken us?"

The sow motions for him to pipe down. "That will become clear the moment you walk outside."

"What do we have to do to pass this test?" Dawson shouts from the back of the room where I can't help but notice he's strategically positioned himself beside the door.

The hare tilts his head in a disapproving fashion but answers the question.

"Simple. To pass the test, you must touch the stone at the centre of the bonfire by midnight."

What? "That's it?"

"Sure," the hare replies with a distorted chuckle that raises the hair on my arms. "Although, I should probably inform you of the one and only rule for this particular test."

Brigid sighs. "For the love of God, tell us the rule and put us out of our misery."

"When you reach the bonfire, all of the members of your respective intake must be with you. You either pass as a team or you fail as one. Attempt to approach the bonfire without each team member accounted for and you'll be denied entry. But as the more astute amongst you have already realised, each intake is down one team member."

"Where are Peadar and the other missing apprentices?" I ask, my heartbeat accelerating. Is this what happened to Muriel? Was she taken during this test and never found again?

The salmon snorts. "It wouldn't be much of a test if we told you that."

Keefe steps forwards and asks the question I should have.

"Are Peadar and the four other apprentices aware of the midnight deadline?"

The salmon and the sow remain silent. But after a moment, the hare answers, "No. The missing apprentices should be waking up at this very moment, lost and alone. It's your job to locate and corral each of the wayward members of your team to the bonfire by midnight or lose."

Keefe looks at his wristwatch, folds his arms, and mutters, "That's a ridiculous deadline."

The hare hears him and says, "No one is forcing you to compete for a place in the SoS. You can refuse to participate and remain in the oratory until the deadline passes. But know that to do so means that you and the other Heron Early apprentices will fail. Without you, they cannot complete the task. Everyone on your team has to pull their weight to win. Those are the rules."

Brigid raises her hand, and I have to stop myself from rolling my eyes at her because it's like she thinks we're in class.

"How did we get here?" She waves her hand at the oratory. "The last thing I remember, we were in Blackhall and then nothing..." Her voice trails off. Frowning, she looks to the masks, me, and then the other apprentices, hoping someone will explain the unexplainable. But no one says a word. We watch and wait, eager to hear what the masks will say.

But the hare simply shakes his head.

"Knowledge is for the worthy. Pass the test, become a member of the SoS and only then will your questions be answered."

"Why us?" The words leave my lips before I can pull them back.

The hare stills and through the slits in his brass mask I watch Oscar's chestnut eyes fix upon my own.

"You underwent a rigorous assessment process to be offered an apprenticeship. In those interviews, each of you said or did something that indicated you may have the strength of character necessary to gain admittance to the SoS. And I for one can't wait to see if we were correct." The hare claps his hands. "From here on out, you're on your own. We will not interfere. You have until midnight."

I search the pockets of my tweed blazer, but my fingers come away empty. Of course, they took our phones. I glance down at my wristwatch. It's 9pm. That gives us three hours to locate Peadar and make it to the bonfire, wherever it is.

Simple.

Out of the side of my eye, I see Dawson make a beeline for the lanterns stacked against the wall. I catch hold of Brigid's and Keefe's cloaks and pull them out of the wave of apprentices streaming through the door. Eager to set off on their quest.

"There," I point at some glass lanterns, an oil-fed flame flickering within. I pick one up by its wire handle and hand another to Brigid while Dawson, Keefe, and a couple of the Nettleford, Costelloe, and Ingram apprentices manage to grab the rest.

The salmon and the sow shove the doors wide open and moonlight streams inside the oratory. But my gasp is stolen by the wind that rushes to greet us.

Brigid halts beside me. Shock written across her face.

"I'm dreaming. This can't be real."

And yet, it is.

We're on top of a mountain. Gusts of wind howl along the mossy, bracken-backed incline on which we stand. The full moon shines down from a patchy, cloud-filled sky and paints the scene before us in a fantastical tableau of grey, white, and black. The moonlight reflects against an inlet. A sea with small islands dotted throughout the distant water.

I take a step forwards and battle against the wind that tries to push me back into the safe sanctuary of the oratory.

Faced with the reality of the task before us, I genuinely consider giving up and going back. But something deep in my bones tells me I'm on the right path. That each step brings me closer to Muriel. Closer to the truth. So, I pull the unwanted, yet maddeningly necessary, green wool cloak closer to my body to ward against the chill October wind and wander out onto the mountaintop.

Keefe walks over to me. Stones crunch under his loafers and he points at the limestone drumlins scattered at the foot of the mountain.

"It's Clew Bay."

It can't be and yet...

"If that's Clew Bay," I reply, not even fully aware that I'm talking out loud, "then that would mean we're in the Nephin mountain range. But that can't be possible. It's all the way over in County Mayo. How on earth could they have gotten us to the west of Ireland without at least one of us waking up?"

"Which would mean," Brigid shouts to be heard over the wind, "the SoS somehow managed to haul us all the way to the top of Croagh Patrick and the dilapidated little room we woke up in was St. Patrick's Oratory. That explains the statue of the green-robed shepherd holding a wooden staff."

My mind races while Keefe runs a hand through his hair. The poor, fact-loving lad looks like his carefully compiled world is falling apart.

"But that's impossible. At six p.m. we were in Blackhall. I remember because I checked my watch when I walked in."

We turn back to look at the plain, white-painted oratory we walked out of. There, the sow, the salmon, and the hare stand by its door, as silent and unmovable as the stone on which they stand. They could be sculpted from the rock of the holy mountain itself. Totally removed and unconcerned about the trivialities of our mortal lives.

They will offer us no help in this trial.

Keefe is on the verge of losing it.

"How are we supposed to find Peadar and the other apprentices in the middle of the night on a god forsaken mountain?"

The moonlight glints off of their strange, brass masks. So sinister looking in the eerie half-light. Yet, they remain silent while the wind rages around us. It nips at our cloaks and threatens to extinguish the meagre flames from our lanterns.

Dawson is the only one who actually looks prepared for this test. He stands tall and surveys the vast expanse of land before us like a grand adventurer of old. He points at Clew Bay.

"Look over there. That must be the bonfire," he shouts.

We follow his line of sight. Sure enough, a flame burns bright against the night sky. Its brilliant colour eats the darkness that surrounds it, imbuing the grey landscape with life.

It kindles a spark of hope within me.

"This is ridiculous," Brigid rages. "We have less than three hours in which to find Peadar and somehow make our way across Clew Bay to the bonfire. Does anyone have any bright ideas as to how we're supposed to do that?"

"As a matter of fact, I do," Dawson says and gestures to a small path meandering around the oratory. "Follow me and I'll show you the quick route down the mountain. I have a strong hunch we'll find our missing intake members somewhere on the beach."

Brigid gives Dawson a hard stare, trying to work out his angle, while Keefe ignores him outright. My annoyance with their childish behaviour rises because I'm forced to be the one to ask, "Why do you think Peadar and the other apprentices are at the beach?"

Dawson points to a series of faint, flickering lights at the base of the mountain. Right on the edge of the bay. They're so faint I'd missed them when I first walked out of the oratory.

"It would appear the other apprentices were also provided with lanterns. So, unless anyone has a better idea, I suggest the Heron Early and Bebb Gwyn apprentices team up and take the shortcut down the reek. That we form a kind of... fellowship. We'd might as well. We're dressed for an adventure," he says with a wave of his hand at our green woollen cloaks.

Brigid regards Dawson suspiciously.

"You mean you want to team up with us because we have three lanterns and your team only has one. You're afraid that, if your oil runs out, you'll be left stranded in the dark with nothing but the moon to guide you down the mountain. And good luck to you if a large cloud rolls over the moon. Then you'd be forced to fumble down the mountain blind."

Dawson stands utterly still while he gazes down at Brigid. His green cloak flaps in the wind and I find myself moving awkwardly from foot to foot. Eventually, he blinks and regains his composure.

"Yep, that's about the gist of it. You know me too well, Brigid. Are you coming or not?"

And with that, he turns to walk away, and the other member of his intake fall into step behind him.

Keefe eyes Dawson's retreating form warily. "What do you think?"

Brigid huffs and wraps her arms around herself for warmth. "I think he's full of it, is what I think."

"But," Keefe persists.

Brigid sighs.

"But Dawson's father made him climb Croagh Patrick every St. Patrick's Day since he was a child. If Dawson says he knows a quicker route down the mountain, then he probably does."

I glance over at the retreating forms of the Nettleford, Ingram, and Costelloe intakes who have decided to take the main path down the mountain, towards the beach. Happy to be rid of us and our constant bickering.

"But what if Peadar comes looking for us and we miss him because we took a different route down the mountain?"

Keefe gives me a hard look before the first grin I've seen him wear all night brightens his face.

"I don't know Peadar Ahern all that well, but what I can say with absolute certainty is that he won't scale a mountain to find us unless there's no other alternative. I think it's safe to assume that, if Peadar and the other missing apprentices aren't aware of the midnight deadline, then he'll sit pretty on the beach and wait for us to come to him."

I can't fault Keefe's logic. And with one last lingering look at the oratory, we commence our descent down Croagh Patrick.

11

DELAY DEFEATS EQUITY

I wore the wrong pair of shoes to work today.

They have no grip, which makes the descent down Croagh Patrick's peak a death-defying experience. Loose shingles, still wet from this morning's rain, slip beneath my brogues. While Brigid, who is a couple of steps behind me, leans into the mountain. Clearly having come to the conclusion she'd prefer to fall on her backside rather than risk a breakneck tumble down the steep decline.

"Hughes, darling," Dawson drawls from where he's perched on a quartz boulder beside Jaya, the other Bebb Gwyn apprentice. "Do you need a hand?"

But Brigid won't allow herself to be helped. Stubborn in the extreme, she snaps, "I don't need a bloody thing from you."

She waves away a similar offer of help from Keefe and crab-walks her way down to where we wait.

My frustration is palpable. This is taking too long. We've two and a half hours left to find Peadar and the bonfire. We're running out of time but, instead of working together like a team, they're bickering like recalcitrant school children. There's too much at stake to let it continue. The other three intakes wisely took the established path down the other side of the mountain and disappeared from sight fifteen minutes ago. Their lanterns lost to the long expanse of night that blankets the mountain. While we stand around like headless chickens.

"Right, this ends now."

Brigid, Keefe, Dawson, and Jaya turn towards me. Their lanterns highlight the startled expressions on their faces.

"There is a literal mountain between us and the finish line. For the love of God, put aside your petty grievances and work together. You two," I gesture at Dawson and Brigid. "I gather you used to date and had a bad breakup. In the greater scheme of things, with everything that's going on, who the bloody hell cares?"

Dawson hops down from the boulder, a wicked gleam in his eyes, while Clew Bay sparkles under the moonlight behind him.

"Finally, someone is speaking some sense. Listen to your teammate, Hughes. You're delaying our quest."

That does it. Brigid loses it.

"Don't you dare speak to me that way. Not after what you did. Because of you, I could barely show my face around town, you spiteful, insecure, little boy."

Jaya makes a tutting sound, picks up her lantern, and walks away. Over her shoulder, she shouts, "Fiadh's right. We don't have time for this."

I watch her retreating back and wish that I too could leave these three to sort themselves out. But we either pass as a team or fail as one. So, I try one more time to understand what happened between them.

"What am I missing from this picture?"

Keefe snorts at that and kicks a shingle loose. I watch it skitter down the mountainside and disappear into the dark.

"Too much to tell. But Fiadh's right, Brigid. It's time we clear the air."

Brigid huffs and walks away. Too stubborn by a mile and unwilling to continue the conversation.

"I mean it," Keefe says and takes a step after her, sending a spray of pebbles down the slope. "No more dodging the issue. No more flying off to the US to forget your problems. I said I was sorry for something I didn't even do. What exactly is your problem with me? Because I'm not Dawson. I don't deserve the grudge you're clearly still holding against me."

I scurry along after them, leaving Dawson behind and follow the light of Brigid's lantern. Keefe leaves our own lantern back at the boulder. While a bitter voice in my head wonders where in my job description was the part about me needing to shepherd uncooperative apprentices into working nicely with one another in order to meet an arbitrary deadline?

"You?" Brigid roars at Keefe and the menace in her voice travels with the wailing wind. "You don't deserve this? You, Keefe O'Kelly, stood back and did nothing, said nothing, when he spread those rumours about me. When he made it so I could barely show my face around town."

My head hurts.

"Who, Dawson?"

"Of course, Dawson," Brigid bites and turns her glassy eyes on me. "And guess who was best friends with the prick who tried to blow up my life?"

"You?" I ask Keefe, who doesn't bother to meet my eyes. The droop of his shoulders indicates he can barely stand the weight of his past indiscretions.

Brigid laughs bitterly at the man standing in front of her.

"Dawson and I dated during our final year of secondary school. When I received my Leaving Certificate results, I told him I'd been accepted to Harvard for my undergraduate degree. And that's when things changed. He grew distant. Ghosted me. And can you believe, I thought it was my fault? That I was the problem? That was until I heard the... rumours." She chokes out the last word.

I wait for her to elaborate, but she doesn't and I don't ask. Because I can hazard a guess as to what those rumours might have been.

"They're the kind of thing that sticks in a small place like Dublin. And they still follow me around like shadows I can't seem to shake. All because Dawson got drunk one night and decided he'd rather attempt to ruin my reputation than deal with the fact that I was leaving him."

"And you were friends with that prick?" I ask Keefe.

He looks up from where his gaze had been fixed on the mountainside. The wind howling around us.

"Not anymore."

"Enough about Dawson," Brigid says and wipes a loose tear from her cheek. "You and I were supposed to be friends. Yet you just stood back and said nothing when he made a mockery of me. When my other so-called friends stopped messaging me back and my phone fell silent, I thought you at least would have had my back, but no. You deserted me too."

Keefe says nothing for a time. His gaze fixed on the distant bonfire. "I'm sorry, Brigid. But it wasn't about you. There were other things going on…"

"Ya," she shrugs, cutting him off. "Well, I'm sorry too. I'm sorry for the young woman who spent her college years desperately hoping she wouldn't cross paths with anyone from home. I'm sorry I took up an apprenticeship at the law firm where I'm constantly reminded of the rumours my ex-boyfriend spread about me years ago. And what I'm most sorry about is that there are no ramifications for him. Oh no. Dawson lives on as the loveable rogue, while I'm supposed to suffer his presence now that he has decided to pursue the career I've wanted since we were teenagers."

Tears stream down her face and neither I nor Keefe stop Brigid when she runs away this time. Her green cloak billowing behind her.

I'm left with a sickening sense of shame that I forced Brigid to relive that. But in a way, I'm sort of glad I finally understand the kind of person Dawson is. I have a newfound sense of respect for Brigid attempting to hold her head high even as others try to drag her down.

Beside me, Keefe sits down on a particularly large piece of shingle. His arms crossed around his knees and head bowed between his legs. While the wind howls with rage along the holy mountain like an angry god seeking sacrifice.

"Keefe," I say after a while.

I receive no response. Not even a flicker of movement to indicate he'd heard me.

"Swan man," I try again and give his knee a shake, but he jerks back suddenly. As though scalded by my touch. Unbalanced, I nearly fall over, arms cartwheeling comically as I regain my footing on the steep incline.

"What the hell!?" I start and then stop. Because a deep frown mars Keefe's forehead and I swear he's staring at me as if he hates me. "Look, I'm sorry if I opened old wounds, but you all need to figure out a way to move on from the past and work together if we're going to pass this initiation test..." I trail off.

His eyes are two dark pits of rage. He has a look on his face that I've never seen before. I can do nothing but stand and stare, transfixed. All too keenly aware that we're alone together. Brigid, Dawson, and Jaya somewhere lower down the mountain.

"This is all your fault."

Malice drips from his words.

What? "That's not fair..."

"I don't want your excuses," Keefe says and places his hand down on the loose shingle beside him and stands. The harsh sound of pebbles grating against one another puts me on edge.

"Keefe, you're scaring me."

My words come out as barely more than a choked whisper. And suddenly, it's difficult to breathe, let alone shout for help. My lungs scream for air that I can't seem to steal from the wind while Keefe's green cloak billows ominously about him. That same wind that cuts through my own clothes and chills me to the bone.

"You ruin everything," he shouts and his broad shoulders heave with ragged breaths. "Where were you when she needed help?"

And just like that my world shatters like the rocks upon which I stand. I stumble backwards. How does he know? How could he possibly know about Muriel?

Keefe takes another step forward.

I attempt to breathe through the intense agony that has taken possession of my body. My left-hand shoots to my chest as though I can cling to the remaining pieces of my shattered soul. The combination of my guilt and Keefe's harsh words fusing together to create a knife that cuts me to my core. My world goes dark at the edges but, under the moonlight, I watch Keefe lift the rock.

"She deserved better than you."

I turn and run.

The rock hits the shingles directly behind me causing some stones to fall loose and skitter down the slope. I stumble forwards. Nearly lose my footing and race down the mountain at a terrifying pace. Tears and panic half-blind me. I run with no particular direction in mind other than the need to get away. To leave behind my suffocating guilt and burn Keefe's face from my memory.

I'm almost through the steepest part of the reek when I see something up ahead. A silhouette under the moonlight. Dark robes dance in the wind, but it's the hair that causes my heart to race. Long, blonde strands, so similar to my own float in the wind. And when she turns around, my heart sings.

"Muriel?" I whisper, barely daring to believe my own eyes. But she stares at me unseeing. As if she doesn't even know me. "Muriel!" I shout and reach out my hand to touch her. But her face morphs into a picture of agony. Surprise and pain shine from her eyes and a single drop of scarlet blood seeps from her mouth and trails down her neck.

"Muriel!" I run towards her. All thought of my own safety forgotten. I career down the mountain in my haste. But no matter how far I run, I can't seem to catch her until a loose slate pulls my legs out from under me and I'm falling.

I experience a brief moment of weightlessness before I hit the stones beneath.

A sharp pain shoots through my limbs. I barely register it amongst the panic and fling out my hands to catch anything that might stop my deadly descent. But every rock I try to latch onto comes away with me. And I'm caught in a terrible cycle of loose shale, pain, and nausea until, finally, something heavy lands on me that knocks the wind from my lungs.

I'm flat on my back, but the world still spins.

"Muriel?" I groan and lift my aching head.

I hope to see my cousin but instead I find Keefe gazing down at me. Worry written across his face and, with a jolt, an image of how he looked at me on our first day of Blackhall surfaces unbidden from my memory. I cough pointedly and Keefe rolls awkwardly onto his side. With his weight removed, I can breathe easier.

"Fiadh, what the hell came over you!? And who's Muriel?"

I sit up and push him away from me.

"The woman you said deserved better than me?"

He stares back at me as though I've lost my mind. The shingles grate noisily when he shifts his weight to stand up. The wind blowing his dark fringe clear off his startled eyes.

"Look, this is going to make me sound deranged…" he starts, but I cut him off.

"You threw a rock at me. My opinion of you is already at an all-time low right now, swan man."

His head droops.

"Something strange is going on. For a moment back there, I thought you were my father."

"What!?"

That is the last thing I expected him to say.

"I know," he says and places his head in his hands. "It sounds mad. But I swear, when I said those things, they were directed at him, not you."

"So... the woman you said deserved better than me was..."

He looks regretfully at me.

"My mother."

Oh.

He takes a step back and brushes some dirt from his green cloak.

"They had a terrible divorce. It was right around the time Dawson and Brigid broke up. It's the reason I chose to go to college outside of Dublin. My mother moved to Galway to get away from my father and I went with her."

Ah.

Keefe runs a self-conscious hand through his hair. "Would you care to explain why you barrelled down a mountain like a woman with a death wish?"

"I also thought I saw someone..." I answer honestly.

In truth, I'm not really sure what I saw. It had seemed so real at the time. But it couldn't have been. I shudder and draw my cloak closer. The numerous cuts and bruises forming across the length of my body scream in protest, vying to make their displeasure known.

"There's something strange happening on this mountain," Keefe whispers, taking a tentative step closer to me. His words almost lost to the wind. "Are you able to walk?"

"Yes," I reply and hobble ahead to prove my point, "and thank you for stopping me from falling down the mountain," I say sincerely, as the moonlight glints against his dark hair and something twists in my gut. I look away, not wanting to examine the feeling any closer than that.

"You almost took me down with you, by the way," he says rotating his right shoulder. "But don't worry, I'll live."

"Shut up," I tell him and shush him when he grumpily tries to respond. "I think I heard something."

We stare at each other in silence as the wind nips at our heels. Gravity doing its best to drag us down the mountainside. The moon highlights a streak of dirt just under his right cheekbone and it takes everything in my willpower not to reach out to wipe his handsome face clean.

The very thought makes me scowl, just as I hear the low-pitched wail again.

"Are there sheep on Croagh Patrick?"

"Probably," he whispers with a concerned frown. "Why?"

"Listen."

He hears it this time. Like a lamb is in distress up ahead and we hurry towards it. Loose shingles slipping from beneath our feet and never have I missed solid ground so much in my life.

"Look," I point at a flock of sheep further down the mountain where the shingle gives way to grass. "Something startled them."

"Dawson and Jaya may have spooked them on their way down," Keefe offers.

"No," I persist. "Look at the stragglers, they're coming from over there. Come on," I say and tug him down the mossy, waterlogged part of the reek. Water soaks through the leather lining of my brogues but still, I thank my lucky stars I didn't wear high heels to work today.

"Look!"

I point at a distressed sheep walking around in circles. Baaing balefully at a lantern perched on a small boulder jutting from the weeds. And there, with her back to the boulder, lying amongst a patch of purple heather, is Brigid. Curled in a ball.

Keefe motions for me to listen. She's saying something. Half of the words lost amongst the baleful baaing of the perturbed sheep.

"They're all talking about me," Brigid mutters, rocking back and forth, as we creep closer. Mindful not to spook the flock.

"Who is talking about you?" I ask, tentatively reaching out my hand to touch her cloak. But she flinches away from me.

"Everyone!" She cries and rocks backwards.

And then I see it. Brigid has a lamb cradled to her chest. But she barely seems cognisant of it. Her eyes completely glazed over like she's somewhere else entirely.

I look over at Keefe, at a loss for what to do.

"Has anything like this ever happened to her before?"

He shakes his head.

That's a no, then.

"Brigid," Keefe tries, adopting a far more patient tone than I've ever heard him use. "Remember how your favourite childhood toy was a stuffed sheep you took everywhere with you?"

This appears to catch her attention. She tilts her head to the side and falls still.

"Well, that lamb you have clutched to your chest is very much alive and you might not have noticed but its mother is, at a conservative estimate, seconds away from attacking you in order to save her offspring from whatever breakdown you appear to be having."

Brigid blinks, looks down and appears as shocked as we were to find a lamb clutched to her chest. She immediately releases it.

With a baleful baa of freedom, it skitters off to its mother, tail wriggling in Brigid's lantern light, while the sheep gives Brigid one final baa of disgust before bounding away to re-join its flock.

Brigid sits up and turns to us. Her tear-stained cheeks glisten under the flickering light.

"Dawson double-crossed us. He stole your lanterns and would have taken mine too, but I ran away before he could spot me."

I place that annoying development to the side for the moment and focus instead on Brigid.

"What happened to you?"

She places her hands on the moss as though to ground herself.

"I thought I was surrounded by people pointing and laughing at me. They were there. I swear, they felt so real." She turns to us, her eyes wide. "What the hell is going on?"

Keefe and I exchange a loaded look before I reply.

"We think something strange is happening on this mountain."

12

No Duty To Rescue

"Never trust a law snake. They'll bite you in the backside every bloody time."

Brigid takes a break from cursing Dawson to pick up a long, thin oak branch a local farmer must have discarded and, having each recovered from whatever in the world had bewitched us, we set off down the mountain at a quick pace. Hoping to make it to the beach before we miss the midnight deadline.

"Dawson did what he always does," Brigid sighs. "He slithered his way into our good graces and then struck the moment we turned our backs to him."

"What exactly is a law snake?" I ask, flinching as needle-like gorse leaves tear at my tights. Exposing the pale skin beneath to the bitter wind.

Keefe raises our lone lantern into the air to help me see the path ahead.

"It's a person who claims they're not going to study for an exam but then you find them swotting away in the library like their life depends on it. Or the lawyer who says one thing but then does another."

"An untrustworthy individual," I surmise.

Brigid snorts her agreement.

"Exactly. A snake doesn't tell the truth; and without truth, how can there be trust? Better to banish the snake into the sea than suffer its poison."

She whips her stick through the air, her green cloak still caked in dirt from her stint with the sheep. And judging by the way she brandishes that branch like a weapon, I have no doubt Dawson will live to regret his decision to double-cross us.

We follow the overflowing stream down the mountain. The distant light of the bonfire in our sights. And eventually, the steep incline turns into a gentle slope. We climb over gates and trudge through fields where cows graze lazily under the full moon. A dog barks from a nearby farmyard and we take great efforts to take the long route through the fields, fearful of a startled farmer pointing a shotgun at us.

We're plodding through a sparse paddock when Keefe spots them.

"There!"

Up ahead I can see the faintest flicker of a lantern. A sparkling moonlit bay behind it.

"Bebb Gwyn have made it to the beach!"

We break into a jog. And even though every bone in my body screams in agony from the tumble I took earlier, I push through the pain. Muriel's image is still fresh in my memory. It's the visceral need to find out what happened to her that drives me past the point of exhaustion and onwards to the bay.

The sound of waves crashing against the shore pulls us closer.

Past a large outcropping of rocks and across a sandy beach stands a long, wooden-framed currach boat. It sits idly on the sand and, in the ocean, a separate boat departs from the beach.

"They must have found Finley, the third member of their group!" Brigid pants from where she runs alongside me.

Up ahead, three apprentices pull frantically at the oars of a currach and fight the shallow waves that try to push them back to shore. Dawson at the helm of their little boat.

"Come on!" Keefe shouts above the roaring wind, pointing to the spare currach sitting idly on the shore.

But we need no motivation and sprint across the beach, even though the sand slows our footsteps. I reach the currach first and catch the canvas-lined starboard side of the boat. Ready to haul it into the water. To give chase to Dawson and the other Bebb Gwyn apprentices as they row across the bay to the bonfire blazing on the nearest island.

Keefe puts his hand on my arm to stop me.

"There's no point, Fiadh. Look."

He inclines his head to the wreckage of the gunwale I'd missed it in the frenzy. Broken pieces of wood scattered throughout the ruined boat. A large hole at the centre.

Someone sabotaged us.

Dawson, now a safe distance away, hands his oar to Jaya as Finley continues to row and turns to face us. He lifts one of our stolen lanterns closer to his face so we can see his smug smirk, even from this distance.

"Snake, you destroyed our boat!" Brigid shouts at him, stick still clenched in her right hand.

"Yes, I did and you're welcome," comes Dawson's reply over the roar of the waves while his teammates paddle furiously beside him.

"For what!?"

"For saving you from yourself. Now you don't have to endure my presence and keep reminding me about a mistake I made when I was only eighteen! And don't look so crestfallen, Keefe," Dawson says with his hand cupped dramatically around his mouth. "You never wanted this career. You're only here because of some misguided act of retribution against your father. I am giving you both an easy out. This kind of career and membership of an organisation like the SoS weren't meant for either of you. Years from now, you'll both come to realise I did you a big favour."

Whatever else he has to say is lost to the wind as the snake slithers out to sea.

"Well, we're royally fucked," Keefe says, running a hand over the damaged currach.

I refuse to give up so easily.

"We could try swimming to the island?"

Even I can hear how alarmingly unsure I sound about the likely success of such an endeavour.

"Through the Atlantic Ocean in late October?" Keefe huffs. "Only if you have a death wish. Look at those swells. The currach boats will have a hard enough time making it across. Attempting to swim would be fatal."

"Well, we have to do something," I shout. "We can't just give up. Not after how far we've come!"

Brigid drops her stick and slumps onto the sand. Defeated.

"There's nothing we can do, Fiadh. It's nearly half eleven and we've no way of getting over to the bonfire on that island. And in case you've forgotten, we still haven't found the missing member of our team. No one knows where Peadar is."

No. There has to be something we can do. I wade into the sea and let the freezing water cool my temper. "I've come too far for this to end now. I need answers!"

"Calm down there, Fiadh," Brigid says with an infuriating sense of defeat. "We all want to figure out how the SoS have been messing with us. No one wants to make it to the finish line more than I do, but I'm not willing to kill myself to get there. What we need is some sort of Hail Mary."

"Shut up," Keefe shouts at us.

"Hey!" I snap back at him, riled up and ready for a fight.

Brigid stands, her eyes wide and mouth open.

"Is that..." she trails off, sand falling from her cloak.

I turn around to see a lone lantern further down the beach. But it's not stationary. In fact, it's coming towards us, swinging wildly and at speed. Held aloft in Peadar Ahern's outstretched hand.

"Hail Peadar!" I shout and throw my arms into the air, only to lower them when I realise he's not alone. A group of angry apprentices appear to be running after him. And they're hot on his heels.

"Is he being chased by the entire Costelloe intake!?" Keefe wonders aloud.

Peadar waves his arms frantically, motioning for us to do something. But what, I don't know.

"Quick," Brigid shouts and leaps away from the water. "He's pointing over there. Run to the rocks!"

Keefe reaches them first. He scrabbles over the sea-worn boulders with an easy grace I didn't know he possessed. When he reaches the top, he shouts back at us.

"There's another boat hidden back here. Help me drag it out. Quick, before the Costelloe intake take it from us!"

Neither Brigid nor I need to be told twice.

We pull with the last remaining strength we have and drag the boat down the beach. Thanking our lucky stars it's high tide and there isn't far to go. We shove the currach into the water, hop inside, and start paddling furiously. I hear a splash behind me and hold my oar out to Peadar. He grips it like a drowning man does a life raft and, with Brigid's help, we grip handfuls of his sand covered green cloak and haul him on board.

Keefe is at the oars. He moves with the practiced efficiency of someone who rowed in college. Peadar ditches the lantern and pulls some painful, ragged breaths into his lungs.

"Go," he gasps.

"Row!" Keefe commands and we comply.

Each of us picks up an oar and puts the last of our waning strength into pulling away from the beach. Trying desperately to put enough distance between us and the shore to dissuade the other intake from swimming to the boat and toppling us all into the freezing bay. Shouts and splashes alert me to the fact that some of the Costelloe apprentices are attempting to do just that.

"Row!" Keefe shouts again and again until his voice along with the wind that howls in our ears is all we can hear.

I turn around and have the misfortune to witness the moment when they give up. Their crestfallen faces barely discernible in the moonlight. Because I know how it feels. I really do. It twists my gut and almost strips the energy from my aching arms, but I also know why I'm here. It's not for personal gain. No, I row for knowledge. I row for truth. I row to get back what was taken from me. I row to right a wrong.

The waves break against the old currach boat, and we dip and bob with the waves. I wonder if the currach can withstand the swell, but the fire in the distance draws us closer. It's all I focus on. Not the split skin on the palm of my hands as I lift the oar and bring it crashing down into the water. Again, and again, and again. Not the nausea that threatens to overwhelm me. Not Brigid's high-pitched shriek every time we take on water from an indomitable wave. And it freezes us where we sit, utterly at the mercy of the sea.

Eventually, I regain the ability to speak.

"Peadar," I shout as I lift my oar into the air. "How did you know there was a boat behind the rocks?" I bring the oar crashing back to the sea.

"Because I'm the one who hid it there."

Another bout of sea water breaks over our little currach that cuts through the waves and I cling to the side to stop myself from falling in. My fingernails chipped and bloody. Our sodden cloaks stick to our skin but we're nearly there. The small island is so close, we can see the giant bonfire on the beach and the black silhouettes encircling it.

"Explain," Keefe shouts but doesn't break his pace.

"I woke up alone on a beach beside two boats and saw the only sign of life was the bonfire over there on that island."

Another wave crashes over us and Peadar is forced to halt as he spits out salty water.

"It didn't take a genius to guess we were going to need a boat to reach that island, so I hid one, just in case there was a shortage. And it was no easy feat, let me tell you. I literally had to hide my tracks by scuffing the marks in the sand. Lucky for us, it was a small currach, so I was just about able to move it myself.

"I don't feel very lucky right now!" Brigid gurgles.

"Then I set off down the beach in search of you," Peadar continues. "And when I saw three new lanterns appear on the beach, I came running. But someone from the Costelloe intake must have guessed I was headed for another boat."

Brigid hacks out a ragged breath and says, "Peadar, if we make it to the bonfire, I owe you a drink."

Peadar beams at her and then points ahead.

"Is that the Bebb Gwyn boat?"

I look over my shoulder and sure enough, Dawson's boat rocks dangerously in the waves up ahead. One of their oars is half-broken and they're having difficulty directing their currach to the beach.

"They have fewer crew members than us, so they're having a harder time keeping their boat steady," Keefe shouts. "Focus on our own raft and hold on to your oars because, if we lose them, we're food for the fish."

I scramble to do as Keefe commands. Oddly proud of him for some reason I don't care to ponder upon right now.

Our currach continues to be battered by each vicious wave. But the Bebb Gwyn boat fares even worse. Their team isn't working together. Dawson is at the gunwale, gesticulating wildly at his crew. And with his back turned, he doesn't see the wave that rises from the sea and rolls towards them. Jaya tries to warn him. I see her point at it. She tries to make him turn around, but it's too late. She grabs holds of the port side as the wave crashes over them and, when the swell dies down, Dawson is gone.

The wave that took Dawson reaches our boat seconds later and it takes all four of us working together to keep our currach from capsizing.

"There!" I shout.

Dawson's head breaks free of the water.

He's like a toy tossed about by the violent force of the sea. We watch him struggle desperately to reach his boat. Arms and legs flailing, but it's no use. The current has him in its clutches and it won't let go. The two other Bebb Gwyn apprentices are unable to help him, doing everything they can to stop their own boat from capsizing and drowning alongside him.

"What the hell are they doing!?" Brigid screams.

Jaya and Finley are rowing towards the beach. Away from Dawson.

"They're choosing one death over three," Peadar grunts, veins bulging in his neck from the strain of keeping our boat afloat. His mop of hair plastered to his face. "They don't have the strength or numbers to save him. If they try, they'll likely drown as well."

But there's something about seeing Dawson in the water, his head bobbing below the surface as he fights for his life. Waiting for a lifeline. Someone to find him, help him, save him. An SOS in the night.

I draw back my on my oar and angle our boat towards him with as much strength as I can muster.

Peadar is the first to realise what I'm doing.

"Stop it! You're going to get us all killed!"

"We can't leave him to die," I shout back as another wave crashes into us.

"Actually," Peadar shouts back, "yes, we can. None of us owe a duty of care to Dawson Garvey. Legally, we are under no duty to rescue him. Especially, if doing so would endanger our own lives. Which, in this instance, it absolutely would!"

Peadar yanks the oar from me and takes the decision out of my hands. He rows in time with Keefe and steers our boat back towards the island and away from the apprentice lost at sea.

I make one last attempt to change their minds.

"What's the point of any of this if we turn our backs on him? If we let him drown, how can we live with ourselves?"

"You had no qualms leaving the other intake back on the shore," Keefe shouts and, before I can refute his argument, he interjects, "yes, I know it's different. For feck sake, I know. But there's still a chance we won't make it through this alive. We're doing the best we can. Let the masked SoS members waiting over there on the beach save him. They put us into this mess, they can get him out of it."

I glance over at the island. But the hare said they wouldn't intervene. We're on our own.

I scramble onto my knees and open the hatch I'd been sitting on. I throw aside the coarse length of rope, take out a scarlet life jacket, shove it over my head, and fasten the straps.

I pull them tight.

"We have life jackets!?" Keefe shouts. "Why the hell didn't anyone tell..."

I dive into the ocean and the icy water closes over me.

It muffles the world above and lulls me down into its quiet embrace. My arms reach forwards on instinct and I kick out. My hands are the first to break free of the treacherous sea. I gulp a blessed mouthful of air into my lungs that constrict from the cold. The salt pours from my stinging eyes and then I see him. His movements have slowed. The ocean has stripped him of the little strength he had left.

A childhood spent by the sea lends surety to each stroke as I fight the frigid water like an old nemesis.

All there is in the world is me, my waning strength, the waves crashing over my head, and the girl in the distance. The one in need of help before she disappears beneath the surface, never to be seen again. Muriel. The name is both a plea and a prayer in my mind as I battle the sea. Each forward stroke a war won and lost to the current. Because Dawson is Muriel. He is every person who has vanished from the face of the earth without explanation. He is my salvation. My penance. My cousin. My family. My future.

He sees me.

Dawson's eyes go wide and he swims closer. Catches hold of my life jacket and, for one terrifying moment, we both go under. Disappear from the land of the living into the numb depths below, until we resurface once more. But the distance to the island seems insurmountable. Dawson is already drained from his prolonged period in the water. And with deadly certainty, I realise; we're not going to make it.

I've damned us both.

Something hits the water and I jolt backwards. But Dawson reaches for it and then I see. It's a lifeline and there is Keefe, holding the other end of the rope.

Another wave crashes against the boat and Keefe is nearly thrown from the currach only for Peadar to grab his sodden cloak and haul him back in.

Dawson wraps the rope around both of us and we're wrenched forwards with each stroke of their oars. The island and the beautiful, roaring bonfire come closer while my fingers turn numb. The rope bites into my skin and somewhere in the back of my mind I experience pain. But it feels far away as though happening to someone else.

The tug of the rope and the insistent pull of the water is all my life has ever been and ever will be.

After an age, Keefe navigates the currach into calmer waters and it's with a befuddled sense of joy that I realise my hands are touching sand. I hear drums and somewhere in the back of my mind I know I've run out of time. Oscar had said when the last drum sounds at midnight, the test will end. And all those who haven't placed their hand on the stone will have failed.

Peadar jumps from the boat and runs to the beautiful bonfire on the beach.

Keefe yells at me to get out of the water while a semi-circle of masked SoS members stand and watch nearby. To see if we'll make it and pass judgment if we don't. But they won't help. It's for us to walk the final steps to the stone.

Brigid catches Keefe by the arm and drags him up the beach. But I am numb. And I know I should care. I can taste the sour urgency in the air. It's mixed with the salt that stings my eyes and coats my throat. There's a reason I'm here. An important one, but I'd might as well be lost at sea for all I care.

Strong hands haul me from the water.

"Come on!" Dawson roars in my ear, and together we stumble from the sea's icy clutches.

His grip is bruising and it's the pain that finally cuts through the fog. I run. Long-legged, clumsy strides. Through the semi-circle of masks and towards an oblong stone, standing upright in front of a blazing bonfire.

The heat spurs me on.

Dawson places his hand on the stone and, as the last drumbeat sounds, I reach forward and graze its smooth, searing surface before collapsing face first onto the sand.

13

INDENTURES

No one parties like a solicitor at closing drinks.

And the dozen or so SoS members gathered round the bonfire whoop and cheer. They celebrate with a wild, sleep-deprived abandon that stems from pent-up energy with no other outlet. Beer bottles are passed around, masks come off, and hoods are taken down. I suppose that makes sense. There's no longer any need to hide their faces from us. We passed the test. We're members of the SoS.

Dawson is the first to recover. He saunters over to re-join Jaya and Finley, the two other sheepish Bebb Gwyn apprentices on the other side of the bonfire, but not before he turns to me and says, "You saved me from the sea and I got you to the stone. Consider my debt repaid."

I'm still sprawled on the sand but I manage to roll over and reply, "Aww, and there I was thinking we'd become best friends. That you'd put your snake-like ways behind you and join our ragtag crew."

He simply laughs and walks away.

With herculean effort, I sink my hands into the silty sand, sit up, and look around. A couple of paces away, some masks clap Peadar on the back for making it to the finish line. But judging by the small number of green-cloaked apprentices gathered on the beach, it looks as though the Costelloe intake weren't the only ones not to make it. There's no sign of the Nettleford or Ingram apprentices either.

I attempt to ignore the distinct twinge of guilt I feel in my gut. They chose to forge their own path down the mountain. But still, I hope they're alright.

My attention snags on an SoS member still wearing the mask of a hedgehog. He herds Peadar and the Bebb Gwyn apprentices over to our side of the bonfire.

"Kneel," he orders us.

"I'm not kneeling just because a hedgehog told me to," Keefe mutters darkly only for Brigid to press down on his shoulder and coerce him to his knees. And with world-weary sighs, Peadar and I follow suit. Shivering in our sodden clothes despite the heat from the bonfire.

The hare steps forwards and removes his mask, revealing the man underneath. With an ear-splitting grin, Oscar Pierce says, "Fáilte to the SoS, little apprentices."

It takes everything in me not to say *I told you so* to Keefe, who stares open-mouthed at his so-called friend.

"You gobshite. How can you stand there and smile knowing what you put us through? How could you keep this a secret from me!?"

Oscar shrugs.

"Sorry, bud. Rules are rules. Couldn't tell you until you passed the tests and proved yourself worthy of the knowledge."

While Peadar whispers loudly to anyone who'll listen, "I knew it was him."

Oscar gives him a dubious look in return. He raises his hands for everyone to settle down. "Nineteen apprentices were tapped to take part in the second initiation test. But only seven of you made it to the Stone of Fáil by midnight."

Am, what?

"Did he just say we touched the Stone of Fáil?" Brigid whispers to me.

"Yes, you did." Oscar replies, clearly having heard her. "This is the Stone of Fáil or 'stone of destiny' as it's sometimes referred to in English."

My gaze flicks from the oblong block of limestone protruding from ground and back to Oscar.

"But that's impossible. The Stone of Fáil is kept on the Hill of Tara, in County Meath. All the way over on the other side of Ireland. How can that be the Stone of Fáil?"

"It's simple really," Oscar replies as if he's having to explain himself to a child. "The stone currently standing on the Hill of Tara, is a fake."

Peadar sucks in a breath. The assertion clearly not having landed well with him. But Oscar continues despite Peadar's discomfort.

"A very long time ago, the SoS arranged for the real Stone of Fáil to be moved to a private island in the middle of Clew Bay. The exact island you currently find yourself on, secretly purchased through a series of shell companies. The general consensus was that the stone would be safer here and that's why it was moved in the dead of night, with the general public being none the wiser."

"You stole the Stone of Fáil and left a fake in its place?"

I can hardly believe what I'm saying.

Oscar shakes his tightly shorn head.

"Not exactly. You can't technically steal what already belongs to you. We merely took full possession of it."

The dozen or so other black-robed SoS members encircling us nod their heads in agreement.

"Explain," Keefe says, his tone brooking no nonsense. "And while you're at it, what's with the creepy animal masks?"

"Oh, these?" Oscar says, looking down at the hare mask clutched in his hand as though he'd forgotten it was there. "It's a tradition dating all the way back to the Celts and the heyday of the Tuath Dé."

"The Tribe of the gods?" I sputter, recognising the old Irish term.

"Yes," Oscar replies. "That is the more literal translation, however the Tuath Dé were not actually Gods but rather, a group of people highly skilled in certain practices. Renowned throughout the land for their wisdom. Making them... a kind of advisor, if you will, to the ancient kings of Ireland. The Tuath Dé were the origins of what we, the Society of Solicitors, became. In fact, the Tuath Dé were the ones who originally brought the Stone of Fáil to Ireland."

"Hold on," Brigid interjects. "I thought the stone of destiny was supposed to have ended up in Scotland. And don't they have a different name for it?"

"They call it the Stone of Scone," Keefe replies. "Which they still use to crown their monarchs in the UK."

Oscar smiles. "That is indeed what they believe. Because God forbid, they're using a fake stone to coronate their Kings and Queens."

Laughter erupts from the other SoS members while the drenched apprentices beside me gaze back at them with mounting unease.

Keefe runs a hand through his hair and blows out a long breath.

"That doesn't explain why you abandoned us on the top of a freaking mountain or how you even got us all up there in the first place!?"

Oscar perks up at that question.

"I imagine the last thing you remember is standing in the members' bar at Blackhall, yes?"

Dawson and the other Bebb Gwyn apprentices nod while Peadar shifts uncomfortably beside me.

Oscar gazes at each of us, until his eyes finally land on mine and he simply says, "magic."

And he actually winks.

"Oh, feck you!" Keefe shouts and in sheer frustration he throws a handful of sand at Oscar which he skilfully dodges. "I've had just about enough of this shite."

"You don't mean that," Oscar replies breezily. "Each of you are now members of an ancient secret society with one fundamental principle at its core. That the law applies to all, without exception."

I let that sink in for a moment, wondering where he's going with this.

"The SoS was originally formed to promote and provide justice for our people and advise the ancient kings of Ireland. We have safeguarded and passed on the sacred knowledge of the Tuath Dé to those who have shown themselves worthy to learn it. To wield its power."

"Well, that explains the cryptic 'knowledge is for the worthy' line they've been parroting," I whisper to Brigid who grins wryly back at me.

"My fellow apprentices, would you like to know one of the most closely guarded secrets in the entire world?"

Keefe leans back on his heels, his interest piqued once more.

"How do you think we got each of you from Blackhall, all the way across the country to the top of Croagh Patrick in a matter of hours?"

Silence greets Oscar's question as we shift uneasily in the sand. Eventually the silence is broken by Dawson.

"By car," he ventures.

"Correct," Oscar replies, "plus the assistance of some off-road vehicles. But shouldn't you have woken up while in transit? I mean the modes of transportation used to place you at your starting positions were not quiet by any means. Why didn't you wake up?"

"Because you drugged us."

Brigid's voice is a knife that cuts through the thick silence.

"Just like you did the night you held us captive in St. Michan's crypt. I woke up in bed the next morning wearing the same clothes I'd worn to Blackhall, with no memory of how I got home."

Oscar shakes his head.

"Incorrect. I promise we did not drug you."

An uncomfortable, weighty silence descends on the beach as we sit with that statement.

"Come on, are you going to make me say it again?"

Oscar continues to goad us into giving him the answer he wants. Until eventually, with a dramatic huff, he gives up and throws his hands into the air.

"We did it using magic."

We all just sit there in silence until the looks of bewilderment on the other apprentices' faces morph into fear. With slowly dawning realisation, we come to accept that we've trapped ourselves on an island in the middle of Clew Bay with a mad man. Or a society of them, judging by the fact that none of the other masks are bothering to correct Oscar or call him out on his bald-faced lie.

I look at the currach boats sitting idly on the beach and calculate the likelihood of reaching one and hauling it into the water before Oscar or one of the other masks can stop me. Brigid catches my eye and it's clear she's thinking the same thing.

Is this what happened to Muriel?

My heart beats rapidly against my chest at the thought. Was she lured to this tiny, remote island and murdered? Did they dump her body in the sea and wash their hands of her? Is that why her bloated corpse visits my nightmares? A restless soul lost at sea. Attempting to call out for help. Trying to come home.

Oscar turns to his henchpersons, the sow and salmon, who, I don't fail to notice, have yet to remove their masks and reveal their identities.

"They still don't believe me," he says to them with a slightly perplexed expression on his face, as though we're the unreasonable ones. He tries one more time.

"The SoS can be traced back to the wise men and women of the Tuath Dé who advised the kings of Ireland. But they were not just advisors, they also practised an ancient form of magic.

"The Tuath Dé brought the Stone of Fáil to Ireland, the same stone each of you touched on the night of a full moon. And there was a reason for that. It's because the Stone of Fáil has special properties."

Despite my better instincts, I'm listening.

"On the night of the full moon closest to All Hallows' Eve, when the veil between our world and that of the spiritual realm is at its thinnest, the Stone of Fáil is thought to be at its strongest. And by touching it under the light of the full moon, you gained the ability to practise an ancient form of magic. Congratulations!"

He looks around the circle as if expecting to hear whoops of excitement from the apprentices gathered before him. Instead, we look everywhere but at the crazy man preaching about the pagan ritual we've unwittingly gotten ourselves caught up in.

Jaya even pushes herself up from the sand and strides purposefully across the beach to the nearest boat. Muttering under her breath about lunatic lawyers operating on zero hours of sleep.

Oscar shakes his head and says, "There's always a runner."

He turns to us, lifts his right hand to his chest, and feigns offence.

"You still don't believe me? Then let me show you."

He pulls a piece of parchment from his robes and scribbles something down using an expensive fountain pen. He takes out the brass stamper I saw him use in Blackhall bar and places it down on the parchment. He nods at the sow and she does the same.

The impact is instantaneous.

Jaya, the wayward apprentice, turns full circle and kneels down between Dawson and Finley.

Dawson touches her gently on the shoulder and asks, "Why did you come back?"

Jaya turns to him and in an oddly flat voice she replies, "I changed my mind."

Oh, feck.

The rest of us are well and truly perplexed by this development. Brigid is the only one brave enough to speak.

"Good one, Oscar," she says adopting a light, playful tone, so at odds with the gravity of the situation we've found ourselves in. "But if you're able to wield magic, then why don't you levitate off the ground and fly us all home?"

Peadar and I laugh but it's a weak, uncomfortable sound.

Oscar grins and says, "Now you're asking the right kind of questions. And the answer is simple. Because, in the Society of Solicitors, our magic is more of the mental variety rather than of the physical. Which unfortunately means no levitating for you."

Peadar raises his hand as though he thinks we're in some sort of nightmarish classroom.

"How can we practise magic?"

Oscar claps his hands.

"Another great question. You, of course, need a certain object to practise magic."

Peadar perks up.

"You mean a wand?"

"Even better. It's called a matrice. But it's probably easier if I show you how it works."

Masked members of the SoS approach the bonfire carrying nineteen wooden boxes, each no bigger than my hand.

"Fiadh Whelan."

I jump when Oscar calls my name. The other apprentices eye me curiously as he holds up a small mahogany box. I rise cautiously to my feet.

"You have been tested and found worthy of learning the knowledge the SoS has guarded for over a millennium. Apprentice, step forwards, accept your matrice, and indenture yourself to the SoS."

I place my hand on the polished box and tentatively lift the lid. Inside lies a round, cylindrical piece of mahogany wood. It curves elegantly inwards before broadening out where a round, brass stamp sits at its base. But the stamper is blank. No image embossed upon it. And beside it lies a piece of parchment, the same texture as the one I found in Muriel's bedroom.

"Read the parchment," Oscar says. "And if you consent, execute the deed of indentures with your matrice and let those gathered here tonight bear witness."

I unroll the parchment to read the letters written in spidery calligraphy.

I, Fiadh Whelan, having been tested and found worthy, hereby acknowledge and agree to become an apprentice of the Society of Solicitors. To be bound by and adhere to their code of conduct for so long as I shall live. May all who read this Deed bear witness to my seal.

For as long as I shall live... hold on, what!?

"Place your dominant hand over the matrice and drip the candle wax onto the deed."

Oh, I don't know if I want to do this anymore.

I glance back at Keefe, worry lining his face as he watches me, and I make the mistake of turning back, only to find myself looking directly into Oscar's piercing gaze. There's a silent plea in the dark depths of them. A raw, untamed desperation illuminated by the moonlight.

Muriel. I'm doing this for Muriel.

Wary, I take out the red candlestick, shove the wick into the bonfire, watch it catch flame, and let the red wax drip onto the parchment. Heart pounding against my ribcage, I press my matrice against the hot wax. And the eyes of the other apprentices are on me as I remove my matrice to reveal the seal of a deer stamped on the parchment.

Oscar picks it up and holds the paper in the air so the gathered masks may see. The SoS members hold their palms out flat in front of their bodies, like the pages of an open book. "We welcome the deer into our ranks."

What the hell does that mean?

Thoroughly bewildered, I stumble back to Keefe and the others.

While my eyes drift to the embossed image of a deer that has suddenly appeared on the brass bottom of my matrice. I sit back down, still reluctant to refer to whatever I just saw as 'magic'. The rational part of me rebelling at the very idea of such a fantastical concept despite everything I've seen and endured.

Oscar brings the other apprentices forward and though there is some negotiation over the terms of the deed, mostly from Keefe, time otherwise progresses quickly.

Brigid's personal seal is revealed to be an image of a sheep. Keefe's is, lo and behold, a swan; and Peadar's personal seal is that of a horse. Which fits considering the way he galloped across the beach earlier. Jaya's seal is a robin, Finley's seal is a hedgehog, while Dawson's seal is a snake.

Brigid, in particular, looks very pleased by this revelation.

"It turns out there is justice in the world after all," she chuckles darkly.

When the last apprentice has accepted their matrice and sealed their indentures, Oscar turns to face us once more.

"You're all likely wondering what exactly your matrice is, other than some old-fashioned piece of stationary. So let me explain. By placing your hand on the Stone of Fáil, you opened yourself up to being able to wield the matrice you are holding in your hand. And the wax you dripped onto the deed is no ordinary, run-of-the-mill sealant wax. It is made of resin extracted from the *pinus sylvestris*. Ireland's only native pine tree which died out thousands of years ago except, that is, for the few remaining pines the SoS continues to cultivate secretly within the Burren. And it was that wax that revealed the animal emblem for your personal seal."

Brigid glances from me to Oscar and asks the question I've been wondering.

"What does a magic matrice have to do with how you got us all the way to the top of a mountain?"

"It's simple really," Oscar says, rather infuriatingly because none of this is simple. "We drafted the deeds or... spell, if that word makes this entire thing more palatable for you, on a piece of parchment. The terms of which stated each of you were to fall unconscious for a period of three hours. I then executed the deed by affixing my personal seal and another member of the SoS witnessed the 'deed' by affixing their own."

"So, you're saying the matrice can make anything we write... become true? Like a magical deed..." Peadar mutters staring at his matrice in awe.

"A dark deed," Oscar corrects him. "And rather than refer to it as practising magic, we, the practitioners, view it as executing dark deeds that implement our will over our adversaries. So long as the deed is drafted with the requisite specificity and in accordance with strict signing formalities required for dark deeds to come into effect."

"This is a lot," I whisper. My mind whirling with possibilities as I rock back on my heels and ponder how this could be linked to Muriel's disappearance.

"So, basically, what you're saying is that the SoS are magic practitioners who can control minds and make people do or believe whatever they want?"

Oscar tilts his head and considers my words.

"Yes. Subject to certain rules and limitations. But I can see some of you are already too tired to fully grasp what I'm saying and I have no intention of explaining myself twice. I will discuss this further at Blackhall on Friday afternoon. Don't be late."

Oscar claps his hands and the other SoS members start packing up their things.

"For the time being, keep your matrices close at all times and enjoy your trip home."

The sound of a motor roars in the distance and five speedboats pull up to the island. Brigid lends me her arm and together we hurry to get as far away from this insanity as possible, but not before I see a mask throw twelve matrices onto the bonfire.

And as I watch the Costelloe, Nettleford, and Ingram apprentices' chances of wielding the power of the Tuath Dé go up in flames, I can't help but wonder who the lucky ones in all of this are.

Them or me?

14

—·—

PRIORITISATION OF COMPETING WORK STREAMS

"You lot don't realise how easy you had it."

The sow grumbles to the salmon.

"When we woke up in the oratory one year ago, they'd taken our shoes. Alby and I had to trek down Croagh Patrick in our bare feet as if we were on some sort of holy pilgrimage. I couldn't walk properly for a month afterwards! I'm still scarred from the experience."

Alby, it turns out, is a burly second-year apprentice at Heron Early. I know this because he whipped his salmon mask off the moment we boarded the speedboat. And the unfortunate individual who was given a sow as her personal seal is Lucile. A petite apprentice I once saw order a skinny latte at the Heron Early canteen.

Alby straps on his life jacket while the driver checks the controls.

"The thing no one tells you about apprenticeships is that you have to be ready for anything. Absolutely anything. Whether it's an impromptu client meeting, a jaunt down to the Four Courts, or even a Tolkien-esque quest down a holy mountain. One of the older members of the SoS said that, back in his day, they weren't even given cloaks.

So, if you turned up to work that day without a blazer, tough luck. You'd just have to somehow make do."

Lucile, the sow, settles herself into a seat beside Peadar on the speedboat.

"I heard he got frostbite in his pinky finger."

Alby nods. "All we're saying is that you should be grateful to us. The people who came before you. We tried to make things better for the apprentices who came after us. Warm woollen cloaks, shoes, lanterns, and even life jackets in the currachs. These are the kinds of safeguards you shouldn't take for granted because we had to fight for them."

The frothy waves of the Atlantic Ocean lap against the speedboat's bow as the driver readies to take off. And it takes everything in my will-power not to push Lucile and Alby into the freezing water and ask how safe they feel then. I even open my mouth to say something to that effect but am saved the trouble when Keefe takes off his sopping cloak and throws it over Alby's head.

The burly man jumps in surprise.

"What's your problem!?" He shouts, ripping the salt-stained cloak away.

Keefe brushes some sand off his trousers before responding.

"They just don't make apprentices like they used to, do they? But tell me this," he says to an uncomfortable looking Lucile. "You faced the mountain last year, yes?"

"Yes...."

"And did you have to sail a currach boat that's so old the local fishermen wouldn't dare step foot in it through a stormy sea?"

Lucile has the good sense to look away while Alby mumbles "No, but..."

"Then consider shutting the fuck up. Sincerely, kind regards," Keefe adds with a huff.

The salmon and the sow stay quiet after that and the journey across Clew Bay that had seemed so long and arduous in the currach is over in minutes with the help of the speedboat. And when we reach the sandy shore, there's no sign of the Costelloe, Nettleford, or Ingram apprentices we left behind, so Brigid, Peadar, Keefe, and I follow Lucile and Alby across the beach to a country lane where two nondescript black cars are waiting to take us back to Dublin.

"What about the other apprentices?" I ask warily.

"They've already been taken home and sworn to secrecy," Lucile replies nonchalantly.

"And you're not in the least bit concerned they might tell someone about the secret society they failed to get into?" Keefe scoffs.

"First, solicitors are supposed to keep information confidential. It's kind of an important part of the job," Alby sneers. "And secondly, the SoS have their ways of maintaining secrecy."

That sounds ominous.

Keefe must think so too.

"Care to elaborate on that rather menacing statement?" He asks, but Alby gets into the first car without so much as a cordial farewell and slams the door shut.

"He's a cold fish, that one," Keefe chuckles.

Lucile at least has the decency to mumble, "See you at work."

"What?"

I halt beside a startled Brigid, certain I must have misheard her.

"It's three in the bloody morning. Why on earth would you think we're going back to the office? I'm going home to sleep."

Lucile shrugs her shoulders as she opens the car door.

"Very few people in Heron Early are members of the SoS. And, seeing as we're not allowed to talk about the secret society, its members, or tests, you don't have much of an excuse as to why you can't come into work in a couple of hours."

She gets into the car, pulls the door shut on our conversation, and drives away.

Peadar opens the door to our car and motions for me to get into the backseat.

"Don't worry, Fiadh. Corporate law firms aren't known for their work-life balance. No one will think it strange if you come into the office with dark circles under your eyes. They'll simply assume you had to work late."

Brigid hops into the backseat beside me.

"I don't think that's what she's worried about, Peadar."

"Do you drink coffee?" Keefe asks as he buckles the front seatbelt.

I shake my head. "No, I don't really like the taste."

I swear, they all stare at me as if I've confessed to murder.

"That's going to need to change," Brigid says and settles back into her seat. "Start off light with a latte and, someday, you'll work your way up to a few espressos a day."

The driver hands out some blankets while grumbling about it being "Eight days to All Hallows' Eve and already I have to ferry around drunk students who ruin my lovely leather seats with their wet costumes."

Ah, the driver must think we came from some sort of Halloween rave on the beach.

I dump my green cloak unceremoniously on the car floor and pull the blanket over my head. And I wake up a couple of hours later when the car stops outside my flat in Dublin. The sun barely risen in the sky. I close the door quietly, leaving Peadar and Brigid fast asleep in the backseat while Keefe walks me to my front door.

My landlady's curtain flickers when we pass. The black beast of a cat gazes down at us from where it's perched on the windowsill. It watches as I slip my key into the lock. Keefe clears his throat as if he has something important to say.

"Look, even if the snake didn't deserve our help, I'm really glad you saved Dawson."

I try to ignore the warmth his words give me and I opt for sarcasm to hide my true feelings on the matter.

"Thank you, swan man. Your approval means the world to me."

He chuckles to himself as he walks back to the car.

I close my door, drop the keys on my desk and throw my battered and bloody brogues into the bin. Completely drained of energy, I hobble into the shower and let the hot jets imbue my tired limbs with some life again. With relief, I watch the sand, dirt, and bits of seaweed float down the drain.

Finally, I allow myself to think about Muriel and the events of the past two days. And in the privacy of my own home, I let myself cry great, heaving sobs that wrack my body. I grieve for the hard choices I had to make while the chill wind from the mountain still howls in my ear. While the bleak, suffocating depths of the ocean still press on my lungs.

I place my palm against the shiny, pink bathroom tile to remind myself I'm no longer stuck on the mountain or drowning in the sea.

I sink down and pull my knees to my chest and let myself grieve. For what Muriel must have gone through when she was forced to face the mountain. To cross the stormy sea. To sink or swim in order to survive. For all of the text messages I brushed off, too engrossed in my own life to ask if she was okay and realise she wasn't.

Eventually, I turn off the water and reach for an old towel the landlady left me. The well-worn fibres nearly strip the skin from my bones and I luxuriate in the harsh feel of it as I towel myself dry.

Afterwards, I rub the mist from the mirror and stare solemnly at the woman reflected in its surface. Haunted, red-rimmed, brown eyes ask if I'm closer to finding Muriel or one foot deeper in a grave of my own making?

Mindful of the time, I throw on a plain black dress and walk to work.

The red bricks of Mornington House loom before me.

It's just gone nine in the morning when I pass the reception area, the staff members already busy fielding calls, and look over at the illustration of Lucifer on his never-ending descent into hell. I trek up the ornate stairs, scan my ID card, and take a deep breath as I wander down the corridor to the M&A department.

The floor hums with activity. Multiple printers churn out documents and the PAs are already hunched over their desks, typing furiously. I attempt to slip by unnoticed, but I must have used up all of my luck last night because Una sees me and her fingers freeze above the keyboard.

"Buach was looking for you last evening."

"Thanks," I mumble and scuttle into my mercifully empty office.

Buach's suit trousers are strewn over his chair indicating he hasn't arrived at the office yet. I sit down at my minuscule desk, switch on my computer, and blanch when I see the number of unread emails in my inbox. It appears we were granted access to the Project Puzzle data room last night. And the email notification arrived just after we left for Blackhall.

Feck.

"You've seen the emails?"

I jump, startled by Keefe's presence in the office doorway.

"I'll take that as a yes," he says and runs a hand over his face.

He looks as tired as I feel.

"Joyce wants us to come to her office now," he continues. "She's fit to kill us for disappearing last night and not staying late to work on the acquisition."

I scramble from my chair and follow him out the doorway and then double back to grab a pen and paper. My heart thundering in my chest.

"But we left after five in the evening and we weren't granted access to the data room until seven pm."

Keefe shakes his head. Genuine concern for me gleaming in his eyes.

"I wouldn't use that excuse if I were you. People here don't work the usual nine-to-five hours. Corporate law firms expect you to drop everything and prioritise the deal until the moment a client says pens down. If you get a solid eight hours' sleep when there's a deal going on, that's considered a good day."

We walk along the corridor towards Joyce's office.

"Wait, how do you know she's in bad form this morning?"

"Because I have the pleasure of sharing an office with her," he responds with a roll of his eyes.

There's a beep and Brigid scurries through the door. She tucks her silk shirt into a houndstooth pencil skirt.

"How annoyed do you think Joyce is?" Brigid asks as she attempts to smooth down her auburn hair.

"For not doing the job we were hired to do? Pretty annoyed, I'd say." Keefe huffs as he opens the door to Joyce's office and Peadar, who is already seated inside, angles his head at the spare chair in the corner of the pokey room. Brigid takes the chair, Keefe sits down at his desk, while I hover awkwardly by the door.

Joyce ignores us and continues to abuse her keyboard while my nose twitches from the stale smell of coffee lingering in the room. Three half-empty disposable cups are scattered across Joyce's desk along with countless documents. One particularly large legal textbook partially obscures a picture of a young girl with pigtails. She wears a navy school uniform and has the same raven hair as Joyce.

It must be her daughter.

Joyce continues to ignore us and taps away at her keyboard until things become so unbearably awkward I cough. Joyce raises a perfectly groomed eyebrow at me.

"Fiadh, can you give me a high-level overview of the documents contained in the Project Puzzle data room?"

Nuts.

I open and close my mouth like a fish out of water.

Joyce, sensing blood in the water goes in for the kill.

"Are there any red flags I should make the client aware of?"

I don't know. I was kidnapped last night. How was I supposed to have completed the due diligence review? But I can't say that because I'm not supposed to talk about the secret society of solicitors that is the bane of my life.

Eventually, my brain unfreezes and I manage to mumble a few words in my defence.

"My apologies, Joyce, I haven't had a chance to look into this yet, but I can prioritise it now."

It's the best response I can come up with on the spot and, out of the corner of my eye, Keefe looks impressed.

Joyce sits back in her chair. Deep frown lines cleave through her thick, ivory foundation.

"And what about the rest of you?"

"Plumbing emergency", "ill dog", "dental appointment," the others mutter in quick succession.

Joyce says nothing for a moment, distracted once more by her own inbox.

"Look," she says when her attention reverts back to us. "When you drop the ball on a project, it delays the deal timeline for everyone else. And our client pays too much money to accept any excuses from us. Una had to pick up the slack and work late when you lot wandered off. Please review the documents and let me know if you have any questions. Thank you."

We're dismissed.

Peadar is the last to leave her office.

"That could have been much worse," he says cheerily and waltzes down the corridor in the direction of his office. I nod my agreement and am on my way to pick up an oat latte from the canteen when Una sticks her head around the corner.

"Buach wants a word with you, Fiadh."

Of course he does.

Keefe throws a sympathetic look my way and with a heavy heart, I walk on leaden legs to whatever fresh hell awaits me in that cold, inhospitable morgue, Buach calls an office. It actually feels as though my blood turns to ice when I press a clammy hand down on the handle and step into my own personal hell.

Buach's suit trousers are no longer hanging over the brown leather chair and are instead, presumably, on his person.

At first, Buach says nothing. His meaty fingers hover above the keyboard while his icy eyes pin me to the wall.

"Take a seat, Fiadh. You and I need to have a chat."

I half-fall into my chair, my legs no longer capable of functioning properly. I glance at the closed door. I can't decide if I'm grateful no one will hear how he's about to speak to me or if I'd rather they did.

A lone seagull breaks the oppressive stillness of the office with a shrill squawk from its perch on the windowsill. I've never been more grateful to be able to hear something else over the thrum of my own blood pulsing in my ears. To feel less alone in this inhospitable office. But Buach gets up and pulls the window closed.

Trapping me alone with him once more.

He settles back in his chair and fixes his disapproving gaze on me.

"I can't believe I have to say this to a Heron Early apprentice, but it's completely unacceptable that you left the office while your team was busy working on a deal. Now, I'm not sure where you've worked before, but let me tell you how things are done at this firm."

I wish I could vanish into thin air and simply cease to exist.

"Project Puzzle is the firm's biggest deal this year. And Hades Partners is one of my most important clients. So, let me spell things out for you. When your associates are working late, you work late. An apprentice on my team should never leave this office until they've asked each and every other deal member if they require any assistance. Have I made myself clear?"

I nod numbly. But I can feel the telltale prick of tears in the corners of my eyes.

"Good," he grunts and turns back to the documents on his desk but he's not done yet. "It's obvious to everyone you're not cut out to be a transactional lawyer but, for as long as you're an apprentice on my team, I expect you to prioritise my work and to do it to the best of your ability."

I feel so small.

Not able to stand being in this room a moment longer, I get up from my chair, open the door, and close it quietly behind me. Una watches me pass by her desk and whispers something to her colleague. I ignore them both, focus my attention on the floor, scuttle down the corridor, push the door to the bathroom open, and, finally, I let my tears fall.

15

THE REGISTRY OF DEEDS

"When common law is unable to fairly resolve a dispute, equity may provide a remedy to avoid an injustice. And in such a scenario, the courts may look to the equitable maxims:

They who seek equity must do equity;

They who come to equity must come with clean hands;

Equity follows the law;

Equity acts personally;

Equity is equality; and

Delay defeats equity."

The lecturer turns from her projector and casts an appraising eye over the apprentices crammed into Blackhall's cavernous lecture theatre on a lazy, Friday afternoon.

"Can someone name an equitable remedy, please?"

I raise my hand.

"Restitution. It requires a defendant to give up a benefit wrongfully obtained. Because no one should be enriched by another's loss."

The elderly lecturer tilts her head to the side and considers my answer with a slight purse of her lips.

"That is the basic gist of restitution, yes. However, it would be remiss of me not to caution that there's more to that particular remedy than your succinct summary implies." She glances over at the clock. "But it's Friday afternoon and I'm sure you all have places you'd rather be. Let's leave it there for today. And at next week's lecture, we'll discuss the rest of the equitable maxims."

Peadar stretches beside me in his chair and yawns loudly.

"Thank God, it's Friday."

He gets up from the seat he's been wilting in for hours and I know how he feels. After Buach's tongue-lashing two days ago, the rest of the week passed in a caffeine-fuelled blur of document review. Every night, Peadar, Brigid, Keefe, and I fell into our beds and, a couple of hours later, we stumbled bleary-eyed back into Heron Early to do it all over again.

The joys of due diligence.

We pack up our books and shuffle past groups of apprentices gossiping and trading war stories about their respective law firms and the projects they've been staffed to. I savour the feel of the crisp autumn air on my skin while other apprentices ask Peadar about his plans for the weekend. They hum and haw over costume ideas for the All Hallows' Eve party next Wednesday.

I spot Keefe and Brigid over by the stone arch and give Peadar's sleeve a subtle tug. We have somewhere to be.

"Have you seen the new law module they've signed us up for?" Brigid says when we catch up to her.

Peadar groans. "Please don't tell me it's more equity."

"Fortunately, not," Brigid replies with a huff. "We've been enrolled in ardchúrsa cleachtadh dlí as gaeilge".

"Advanced legal practice Irish?" I ask. "Why?"

"That's the secret name the SoS are calling our clandestine tutelage," Keefe replies dourly, before glancing at his wristwatch. "And we're already five minutes late. Come on."

We hurry after him down the corridor. Worry eats away at my insides as I wonder what fresh hell awaits us. But Peadar has other things on his mind.

"We still haven't had a proper night out in Dublin. So, we are going out tonight, my friends. And you'd better prepare yourselves because it's going to be loose."

"I'm in," Brigid says with a toothy grin that disappears the second she walks into the members' bar and spots Dawson and the other Bebb Gwyn apprentices inspecting the whiskey collection.

"The latecomers have arrived at last," Dawson says snidely to Oscar who is dressed in plain clothing today. No hare mask or robes in sight.

"Please can we get this lesson over with? I have a pint of the black stuff waiting for me at a pub down the road and I'd hate to see it go to waste."

Oscar stares stonily at Dawson and points to the door.

"By all means, don't let me stop you. The exit is right there if you'd prefer to leave the SoS and re-join the ranks of the laity?"

Dawson, the smart snake that he is, remains silent and stays where he is.

"No? Then pipe down and follow me."

Oscar leads all seven of us through a side door and down a corridor hemmed in by crates of bottled beers and every spirit under the sun. He shifts one of the larger crates aside to reveal a broken sconce attached to the bare brick wall. He gives it a pull and a series of clicks ensue. I stare open-mouthed as a portion of the wall swings inwards.

Peadar whistles.

"Secret door, nice."

Oscar disappears into a dimly lit stairwell.

"Quick now," he whispers. "There should be no dilly-dallying outside the Registry of Deeds."

Cautiously, we follow him down the stone staircase. Oil lanterns hang from the ceiling and, as I trail my fingers along the dust-lined wall, I ask Oscar, "How are you here? I thought you're supposed to be on secondment at Hades Partners? Buach's most prized client. I'm surprised they don't have you chained to your desk."

Oscar pauses at the foot of the staircase. His eyebrows raised in surprise at my question.

"Ordinarily, I am. But I'm also this year's apprentice representative. And it's my job to teach you newbies the knowledge our society has guarded all these years. Lucky me."

Oscar pushes open a red door at the foot of the stairs and we follow him into a high-ceilinged room with rows of filing cabinets. It's basically a basement library. The smell of musty pages and candle wax gives it away. Shelves line every wall. Practically overflowing with dust-covered, leather-bound books. But when Oscar halts before an imposing desk, I nearly fall over. Because Una Bewley, Buach's part-time PA, with her thick glasses, severe bob, and disapproving aura, sits behind the desk, reviewing a stack of deeds.

I can't catch a break.

"Registrar, let me introduce you to this year's intake of SoS apprentices," Oscar says with a flourish of his hand in our direction.

Registrar?

Una glances up from her work with the annoyed expression of someone who's been interrupted from a very important task. She puts a delicate finger to her mouth, makes a shushing noise, and goes back to inspecting the deed in her hand. To my unending delight, heat rises to Oscar's cheeks at the rebuff. He hastily leads us down a stone corridor and into a classroom complete with desks, chairs, and chalkboard.

The room is chilly. With no visible sign of central heating, the only source of warmth comes from the oil lanterns hung along the wall. I pull my cardigan closer and sit down beside Brigid. While Keefe ignores the perfectly fine chair and plonks himself on the table to our left. He doesn't even bother to take off his wax jacket.

"Oscar, my supposed friend. Why don't I kick off this class with a couple of questions. A few soft balls like... what is this place, why did you refer to Buach Scannell's PA as the 'Registrar', and does the SoS not believe in electricity? Or do you prefer to live life on the edge by having lanterns in outrageously close proximity to vast quantities of highly flammable paper?"

Oscar chuckles and sweeps out his hands in a wide arc.

"Fáilte to the SoS where knowledge is only for the worthy and dark deeds are afoot."

That was clearly a rehearsed line and judging by the ear-splitting grin on Oscar's face, he's wanted to say it for a while now. Keefe rolls his eyes in response.

"This is the SoS Registry of Deeds where every dark deed must be filed with Registrar, Una Bewley. They say she's the best Registrar we've had in years. Her attention to detail is unrivalled. The Registry of Deeds itself is off the grid in every sense of the word. We don't want the administrative staff in Blackhall wondering why their electricity bill is higher than it should be. Because for anyone outside of the SoS, this place does not exist. There is no cell reception down here and don't even waste your time trying to access a wifi network."

Oscar moves to the front of the classroom and flicks Keefe's ear to make him get off of the desk and take a seat like everyone else. Keefe swats his hand away and pulls out a chair.

"I hope each of you brought your matrices to class today. Because if you look inside of the wooden box, you'll see there's a false bottom."

I do as Oscar instructs and pull out an expensive fountain pen. It's made of solid silver and even has my initials embossed on the side along with an image of two Irish wolf-hounds supporting the lady of justice. The words 'VERITAS VINCET' imprinted on the finial part of the pen. A glob of black ink stains my finger.

"The truth will win," Brigid mutters beside me. "For a secretive society, they have a rather odd obsession with the truth."

I nod silently in agreement as Peadar holds the fountain pen flat on the palm of his hand as though he's trying to weigh it.

"Is this a magic pen?" He asks, in all sincerity.

Oscar snorts.

"No, it's just a pen. But they're pretty slick, right?"

"Excuse me," Jaya says as she holds up a piece of parchment. "Is the parchment made of animal skin? Because if so, I'm flagging now that I'm uncomfortable using it."

Oscar waves her off.

"Years ago, that would have been a problem but, these days, it's made from wood pulp and cotton fibre."

Oscar folds his arms and gazes at all seven of us expectantly.

"Who here would like to know how to execute a dark deed and enforce their will over another person?"

All of the apprentices lean forwards in their chairs. Eager to lap up any knowledge Oscar is willing to impart.

"All you have to do is draft the specific terms of the hex on a piece of parchment, seal the dark deed using your matrice, and have a second SoS member witness the deed by affixing their own seal as well.

"And there you have it. Signed, sealed, delivered — and they're yours to control."

He walks over to the wooden lectern and places his hands on both sides of it.

"But if you take anything away from this class, remember; specificity is key. When you draft a dark deed, you need to be specific as to whom it should affect, for how long should it affect them, and what you want them to do or believe for the duration of the dark deed."

Huh. Law school did not prepare me for this.

"Hold on," Dawson says like a man who thinks this is too good to be true. "Are you saying that I can make anyone in the world do or think whatever I want?"

Now that's a terrifying thought. And judging by the shudder that goes through Brigid, she must think so too.

"Absolutely not," Oscar responds flatly. "First, as apprentices, none of you are authorised to execute a dark deed without the guidance of a more senior society member and, second, you have to be able to physically see the person who is the subject of the deed, in order to hex them."

Annoyed tuts echo around the small classroom.

"What's the point of teaching us about dark deeds if you're not going to let us execute them?" Finley asks, frustration leaking from his words.

"Because the SoS isn't going to unleash you on the world without training you first. And I encourage all of you to take the time to review the precedents stored in the Registry of Deeds. Familiarise yourselves with the clauses contained within the different types of dark deeds."

I stick my hand in the air and Oscar nods for me to speak.

"Why do you call them dark deeds?"

Like a switch has been flicked, immediately, Oscar turns more serious. Gone are the jokes and banter.

"Because executing a dark deed comes at a cost."

Keefe's hand shoots into the air.

"But under common law, ordinary deeds don't require consideration?"

Oscar pinches the bridge of his nose and to the class at large he says, "I ask you, is there anything more dangerous than a law student who thinks they know it all?"

A hint of colour graces Keefe's cheeks and I find myself feeling sorry for the swan man. Still, he persists.

"But you said executing dark deeds comes at a cost and consideration is essentially a cost."

Oscar gives him a long-suffering look.

"Tell me, Keefe. Does your standard, run-of-the-mill deed enforce your will upon another person?"

"Well," he flaps, "it does create a binding obligation."

Oscar crosses his arms stubbornly.

"Let me rephrase my question. Does a typical deed have the ability to make someone take a long walk off a short bridge?"

"No..."

"Then would you care to stop showing off," Oscar gestures at me for some unknown reason, "and let me instruct you in the proper execution of dark deeds?"

Dawson sniggers from his seat in the corner of the classroom.

"Keefe O'Kelly, once a swot, always a swot. And even more so in the presence of his lady-friend."

Now my face is turning red.

Keefe rolls his eyes and ignores Dawson.

"What's the cost of executing a dark deed, Oscar?"

Oscar stares back at him solemnly.

"A piece of your soul."

What!?

My sentiments are echoed by the other apprentices. Whispered conversations break out all around and, in Dawson's case, curses that don't bear repeating.

"Calm down!"

Everyone ignores Oscar. Brigid even looks like she's about to walk out the door and never come back.

"Sit down," Oscar shouts at her and eventually, the noise dies down. "Did any of you ever consider where the word 'hex' comes from?"

Silence greets his question, which is answer enough.

Oscar picks up a chalk stick and writes on the blackboard:

H + execute = <u>hex</u>ecute = to hex

"To enforce your will over another person is to hex them and the cost is a piece of your soul. That is why we call them dark deeds."

Peadar asks the question I personally, want an answer to.

"Let's say, hypothetically speaking, of course. That some of us, might prefer to keep our souls intact? And that, having learned the price of performing this magic, one or two of the others would like to rescind their indentures of apprenticeship to the SoS?"

Oscar glowers at him, which causes Peadar to hastily add, "Not me. I'm totally committed to the cause and the quest for truth and justice. However, whether I even had a soul to start with is debatable. Meaning, that I may unfortunately be of no use to you. But Dawson over there is definitely having doubts."

If looks could kill, Peadar would be dead on the floor from the death stare Dawson gives him.

Oscar rolls his eyes, utterly unperturbed.

"I know it sounds awfully dramatic but look at it this way. Your soul is essentially your energy force. An unquantifiable willpower unique to each individual. And before you run screaming from the room, it's not as finite an energy source as you may think. And you'll be glad to hear, you have a lot of willpower."

Peadar nods as though this makes perfect sense.

"Think of your soul as an energy source found deep within yourself. You draw from that well every day and, if you take too much, you risk depleting it and burning out."

Brigid remains in her seat, but she doesn't look convinced.

"Is there a way to replenish the well or soul or whatever mixed metaphor we're using?"

Oscar grins.

"Rest, exercise, laughter, reading a good book, petting a puppy. Whatever works for you. How one replenishes their energy and rejuvenates their soul is unique to each individual."

I suppose this sort of makes sense.

"Is the cost of executing each dark deed the same?"

"No. Some deeds are darker than others and exact a higher cost from the executor and their witness. Some things are harder to make people do or believe and require more energy from you to exert your will."

That doesn't sound good.

"And why do you need two people to affix their seals? Why isn't one person and their matrice enough?"

"Because when a witness affixes their seal, they lend a small part of their own soul to strengthen the magic of the deed. And it reduces the likelihood of any SoS members using their powers for nefarious purposes. The fact that we need another SoS member to agree to witness our dark deed reduces the risk of a member going rogue. That and the fact that every deed has to be registered with the Registrar and made available for inspection in the Registry, should any SoS member wish to review its terms."

Dawson drums his fingers absentmindedly on the desk in front of him.

"But let's say, in a strictly hypothetical situation, someone was to execute a deed and not have it witnessed. What would happen?"

Oscar says nothing for a moment, as though considering his response.

"There are three likely outcomes. In the best-case scenario, the hex simply wouldn't work. Or the dark deed could partially come into effect with unexpected consequences for both the executor and the subject of the deed."

"And what's the worst-case scenario?" I ask tentatively, already dreading his response.

Oscar responds with barely more than a whisper.

"The dark deed could drain the entirety of the executor's soul from their body and kill both you and the subject of the deed. So don't do it."

He points his finger squarely at Dawson.

"And if the reasons I listed aren't enough of a deterrent, executing an unsanctioned dark deed could get you struck from the SoS register. Remember, there are checks and balances on our power for a reason and any member of the SoS found to break its rules will find themselves hauled before a tribunal of investigation led by our society's most senior members, the Council of Hons."

My heartbeat quickens. Is this what happened to Muriel? Did she break the rules and the SoS excommunicated her?

"Now, if there's nothing else, I plan on enjoying my weekend. Class dismissed."

The room is a cacophony of screeching chairs and hushed conversations as the apprentices rise from their seats.

I see my opening and take it. I hurry from the room before anyone can stop me and duck behind a large bookshelf. I peek my head out again, only once the sounds of the departing apprentices' footsteps fade up the stairwell.

Not wanting to draw Una's attention, I tiptoe to the back of the Registry and pass row upon row of filing cabinets. The dark clings to the old-fashioned drawers, the teak wood warped from years of use. I place my hand on a brass handle and pull. The cabinet makes an alarmingly loud creak as I pry the stiff drawer open. The smell of dusty, old parchment wafts up from the ancient deeds stacked inside.

I pull out the closest deed. The parchment so old it could disintegrate in my hand. The spidery writing is faded and the edges worn away. But from a quick perusal, I see the terms refer to the transfer of Mornington House.

But that isn't what I came here for.

I rush along the cabinets and hope surges within me as I look for the letter 'H' and eventually I find it. Hazarding a guess that the newer cabinets will house the most recent dark deeds, I pull open a drawer and riffle through parchments from the past two years. But when I get to the bottom of the bundle, my heart sinks because there's no deed of indentures executed by Muriel Hunt.

The disappointment feels bitter on my tongue.

"You know…"

I jump and slam the drawer shut.

Keefe O'Kelly leans against a nearby cabinet, his gaze fixed on the drawer I just closed.

"When Oscar told us to peruse the Registry, I don't think he meant for you to do it on a Friday afternoon."

I try my best not to look shifty as he walks closer.

"Find anything interesting?" He asks. And despite his feigned non-chalance, I can tell he's more curious than he's letting on. I know the swan man far better than I'm willing to admit.

"Not really," I reply breezily. "Although, I found the dark deed that was used to force the previous owner of Mornington House to transfer the freehold to Heron Early's partners."

I offer this tidbit of information, knowing a curious mind like his will lap it up.

"That is rather interesting," he murmurs. His fingers twitching with the need to peruse the terms of that deed himself. "I wonder what other secrets are hidden down here."

I shrug my shoulders as if to say 'who knows' and walk away. But much to my annoyance, Keefe glides after me. I can never seem to shake the swan man off. Somehow, he has become a near-constant companion during this tumultuous apprenticeship.

"What are you doing down here?" I ask, hoping my nosiness will scare him off. I've come to realise he doesn't like answering questions about himself. For a man who loves nothing more than to stick his beak into other people's business, he shies away from talking about himself.

"I just learned that I have the ability to hex individuals to do or believe whatever I want," he grimaces. "How could anyone walk away after being given the key to this treasure trove?" He gestures to the Registry of Deeds and its rows of cabinets in all of its shabby glory.

I shrug, unconvinced. Each to their own, I suppose.

"This place is unbelievable," Peadar says, sticking his head around the corner.

I sigh. So much for my covert investigation.

"What are you looking for?" I ask him, deciding to give up on my quest for solitude.

Peadar rummages through a cabinet. His fingers disturbing the dust.

"I'm looking for the indentures we executed last night."

"The ones we sealed by the bonfire?"

"Yep."

He trots down another aisle. Keefe and I follow him.

"I want to see how long it takes them to file a dark deed."

He tugs open another cabinet and riffles through another bundle of deeds until he pulls out the one with an image of a horse on it. Peadar's personal seal.

"Here they are!"

And then an idea hits me and I push Peadar aside.

"Your deed is here, Fiadh!"

Peadar holds up my indentures executed with my deer seal. But that's not what I'm looking for. And after a couple of heart-wrenching minutes, I find it.

Near the back of the bundle is a dark deed signed and executed by Muriel Hunt. A red seal with the image of an owl embossed on it. I pull her deed of indentures free of the bundle, hold it to my heart, and nearly weep with joy.

She was here!

Muriel was here and she was a member of the SoS. This is irrefutable proof. I was right. I was right all along that the SoS had something to do with her disappearance.

A cough sounds from behind my shoulder.

"Who's Muriel?" Peadar asks.

"No one," I choke, inwardly cursing myself for not being more discreet.

Peadar looks less than convinced, but he must see the pained expression on my face and chooses not to pry. I'm grateful to him for it.

"Hey, come over here and take a look at this," Keefe whispers an aisle over.

I place Muriel's indentures back into the cabinet where I found them and walk over to Keefe. He's holding a piece of parchment.

"I thought Oscar said apprentices aren't allowed to execute deeds?"

He hands me the parchment. A deep frown marring his handsome face.

It's like the deed was dropped in water. The ink is so smeared, it's impossible to read. All we can see are two seals. A hare and a fox. Oscar and an unknown SoS member. The names and signatures at the bottom of the dark deed are so smudged, it's impossible to discern who the fox could be.

"What do you think this is?" Peadar muses.

"Impossible to say," Keefe replies.

But I know what it is. I feel it all the way down in the tattered remains of my soul.

It's a clue.

16

TO THE BAR AND NO OBJECTIONS

"You made it!"

Peadar waves me over to where he and Brigid are queuing to get into one of Dublin's liveliest pubs. I join them underneath a rainbow assortment of umbrellas suspended by wires running the length of the lane. It does a reasonable job of keeping the drizzle from ruining my makeup.

"Check you out," Brigid says and runs an approving gaze over my outfit while I tug at my low-cut velvet dress, uncomfortably conscious of how form-fitting it is. Brigid, on the other hand, has forgone her usual preppy attire in favour of a gothic-looking chic leather dress paired with a femme fatale lipstick.

"Who did you dress to impress, hmm?"

Thankfully, I'm saved from answering when the bouncer opens the pub door for some drunken patrons to stumble out onto the cobblestone street.

"Ugh, I hate trad music," Peadar says when the melody from inside the bar floats out of the open door. "I'd suggest we go somewhere else, but the other apprentices are already inside."

Brigid's mouth hangs open at his revelation.

"I'd be careful who you say that to, Peadar. I'm fairly sure anti-trad sentiment is reasonable grounds to have an Irish passport revoked. And you're wrong, by the way. The music they're playing isn't trad, it's actually Celtic fusion. It's like trad mixed with electronica. You can dance to this."

I let them bicker while I cast an appraising eye over the long line of poor souls, not at all dressed for the weather, queuing to get inside. But I can't see Oscar anywhere. And he's the sole reason I agreed to come out tonight. I need to question him about the dark deed we found in the Registry.

Oscar and the fox, whoever that is, tried to cover their tracks by making the terms of the deed illegible. And I intend to find out why. It's a wonder the deed made it past Una. Does she not inspect every dark deed that gets filed in the Registry? Or is she working with Oscar...

The bouncer waves us through and Peadar, Brigid, and I stroll into a dimly lit bar where countless familiar faces from Blackhall are already well into their cups. A group of women are sitting around plush couches with extravagant cocktails in hand. They pause their conversation to wave Peadar over and pose for a few pictures.

We shuffle past the ladies and stroll over to the bar where an impressive selection of gin is stacked in a pyramid under bright, neon lights. And while Peadar places our order, I scan the room for any sign of Oscar.

"Searching for anyone in particular?" Brigid says with a quirk of her lips. Her heavily mascaraed eye-lashes flutter with silent insinuation.

"Who do you think the other masked members of the SoS are?" I ask her in a blatant attempt to change the subject.

Peadar, having overheard my question, runs a hand through his slicked-back hair.

"I haven't really thought about it."

I'm not sure I believe him.

"But isn't it a strange coincidence that Una Bewley, Buach Scannell's PA, is the Registrar? Does that mean Buach and Joyce are members of the SoS as well?"

Brigid chuckles darkly as she pays the bartender.

"After the dressing down Joyce gave us for leaving work the other night, I sincerely doubt she knows anything about the SoS."

Peadar nods to one of the Nettleford lads over by the bar, a massive smile on his face before he turns his attention back to me.

"Judging by the stack of deeds we saw on Una's table, I doubt she even has the time to review every single deed that passes her desk. There's too much work for one person to do."

Brigid taps her fingernails to the beat of the music.

"On the topic of dark deeds, am I the only one who's not keen to lose a piece of my soul every time I have to hex someone? That cannot be sustainable over the long term."

Its my turn to laugh.

"Maybe that's why law firms have such high attrition rates. Perhaps the SoS will chew us up and spit out the soulless husks of our bodies once they no longer need us."

The other two do not find this funny.

"Nah," Peadar shakes his head as he hands out our drinks. "As long as we don't do anything to get ourselves struck from the SoS roll of solicitors, we're members for life."

Brigid twirls the straw in her drink thoughtfully.

"And what exactly would get a person struck off?"

Peadar shrugs.

"If they bring the society into disrepute, I guess."

I snort and the ice jiggles in my glass.

"A rule that vague means we could be struck off for doing almost anything."

Peadar sets his drink on the counter and raises his hands in a placating manner.

"You're looking at this all wrong. We are members of one of the most exclusive societies in the world and, if that weren't enough to put us in a good mood, it's Friday night, we're out on the town, and we're surrounded by other apprentices. And need I remind you, that solicitors are sexy as hell. So, chill out, let loose, and enjoy yourselves."

"What's this?" Keefe asks as he sidles up to us. A half-pint already in hand.

I can't help but notice he's looking well. Hair slightly ruffled, white shirt rolled up at the sleeves, his wax jacket nowhere in sight.

Brigid brings him up to speed.

"Peadar's trying to argue that solicitors are sexy. But I personally didn't suffer through years of study to have my physical attributes or perceived attractiveness tied to my career."

"Loosen up," Peadar says as he shimmies to the music. "Studying is sexy and books are hot. Lean into it and have some fun. Love, life, law!"

Brigid watches in horror as he proceeds to make the sign of a heart, an 'L' and opens the palms of his hands to mimic a book. And having said all he has to say on the matter, Peadar saunters onto the dance floor to join the Nettleford crowd.

Keefe takes a sip from his drink and remarks, "I sometimes forget there are twenty-six other people in our intake."

His gaze is fixed on a large group of apprentices merrily chatting together at the other side of the dance floor. I've seen some of them around the Heron Early canteen and a twinge of jealousy tugs at my gut. They look so happy and carefree. Utterly unburdened by the need to find their missing cousin. Unconcerned by the machinations of the SoS. And not one of them has to share an office with Buach Scannell.

They don't know how good they have it.

Brigid hands me another drink and, seeing as I still haven't spotted Oscar skulking amongst the apprentices, I ask her the other question that's been weighing on my mind.

"What happens to the people who fail the initiation test?"

She arches her eyebrows, clearly not having expected the question.

"Nothing, I guess. The Ingram apprentices didn't make it into the SoS and the four of them are over there doing shots by the dance floor."

Keefe nods his head in their direction and says, "I tried to speak to one of the Costelloe apprentices earlier, but they completely blanked me. There may be some lingering resentment on their end. Although, considering we nearly drowned trying to reach that island, perhaps they should be thanking us for taking the last boat."

Brigid blinks in surprise.

"Careful, Keefe. You're beginning to sound an awful lot like Dawson."

"Nonsense," Dawson says, as he leans over Brigid's shoulder and causes her to jump, spilling half of her drink on the sticky wooden floor. "No one can imitate a once-in-a-generation genius like me."

Finley, one of the other Bebb Gwyn apprentices, strolls over while Brigid pushes Dawson away, muttering about the need for personal space. Dawson gives her a quick smirk and turns his attention to Keefe.

"I hear you're living with Oscar, our tight-lipped apprentice representative, these days. Pray tell, what secrets has our SoS representative revealed to you? Because there's no way you haven't been pestering Oscar for information."

My ears prick up at this.

"Honestly, Oscar hasn't told me a thing about the SoS that you don't already know and, whenever I try to pull the smallest scrap of information from him, he fobs me off and says his lips are sealed."

Dawson pretends to hit an imaginary drum.

"Great pun, should have thought of it myself."

Brigid scowls at him.

"Dawson, no one here has forgotten how you sabotaged us on the beach. So why don't you slither off and go bother someone else."

Dawson rolls his eyes, but her comment seems to put Finley's nose right out of joint.

"You should be thanking him. Dawson basically carried Fiadh to the bonfire. If it wasn't for him, none of you would have passed that test."

Dawson puts down his empty glass and surprises me by coming to my defence.

"To be fair, Fiadh saved my life while you, my dear unfaithful Finley, left me to drown."

Finley stutters, at a loss for words. His face turns beet root red. But after an awkward moment or two, Dawson barks out a laugh and pats him on the back.

"Buy me a drink and all will be forgiven."

The two Bebb Gwyn apprentices stroll over to where Jaya is queuing by the bar. While Keefe is called over to down a shot with some of the Nettleford apprentices.

Brigid comes to stand beside me, her eyes on Peadar and the others making shapes on the dance floor. And out of nowhere she blurts, "It's kind of surreal, isn't it?"

"What?" I ask genuinely puzzled.

"The fact that every solicitor who completes an apprenticeship in Ireland has to attend Blackhall. Where we have to study, take exams, and qualify together. I mean look at them." She gestures to the impromptu line of apprentices that snakes its way over to a concerned bartender shouting, "Love, Life, Law, Shots."

"The solicitors' profession is like an odd sort of beehive. Each member is capable of wounding another with a stinging comment one moment and then, when the need arises, we have to be capable of working together with a singular, intense focus to achieve a common goal. It's bonkers when you think about it."

I smile at that because she's right. It is bonkers.

Peadar catches my eye from the dance floor and waves us over. I'm tempted to decline, but Brigid catches my arm and drags me down into the mosh pit of apprentices jiving to the beat of the music. Peadar at its epicentre. Moving like the lord of the dance himself. He's getting saucily close to the Nettleford lad. So, I resolve to be more like Peadar, plaster a smile on my face and dance.

At some point, long after the alcohol has placed me into a more jolly state where my worries seem far away, Dawson, of all people, shimmies up to me. I decide to take Peadar's advice and go with the flow. Love, life, law, right? And we dance together for a bit. He's actually pretty good. At one point, he even slithers on the floor like a snake. It's rather amusing. And eventually, I realise I'm not pretending anymore.

I'm actually having fun.

Dawson places his hands on my shoulders and attempts to draw me closer. His cologne is spicy. He tilts his head and leans down...

"Abso-fucking-lutely not."

I stumble back and, in my haste, I slip. Keefe catches my arm before I fall.

"The hell are you playing at?" Dawson shouts at him while I ungracefully regain my balance.

Keefe squares his shoulders and I swear to God, the swan man actually juts out his chin.

"Fiadh and I have something very important to discuss and, soz, but no snakes allowed."

Dawson's eyes dart from Keefe to me and for a moment, I honestly think he's going to deck him, but then he must change his mind. Because he simply smirks and walks away. And then I hear the whispers. Distinguishable even above the music. I sober up quickly and turn around. It feels like the entirety of Blackhall is staring at us. Had they been there this entire time, watching me dance with Dawson?

Oh God, did Brigid see?

I pull free of Keefe's grasp and storm off the dance floor. The former feeling of jubilation gone as though it had never existed. I'm crashing back to reality, and it's not an easy landing. I stride into the hallway, past the cloakroom and out onto the umbrella-lined lane.

The evening air greets me like an old friend. I welcome its cool embrace after the stuffy dance floor and at the end of the lane, fortunately a line of taxies stands ready to take me away from this nightmare.

"Fiadh."

For feck sake. I plaster my best stay-the-hell-away-from-me look across my face and stare him down. But it seems to have the opposite of my intended effect because he bites down on his bottom lip. Like he's trying not to laugh at me.

"Are you okay to get home?"

"Yes, Keefe. After all of two drinks, I still maintain the ability to instruct a taxi to take me home."

I walk away, only to turn back a moment later because I'm bloody annoyed about what he did. So, I walk right up to him and stare directly into his eyes. Those beautiful, bottomless eyes.

"In the future, consider asking for permission before you decide to intervene on my behalf."

But he just stares back at me with a stupid smirk on his face. Not in the least bit put out by my comment. And with an infuriating kind of calm, Keefe leans down, his eyes focused on my own, and whispers, "May I?"

Oh feck.

My eyes trail down his jaw, barely daring to breathe in his coconut cologne. But my body betrays me. And when my gaze wanders down to his lips, I feel my own part. My head tilts to the side and then he's there. His cold hands press against my cheeks, so at odds with the soft warmth of his lips. He increases the pressure of the kiss. Warmth radiates from him as I slip my hands along his shirt and feel the stiff cotton as my fingers lightly graze the surprisingly firm muscles beneath. His hands pull me in until our bodies are pressed against each other. With each movement he angles himself closer, sending a pleasant thrill through my frayed nerves.

And I stay like that, locked in his soft embrace until the pub door swings open and knocks me out of the trance I'd slipped into. And with a jolt, I'm back to a reality where I've just kissed my colleague. I blink and pull away. Catching the barest flicker of hurt in Keefe's eyes as I do. Suddenly horrified by what I've done, I turn away and flag a taxi. Keefe stays silent as I slam the door shut on whatever madness subsumed me.

And as I fly off into the night, I refuse to look back at the swan man I left behind.

17

In Good Faith

It's All Hallows' Eve and I'm stuck in Buach's office reviewing the latest draft of the Project Puzzle purchase agreement. The due diligence review has stalled and I have the office to myself. A large mug of Irish breakfast tea is steeping nicely on my dinky desk while I wait for the sellers to upload more documents to the data room.

I flick the last chunks of my sad egg sandwich onto the cement ledge, close the sash window, and bolt it shut. Outside, the sun sets over Merrion Street. The road is already backed up with commuters driving home to take their kids trick-or-treating. And as I take a swig of hot tea, sweetened with a spoonful of sugar, I watch a dozen zombies stroll out of the Department of An Taoiseach in search of a pint over at Doheny & Nesbitts pub.

Hurried footsteps from the hallway followed by the screech of the door handle are the only warning I have before Buach bustles into the office, mobile in hand. Without acknowledging my presence, he plonks his phone down beside a stack of documents and places it on speaker mode while he logs into his computer.

"You're making me look like a laughing stock," the disembodied voice on the other end of the line says. "Do Hades Partners not pay enough to have our deals prioritised?"

"Conn, you know you're a valued client to the firm. I came back to work the day after my first child was born so I could close Project Green for you. But the sell side are stalling on the sale of the publishing house. We need them to provide the remainder of the documentation. We can get a draft due diligence report out to you in the interim but we can't sign off on the finalised version until we receive answers to our outstanding questions. No counsel could, in good faith, advise you to sign a deal on the basis of the limited due diligence carried out to date."

"Buach, I need solutions not problems. This has become a bone of contention over here. The other directors want to switch legal advisors. Apparently, Phelim O'Kelly, the managing partner over at Bebb Gwyn, brought them out to dinner last night and went on about how his law firm can provide a more cost-effective service than Heron Early."

"And you know we appreciate..." but whatever Buach was going to say next is cut off.

"Stop with the excuses, Buach. Pick up the phone with the sell side's legal counsel and get it done. Enough is enough. Word on the street is the sellers are reconsidering their position and the longer this drags on, the more likely they'll be talked around by the next highest bidder. We need to show we're committed and keen to close."

"Right you are, Conn. Message received."

"Then pull your finger out and get it done. And Buach?"

"Yes, Conn?"

"Please don't give me cause to call you again."

The line goes dead and Buach just sits there, looking down at his keyboard.

The silence is almost suffocating in its stillness. I pretend to read the document open on my screen. Afraid to type, to press my finger to the mouse, reluctant to even breathe for fear I'll catch his attention and remind him there's another person in the room. That someone else witnessed the way that man spoke to him. As if Buach isn't an incredibly wealthy and powerful person in his own right. As though he were nothing.

Like the way he treats me.

"Heard all of that, did you?"

My heart sinks even as my mind tries to conjure up a more hopeful scenario. One where this unfortunate situation melts the frost between us and creates some common ground. Because Buach clearly knows what it's like to work for a short-tempered taskmaster.

"I'm sorry he spoke to you like that."

Buach huffs out a laugh, rubs his eyes, and sits back in his chair.

Every nerve in my body is on high alert while I try to pre-empt what he'll do next. How he'll react. How I can limit the fallout from the situation and attempt to keep my career and good standing at this law firm intact.

"Rather than be sorry, which is utterly unhelpful to me, could you tell the other apprentices that I'd like to speak to them in the meeting room?"

The muscles in my neck are so tense I'm surprised they don't snap when I flinch at his verbal rebuke. I turn back to my monitor and shoot off an email relaying Buach's message. Feeling like my head is underwater. I get up from my desk and clutch my pen and notepad to my chest as if they're an anchor that will save me from getting swept up in the tempest of Buach's vitriol. As for the man himself, he just sits in silence and stares out at Merrion Street while a lone seagull perched on the windowsill stares in at the man, warm and dry in his luxurious office.

The door closes behind me with a soft click.

I walk down the corridor, past Una who's elbows deep in a pile of documents and disappear into the kitchenette. I attempt to calm my frayed nerves by box-breathing but the reflection in the kettle catches my eye. My face is pale and drawn, my eyes are red-rimmed. At a cursory glance, I look like someone who's done a few too many late nights. And it doesn't help that I spent every spare hour I could eke out riffling through the Registry of Deeds in search of anything that could help me figure out who the fox might be.

"Are you okay?"

I sigh. Somehow, the swan man always appears when I least want him to.

With a flick of my fingers, I turn on the tap and reach for a glass of water. I bite the inside of my cheek in the hope it'll keep the tears at bay. It has the desired effect.

"I could ask you the same question."

Keefe's face is drawn and his normally pristine shirt is creased. I take a steadying gulp of water and swallow a painkiller. He gives the packet of tablets a pointed look.

"Headache," I shrug.

He leans back against the countertop. "You've been avoiding me all week."

"I have not."

That is such a lie. I absolutely have been avoiding him. Mortified that I not only kissed my colleague but the most opinionated and arrogant apprentice I've ever met. Even if he is very good-looking. Objectively speaking, that is.

Keefe, for his part, seems to want to say more, but Brigid sweeps into the little kitchenette and pushes him aside.

"This is where you're hiding! That email you sent round. Any chance it's because Buach wants to thank us for all the late nights and hard work we've put into his deal?"

I grimace and shake my head, not trusting my voice to speak.

"I suppose that would be too much to expect," she says with a frown and we walk rather dejectedly down the corridor and into the meeting room. Inside, we find Peadar slumped in a brown leather chair, his forehead pressed against the table.

He looks miserable.

I pull out a seat while Keefe pours a glass of sparkling water. The bubbles fizz and pop and it's the only sound in the room until, with a quick glance at the open door, I whisper, "Hades Partners are not happy. They want the finalised due diligence report, yesterday."

Brigid leans back in her chair like the wind has been stolen from her sails.

"I've gotten no more than a couple of hours sleep every night since I was staffed on this project. Do you know how bad that is for your body? What more does he want from us? Our blood, sweat, and tears?"

Peadar reaches for a glass of water but his hand shakes and some of the contents spill onto the marble surface. "You slept? I've been awake for thirty-three hours straight."

Keefe takes a sip of water and wraps his arms around his stomach. His brows furrowed as though he's in pain.

"No one wants to have to pick your body off the floor when your heart gives out, Peadar. Do us all a favour and find an empty office, lie down under the desk, and take a nap."

Brigid nods her head in agreement.

"Not only would you be dead, but all your work would have to be re-assigned to another apprentice. Imagine how annoyed Joyce and Buach would be by the delay."

"That's dark," I say and open my notepad. "Although given the ridiculous amount of hours we've spent immobile at our desks while we review contracts, one of us suffering a blood clot isn't as far outside of the realms of possibility as it should be." I place my pen down on the table and turn to Peadar. "I heard one of the partners keeps a sleeping bag in his office. Maybe ask if you can borrow it?"

Peadar looks up from the table. His eyes are bloodshot.

"I'm so tired I've forgotten how to sleep. I don't know how much more of this I can take. I ache all over. My stomach is in knots and I feel nauseous. This is the worst I've felt in my entire life."

I fully expect Keefe to scoff at Peadar like he normally does, but the swan man surprises me. He places his hand on Peadar's shoulder and in a surprisingly empathetic fashion says, "I'm feeling pretty rough myself," and then he stops asks, "By any chance, do you also have a pain in your stomach?"

Peadar manages to nod his head even though it's pressed against the table.

"The pain comes and goes in waves. I've never experienced such a strong urge to curl into the foetal position and welcome death."

Brigid and I exchange a sceptical look before she walks out of the meeting room and I slide my painkillers across the table towards the two suffering men. Brigid returns a minute later and throws a small, rectangular hot water bottle at Peadar. The water splashes around inside its plastic container.

He blinks at it.

"What's this?"

She looks at me conspiratorially before turning back to Peadar.

"Hold it against your stomach for a couple of minutes and let's see if the heat eases your pain."

Peadar does as instructed while Keefe helps himself to a painkiller.

"Brigid, the insinuation that by showing our vulnerabilities and being open about our collective suffering it somehow makes us feminine is offensive. That kind of reasoning is reductive and quite frankly beneath you..." he trails off as Peadar lets out a low groan.

Brigid's hot water bottle clutched to his stomach.

"What kind of witchcraft is this? Keefe, get yourself a hot water bottle; it's really taking the edge off the pain."

I take off my dark, woollen shawl and wrap it around Peadar's shoulders.

"This will hide the telltale bulge of the hot water bottle."

Keefe runs a hand over his face.

"What's going on?"

"If I were to hazard a guess, I'd say someone in the SoS is messing with us."

My mind immediately turns to Oscar as the likely culprit.

"Hold on," Keefe starts and then pauses as he clutches his stomach again. His faced scrunched as he waits for the wave of pain to pass. "Do you think someone hexed us?"

"Well, this seems like too much of a coincidence for someone not to have hexed you both," I gesture to the two men who can barely function from the pain they're experiencing.

"Yep," Brigid says with a smirk. "Looks like someone hexed you to experience the joy that is dysmenorrhea."

"And what in the world is that?" Keefe asks.

Brigid and I answer at the same time.

"Period pain."

18

STET

The revelation sinks in and the swan man flips out.

"That can't be right. Oscar said members of the SoS have the power to force people do or think whatever they want. He said nothing about dark deeds making people physically ill."

I hand him another glass of water to help the painkillers go down. Although, now that I think about it, I'm not sure if painkillers can help against the effects of a dark deed.

"They can control minds, Keefe. And there are pain receptors in your brain. Therefore, it's not beyond the realms of possibility to assume they can make you feel like you're experiencing some sort of phantom pain."

Brigid snorts.

"Which is ironic because that's exactly what some women are told when they seek medical help for dysmenorrhea or even endometriosis. They're often misdiagnosed and told they're experiencing phantom pain and a proper investigation into the root cause of it is never carried out."

Peadar lets out another groan from where he's still slumped pitifully in his chair.

"I wouldn't wish this on my worst enemy." He glances up at Brigid and me. "How can you work like this?"

Brigid leans back in her chair and to me she says, "It appears Peadar has come to the realisation that many women in the workplace have to deal with this every month." She turns her disapproving gaze back on Peadar. "It is astonishing that you've never thought to ask that question before."

Rather than snap at him, I try to answer his question honestly.

"We throw maximum strength painkillers down our throats. Clutch hot water bottles when we think no one is looking or apply heat patches to our skin."

Brigid huffs and continues the long list.

"We use self-adhesive pulsating devices that stimulate the abdominal nerves in an attempt to confuse our pain receptors. While others take the combination contraceptive pill. That is, unless someone in your family has suffered a blood clot and then the doctors probably won't prescribe it to you. Instead, they might put you the progesterone-only pill instead. And God help you if you take that pill even a couple of hours late because then chances are that you've just bought yourself a one-way ticket to cramp town. First stop, low energy levels. Second stop, pain. With a potential layover in hormonal acne village where picture taking is not advisable."

The door slams shut.

"You're all here, good."

And even though every cell in my body urges me to run, I can do nothing but remain where I'm seated as Buach storms into the meeting room. Joyce close on his heels.

Buach pulls out a chair with brisk efficiency.

"I'm sure Fiadh has already informed you the client is not happy with the level of service they've received. The relationship has been strained since a former apprentice, who went by the name of Muriel Hunt, messed up the original deal term sheet and left the rest of us to clean up her mess."

Underneath the desk I clutch Muriel's claddagh bracelet. I have to literally bite my tongue to remain silent.

"As far as Hades Partners are concerned, the due diligence is taking too long and I'm not inclined to disagree."

His beady eyes rove around the room and settle on the shawl wrapped around Peadar.

"What in the world are you wearing?" He says with a scowl but, before Peadar can hazard a response, he cuts him off. "Never mind. Your choice of clothing is the least of my concerns today."

He reaches forwards, unscrews the cap on a new bottle of water, and pours himself a glass. "Why don't I let you all in on a little secret."

The others lean forwards while I press back into my chair.

"The client doesn't really care about your legal due diligence report."

I blink, startled by this statement. Of all of the things I'd expected him to say, that was not one of them and, by the confused expressions on the others' faces, they weren't either.

"The only people who really care about a legal due diligence report are us, the solicitors and the insurance providers. Do you know why that is? One of the key functions of a DD report is to pinpoint any red-flag legal risks the buyer will face if they purchase this publishing house. But unless there's a multi-million-euro lawsuit, a governmental or regulatory investigation, or antitrust concerns, chances are that Hades Partners aren't going to be particularly concerned by the issues we flag in the report."

Peadar raises his hand tentatively into the air.

"Then why bother engaging expensive solicitors to carry out a legal due diligence review on the target at all?"

Buach steeples his fingers on the table.

"Because it would be too risky not to. A sophisticated buyer, such as a private equity house, could not in good conscience deploy the dry powder fundraised from investors to acquire a multi-billion-euro asset without having first engaged an elite law firm to pore over the legal affairs of the target. To have us put in place all of the customary warranties, indemnities, and any other legal documentation necessary to limit the risk to the buyer."

Silence, thick as a Blarney Woollen Mills blanket falls over the room until it's broken by shouts of "aaaarrrrghhh" as a Viking Tour Bus rolls down Merrion Street. The guide loudly encouraging his passengers to scream like raiding Vikings as they pass the governmental buildings located across the road from our office.

Buach walks over to the window and mutters something about needing to investigate their licence to operate.

Meanwhile, Joyce capitalises on Buach's distraction to speak for the first time.

"Unfortunately, the client would, in all likelihood, prefer for us to simply rubber-stamp the transaction and have Heron Early face the risk and repercussions, should we be found to have failed to fully review the legal affairs of the target. But we cannot rubber-stamp this transaction because we must adhere to our regulatory body's high standards of conduct."

"So here's the inconvenient truth of the matter," Buach says as he walks back from the window and sits down. "You have to strike the right balance between being commercial enough to meet the demands of powerful clients, while also upholding the strict standards our own professional regulatory body places upon us."

Keefe shoves his glass away from him and speaks up.

"That sounds like a nearly impossible balance to achieve, so I assume the client is going to be left unsatisfied because, at the end of the day, we have to perform our role to the high standards required of us."

Buach rubs a hand over his face and casts an annoyed look in Joyce's direction.

"Where do you find these apprentices? They don't have what it takes to survive in corporate law I mean would you look at him. That one over there looks like he's fit to cry," he says with a wave of his hand at Peadar, who does appear rather glassy eyed, slumped over in his chair.

"Look," Buach says, laying his hands flat on the boardroom table. "It's been a long day and I was up late last night with a sick toddler at home. I don't have time to hand-hold apprentices who should be savvy enough to perform the tasks they were hired to do. Or did you mislead us during your interview process and the reality of the situation is that you can't actually do this job?"

This earns him a sharp look from Joyce, but she remains silent.

Buach casts an annoyed glance at his watch.

"You've had long enough to check for skeletons in the closet. It's time to hurry the hell up so we can finalise the transaction documents, close this deal, and get paid when the funds flow."

Peadar, the bright and irritatingly optimistic apprentice who can normally light up a room with his enthusiasm, slumps, grey-faced in his chair. His outlook dimmed. Even Keefe, ordinarily so fierce in his convictions, stares bleakly at Buach. And I see myself in them. The girl who hides in the corner, terrified that even the slightest provocation will upset this angry, man with far too much power over our careers. Because at the end of the day, a word from him in the right ear – and I won't be hired on qualification. A lacklustre reference from him – and I may never work in another law firm again.

Is this how he treated Muriel when she was his apprentice?

And for the first time since I stepped foot in Heron Early, I'm no longer afraid of Buach Scannell. No, that feeling is replaced by a red-hot rage that burns through my veins and overpowers the internal voice that advises I proceed with caution.

"How dare you."

My voice is steady and unwavering.

"Excuse me?" Buach's response is a deadly whisper that threatens severe reprisal.

Fuck the repercussions.

I clench my trembling hands under the table where no one can see them. But my gaze is unfaltering.

"Your little temper tantrum. The point of it was to whip us into shape, right? To get the adrenaline pumping and push us to get this deal over the line. Regardless of the impact on our mental and physical health."

I wave a hand at Peadar who looks so unwell, he might throw up.

"And perhaps, if you undermined us enough, we'd doubt our own capabilities and work twice as hard. Because that's what your strop was really about, yes? In a competitive services market where each of the big law firms pitched for the mandate to advise on one of the biggest deals of the year, you won the work by agreeing to a fixed fee.

"And now we're caught between a rock and a hard place, because you'll have to answer to the rest of the partnership for staffing four apprentices to this deal, only to write off our billable hours and tank our respective utilisation rates. Metrics that will be looked at unfavourably when bonus season comes around and decisions are being made as to whom to keep on and whom to cut. All because your prized client, who treats you abominably by the way, bullied you into doing it."

Angry, purple veins protrude in Buach's neck. He pushes back his chair and stands like an Aberdeen Angus ready to charge. His beady eyes promise retribution.

"Now you listen to me, you little miss…"

"Don't speak down to her like that."

Brigid points a perfectly manicured, albeit shaky, French nail at Buach.

"Everything she said is true and you know it."

Buach takes a different tact with Brigid. He visibly takes a deep breath and, in a more reserved tone, replies, "I would have thought the granddaughter of a former partner would conduct herself with a modicum of more decorum. Be careful, Brigid. Once your good name is tarnished, it's hard to get it back. And out of respect for your grandmother and her legacy at this firm, I'll pretend not to have heard you."

That was the worst thing he could have possibly said to Brigid Hughes.

"That doesn't sound like much of an apology," she says and rises to her feet. "And if we've made such a terrible mess, then I guess we'll just have to tear it all down and start from the beginning, won't we?"

She picks up a coatrack from the corner of the room and dumps its contents on the floor. Keefe saves his favourite wax jacket from the pile while Buach takes a step back. He looks worried. The situation has spiralled out of his control.

I see what Brigid has planned and gleefully pull open the meeting room door. I pluck an empty coatrack from the hallway and set my sights on the main thoroughfare of the M&A department. Where boxes upon boxes of the Project Puzzle data room documents, which we've spent days poring over, are stacked behind Una Bewley's desk.

Slowly, I re-adjust my hold on the coat rack. Knowing I'll only get one shot at this, I charge towards them like a jouster from the Middle Ages.

Startled by the noise, Una removes her earphones and looks up. She sees me charging towards her and falls backwards off the chair. I leap over her splayed legs, lunge for the epicentre of the boxes, and bring the pyramid of misery toppling down.

They crash open on impact and loose papers fly through the air. Brigid is at my side a moment later and swings her coat rack at the boxes like the Dublin secondary school's all-star hockey player she once was.

Out of the side of my eye, Keefe reaches out to try and stop me, but then appears to think better of it. He moonwalks back to the kitchenette, closes the door behind him, and watches the destruction unfold through the safety of the clear glass.

Peadar, on the other hand, attempts to calm Brigid down by making the kind of 'shushing' noise one would ordinarily use on a baby. This elicits the outraged reaction I would expect from a twenty-three-year-old woman. So, when Brigid hoists the coatrack threateningly in Peadar's direction, he wisely turns tail and clambers to the top of a nearby bookshelf where he watches the remainder of the rampage from a relatively safe height.

But we're not done yet.

Above Una's desk sits the Project Puzzle deal board where numerous structure charts of target entities, their subsidiaries, imprints, buy-side fund vehicles, and deal lists are painstakingly pinned to the board. Una must sense our intent because she crawls towards the notice board as though she plans to place her body between us and her precious charts.

But Joyce stops her. She places a hand on Una's shoulder as Brigid and I sweep past and in a sombre voice she says, "It's not worth it."

We bring the deal board tumbling down with a wild fervour I didn't know was in me.

The other PAs and paralegals shield their eyes as shredded paper and lethal thumb tacks spin through the air. And when it's done, Brigid and I stare at each other. Eyes bright, grins wide, and our shoulders heave from the heady exertion of acting on our baser impulses without any care for the consequences. Without any inhibitions.

And with each ragged lungful of air I pull into my lungs, I see my own reactions reflected in Brigid's face as if it were a mirror of my own. Eyes that were so bright a moment ago dim. Wide, toothy grins drop into a grimace and, slowly, we turn to survey the paper scattered about the open-plan area like a blanket of fresh snow.

And take in the chilly reception that awaits us.

Suddenly and, oh, so devastatingly, the red-hot rage that had fuelled my actions only moments ago freezes. And in its place, all I can feel is an overwhelming sense of shame at what I've done. I'm left to wonder when I became the villain of this story. Because I'd give anything to write 'stet' in the margins and put everything back to the way it was before.

Una cries softly. Tears spilling down her cheeks at the mess we've made of all her hard work.

Buach offers her a handkerchief, which she gratefully accepts; and with a sniff, she speaks.

"You lot have another thing coming if you think I'm printing all those bloody documents again."

19

PRIMA FACIE EVIDENCE

Brigid strolls into Keefe's kitchen wearing an ebony lace dress that belonged to her great grandmother.

It fits her like a glove, displaying her trim, neatly tapered waist. The long skirt trails around her ankles as Brigid opens the fridge and pulls out some drinks. She looks like she's just walked out of 1920s Ireland. As do I. It's the theme of tonight's All Hallows' Eve Party at Blackhall.

"Who do we think hexed us?" Brigid asks as she hands the mixers to Keefe, our self-appointed bartender for the night. He tips his old-fashioned flat cap to her in thanks. Then pours some peach schnapps into a large shaker over by the sink.

Peadar takes off his bowler hat and runs a hand through his hair. He visibly shudders at the memory.

"Not a clue. It was only after a nap that I felt like a fully functioning human being again, you know?"

"Yes, I do know something about that," I tell him and try very hard to keep the sarcasm out of my voice.

One of the other Heron Early apprentices walks into the kitchen, dressed in a pair of old-fashioned overalls. He gratefully accepts a cocktail from Keefe's outstretched hand with a tip of his hat and strolls back into the living room where the rest of our intake are getting ready for the fancy dress party.

"Here," Brigid says and hands me a cocktail. "I think you need this more than I do."

"Thanks." I take a sip of the supremely sweet concoction. "What is it?"

"Sex on the beach," she says with a wink.

I laugh. It's probably the first time I've smiled all day and swivel in my chair so I can face Keefe as he chops fruit over on the counter.

"How are you so good at cocktail-making?"

He looks up from slicing lemons and grins at me.

"Because I used to bartend."

"Where, in Dublin?"

"Nope, Galway. In a lively little pub near Salthill. I lived with my mother for the first year of college and it helped pay the rent."

Oh.

"On the mountain you mentioned your parents went through a bad divorce?"

Keefe picks up the mixing glass, clamps a lid on it, and shakes its frothy contents.

"That's putting it mildly. My father's a bully. Somehow, he manipulated my mother into signing all of their assets over to him in the separation agreement."

He hands Brigid a pink cocktail. His face grim.

She places her hand on his shoulder and says, "I'm sorry, Keefe. I had no idea."

"Don't worry about it," he says and takes an ice tray from the freezer. "Focus on yourself. After the stunt you two pulled this afternoon, you're lucky to still have a job. Thank goodness, Joyce managed to calm Buach down and told everyone to take the night off."

I place my drink back down on the counter.

"I still have a job because they need us to finish the deal. Otherwise, they would have booted me out the front door."

Peadar plays with his bowler hat, spinning it on the tip of his index finger.

"Fiadh's right. Buach's not going to fire any of the apprentices working on his big project. It would take too long to train someone else."

Brigid leans against the countertop, her expression thoughtful.

"But we're all agreed that someone must have hexed us? I mean, I don't usually fly into a fit of rage and annoy the paralegals so much they take an extra long tea break in protest."

I rub a weary hand over my eyes and mutter, "Una was on the war path the rest of the day. Telling anyone who would listen about the sorry state of the legal profession."

Brigid shakes her head regretfully and asks, "Why does Una bother to work for Buach? She's been with Heron Early for years. One of the other partners would gladly poach her for their team."

"And they'd risk falling out with one of the most powerful partners in the firm," Keefe grunts as he mixes the next drink. "Who do you think hexed us?" He asks, clearly intrigued.

Brigid throws a surprised look at him.

"Can't you guess? The same snake who sabotaged us on Croagh Patrick, of course."

"Dawson," Keefe says and places his shaker down on the counter.

But something isn't sitting right with me.

"What if it wasn't Dawson?"

"What do you mean?" Brigid half-shouts. "He bashed a hole in our boat. And a couple of days after he learns how to execute a dark deed someone hexes us. He probably did it to get back at Keefe for pulling Fiadh away from him at the pub last Friday."

I will my face not to go red and look everywhere but at Keefe.

"I don't think today was the first time we were hexed. I think someone has done it to us before."

Brigid looks at me sharply.

"When?"

"On Croagh Patrick. Don't you remember how each of us saw things that weren't really there?"

Brigid squirms in her high stool, looking distinctly uncomfortable.

"I just assumed I had a panic attack brought on by the high altitude."

I shake my head.

"No, I think we were hexed with a dread deed."

"A what?"

"The SoS call it a dread deed. It makes you experience or see the thing you dread most. Think about it. Keefe, you said you saw your father; and, Brigid, you thought everyone was talking about you behind your back. And I'm willing to bet that, as a result of past traumatic experiences, those are the things you dread most in the world. Am I right?"

"Hold on," Keefe says. "If that's the case, what did you see?"

I hesitate. I want to tell them the truth, but something niggles at me not to.

I simply whisper, "I thought I saw a dead body."

Keefe leans against the kitchen counter and considers my theory.

"But when we faced the mountain, Dawson didn't have a matrice. He couldn't have executed a dark deed because he hadn't yet touched the Stone of Fáil. How could he have hexed us with a dread deed?"

Brigid folds her arms.

"Who's to say Dawson didn't already know about the SoS? He's connected to everyone in Dublin. Maybe he bribed someone else to hex us."

I mumble that I need to use the bathroom and leave them to their debate.

I weave through the living room, where the male apprentices wear varying assortments of 1920s-style day suits or overalls while the female apprentices, much like me, have opted for long dark lace dresses, high-heeled boots and an assortment of black shawls to keep the October chill at bay.

In the hallway, I find three closed doors. Gently, I open the first door on my left and spot a familiar wax jacket strewn across a king-size bed. Quietly, I close that door and cross the hallway to the other. I knock but there's no answer. Praying the room is empty, I turn the knob and slip into Oscar Pierce's bedroom.

The first thing that hits me is how immaculate it is.

Books are stacked neatly on top of a high shelf. A plain reading desk with a lone yellow lamp is situated in front of a window with a view of Smithfield Square. The bed is neatly made with the corners of the sheets tucked in.

And for one blissful moment, I savour how the tides have turned.

I'm now the trespasser standing in Oscar's room. Ready to tear the place apart to find anything that might incriminate him in both Muriel's disappearance and the dread deed I'm almost certain he hexed us with on Croagh Patrick. But I need to find prima facie evidence to prove my case to the others.

I hear hushed voices in the hallway and freeze.

"I heard she's mental."

"Who, Brigid?"

Two female Heron Early apprentices must be chatting in the hallway. I don't know them well enough to determine who.

"No, her sidekick. What's her name... Fiadh! Someone said they heard her crying in the bathroom at work the other day. Apparently, her partner, Buach Scannell can't stand her. Complains to anyone who'll listen that she's brutal at her job. And did you hear about what she did this afternoon?"

"Ya, I did hear something about that. The PAs are livid. But I do hate to think of someone being upset at work. If she's having a hard time, I hope she talks to someone about it."

The other woman laughs.

"Fat chance of that. I heard the waiting list to see the Blackhall therapist is so long you'll be dead and buried by the time you reach the top of it."

I place my hand against the cold wall to steady myself. It feels like my chest is caving in, but I ignore it. They don't matter and neither do their opinions.

It's already eight p.m. and I'm running out of time.

I open Oscar's wardrobe. Ironed shirts hang from individual clothes rails. Jumpers stacked on the right and trousers on the left. And as the faint smell of fabric detergent reaches my nose, I'm struck by how much of a violation of his privacy this is. But any lingering doubts I may have about the ethics of what I'm doing vanish when I recall the expression on Oscar's face when I saw him sneak out of Muriel's bedroom five months ago. The same expression he wore the night we faced the mountain.

He's a man drowning in the guilt of his dark deeds and it's up to me to uncover his secrets.

I rummage through the drawers but find nothing out of the ordinary. And it's only as I consider giving up that the light flickers, causing me to look up. Then I see it.

The edge of a wooden frame, tucked away behind a stack of books. I reach for the photograph taken outside of Blackhall and stare down at four Heron Early apprentices I know all too well. Alby, Lucile, Oscar, and Muriel smile back at me. The salmon, the sow, the hare, and the owl.

They must have been friends.

"Oscar?"

Quickly, I shove the picture back where I found it, just as Keefe opens the door.

He squints at me in surprise.

"I saw the light on in the room. What are you doing in here?"

I paint an easy smile upon my face.

"Looking for the bathroom," and breeze past him to find Peadar and Brigid still bickering in the hallway.

They must have been at it for a while because Brigid is almost spitting with rage.

"Dawson used his newfound abilities to jeopardise my career. He cannot be allowed to get away with this."

"But what if it wasn't Dawson?"

Peadar's and Brigid's heads snap to me.

"Who else could it have been?"

Keefe watches me warily. The swan man sees far too much for his own good.

"What if Oscar was the one who hexed us?"

Silence. Then they each speak over one another, all at one, but it's Keefe who eventually wins out.

"Why on earth would Oscar do that?"

But I'm still not ready to divulge my suspicions about Oscar's hand in my cousin's disappearance. Especially given the disparaging way in which Buach spoke about Muriel earlier today. They probably wouldn't believe me even if I tried.

"How well do you really know Oscar?" I ask, turning the tide on the swan man. "How much do you really trust the person who locked us in a crypt?" I stare at Keefe incredulously.

"Why am I the only one who suspects him of hexing us?"

Keefe moves aside as one of the other Heron Early lads passes us in the hallway and shuts the door to the bathroom.

"Because there's no way Oscar would do that to me. Dawson, on the other hand, would turn on his own mother if he thought it would advantage him in some way. And I wouldn't be surprised if he convinced one of the other SoS members to help him hex us."

"Fine," I say and decide to take a different tack. "Bullies don't tend to go away if you ignore them. And a problem like Dawson will only get worse if we don't retaliate."

"Well, come on then," Brigid says, clearly impressed. "Sounds like you have a plan. What is it?"

She's right, I do.

I pull out two pieces of parchment I'd taken the liberty of drafting earlier. The others read the first piece of parchment and stare back at me with mixed expressions ranging from apprehension to excitement.

"Is that why you've been spending so much time down at the Registry of Deeds?" Keefe asks.

Like I said, the swan man is far too perceptive for his own good.

"Yes," I respond, somewhat grudgingly. Although it's only part of the truth.

"What is it?" Peadar asks and takes a step away from the parchment as if he's afraid he may get hexed by sheer proximity to it.

"The SoS calls this type of dark deed a gag order."

I hold up the first piece of parchment.

"Given that Dawson is the head of the party planning committee for tonight's festivities, I suggest we execute it when he walks on stage and enjoy the show."

"I like it," Brigid says with a grin. "Nothing like a bit of public humiliation to bring Dawson down a peg or two."

Keefe still looks unconvinced.

"And what about the other deed you drafted?"

I hold up the other piece of parchment.

"This is a veracity deed. When executed, it compels the subject to answer questions truthfully."

Brigid looks at them both, calculatingly.

"Personally, I preferred the gag order."

"Hold on," Keefe says and attempts to reach for the veracity deed but I pull it back to my chest before he can grab it.

"Who is it you intend to use the veracity deed on?"

Too smart for his own good.

"Oscar Pierce. And I need one of you to witness it."

20

EQUITY LOOKS TO INTENT RATHER THAN FORM

"Here's a radical idea. Why don't we enjoy the party and take a couple of days to think through any drastic acts of retribution?"

Keefe turns to Peadar and looks at him with something akin to respect.

"I'm surprised to say it, but Peadar has a point. There's no way I'm going to hex Oscar. I barely feel comfortable doing it to Dawson."

Brigid throws her hands into the air and leads us through a group of drunk Heron Early apprentices loitering in the living room. Once back in the quiet confines of the kitchen, she says, "Fine. We'll hex Dawson and leave Oscar alone for the time being."

We'll see about that but I keep my mouth closed and help myself to a glass of water.

"Aren't you forgetting something?" Keefe asks. "All dark deeds have to be filed with the Registrar. But as first-year apprentices, you're not authorised to execute dark deeds without permission."

"Dawson and Oscar did," I point out.

Keefe rubs his hands over his eyes like he has a headache coming on.

"And if the SoS ever figure out they did that, they could be struck off."

Brigid shrugs.

"You worry too much. If Dawson did it, that means we can too."

"So, what? You're suddenly fine with giving up a piece of your soul?"

Brigid shrugs. "I was going to have to do it sometime. Might as well get it over with sooner rather than later."

I try and fail to stifle a laugh.

"Aww, Dawson's going to be your first."

This earns me an immediate scowl from Brigid, while Keefe continues to try to talk us down.

"And what if you get struck off for this."

Brigid takes a sip of her drink before responding.

"How would the Registrar ever find out? Look, Dawson started this, so we're finishing it. We're simply taking justice into our own hands."

Keefe looks at her in disbelief.

"That's not a good thing, Brigid."

"Keefe!" Comes the voice of a lad from the living room. "We're leaving, come on!"

"Let's get going then," Brigid says and strolls into the living room. She comes back carrying four crudely carved turnips and hands one to each of us. Begrudgingly, I take mine and shudder. If I never see another turnip before the day I die, it'll still be too soon.

Keefe must share my sentiments because he turns to Brigid, a forlorn look upon his face and says, "Why do we have to dress up like we're living in a gothic version of 1920s Ireland? And please explain, what turnips have to do with our costumes?"

Keefe holds the purple root vegetable by the long, green-leafed stem that sprouts from its head like hair. The body of the turnip has been gutted like a pumpkin, with features hacked into it to resemble a deformed face.

It's truly horrifying to look at.

"Because we're supposed to be dressed like Stingy Jack," Peadar says as he pulls on his suit jacket.

I wrap a black shawl around my shoulders before Brigid leads us into the living room, a tea candle lit inside her turnip's gaping mouth. We follow the other Heron Early apprentices down the stairs of Keefe's apartment and out onto chilly Smithfield Square.

And together all thirty of us, black-clothed Heron Early apprentices, walk across the square with turnips clutched in our hands. Drawing surprised looks from superstitious locals who stumble upon us, on this foggy All Hallows' Eve.

Keefe and I pass under a flickering streetlamp, bringing up the rear of our little group, when Keefe turns to Peadar with more questions on his lips.

"Would you care to tell me, who exactly Stingy Jack is? Other than a man with an unfortunate nickname."

Peadar pulls his bowler cap lower down his forehead and obliges.

"A long time ago, a man called Jack walked into a pub. There, he met a well-dressed gentleman and invited him for a drink. They got chatting and when it came time to pay, Jack looked to his companion.

"Because Jack was known for two things around town. And the first was being as cheap as they come. But Stingy Jack was in luck because it was All Hallows' Eve, the night when the veil between the dead and the living is at its weakest. And the gentleman sitting before him was no ordinary soul. No, he was Lucifer himself, disguised as an ordinary man. But the devil, as you can well imagine, did not have money on his person. And all Jack had on him was the holy cross he wore around his neck and a turnip he'd stolen from his neighbour's field.

"Jack pondered their predicament and then the solution hit him.

"He told the devil to turn himself into a coin and Jack would use it to pay for their drinks. The devil thought this a marvellous plan and shape-shifted into a silver coin. But then Stingy Jack did the second thing he's known for. He played a trick on the devil and placed his silver cross on top of the coin."

We cross the road to Blackhall's iron gates. Keefe strolls beside me, looking confused.

"Why would he do that?"

Peadar opens the gate and we walk up the leaf-strewn driveway.

"Because it prevented the devil from changing back into his original form. And legend has it that Stingy Jack kept the devil's coin in his pocket alongside the holy cross right up until the day he died."

I'm invested in this tale and, when we pass under the old arch and walk towards the back of Blackhall, I ask Peadar to finish the story.

"Well, Stingy Jack had hoped that, by keeping the devil locked in his pocket, God would unlock the pearly gates of Heaven for him when he left this plane of existence."

"Did he?" Keefe asks as we approach the GAA pitch at the back of Blackhall.

"Quite the opposite. God had heard of what Jack had done to the devil and wanted no tricksters in Heaven. So, he cast him down to

Hell; and there, after all those years, Stingy Jack was re-acquainted with the devil.

"Free at last, Lucifer was ready for revenge. But the devil is as cute as they come. He plucks a burning piece of coal from the fiery pits of Hell and banishes Stingy Jack to walk the earth for all eternity. And legend has it that, if you look out your window on All Hallows' Eve, you might see Stingy Jack, holding the carved-out turnip he uses to carry the devil's burning piece of coal. The only light in the dark of his endless purgatory."

I shiver and pull my woollen shawl closer.

Before us, carved turnips line the length of the grass pitch. Their gruesome faces lit up by the candles inside, casting an eerie glow over the foggy field. A lone floodlight is focused on a stage erected at the centre of the pitch. Over a hundred apprentices crowded around it. They drink, chat, and dance while Halloween music pumps from the stage's speakers.

"Remind me to say 'well done' to the planning committee," I remark to Brigid. "I don't even want to think about how much time they spent carving faces onto all of these turnips."

The Nettleford lad, who I suspect may be Peadar's boyfriend, waves him over while Keefe, Brigid, and I gratefully accept a beer from a passing apprentice. Her long lace skirt trails in the wet grass behind her.

Brigid catches my eye and nods to where a group of lads are huddled by the side of the stage.

"There's the man of the hour himself."

And, true enough, Dawson is surrounded by the rest of the planning committee. Clad in a dark suit, dickie bow tied smugly at the front of his shirt and matching bowler hat on his head, Dawson takes the stage.

"Hello, Blackhall!" He shouts into the mic, riling up the gathered crowd who cheer and whoop back at him.

"Tonight is a very special night and do you know why?"

This elicits some shouts from the animated crowd as Dawson puts his hand to his ear.

"Yes, that's right! Tonight is All Hallows' Eve. When the absolute legend, Stingy Jack, is set to walk the earth."

He pauses dramatically.

"And what better way to pay homage to the man who did a deal with the devil himself and came out on top than to light it up tonight! Blackhall, make some noise!"

All of the gathered apprentices raise their turnip heads to the night sky and roar their approval.

Keefe turns to me, his eyes as dark as the sky above.

"Please say you've changed your mind. What you're about to do is against the rules."

I plaster a devilish grin on my face.

"Solicitors don't break rules. They simply interpret them in a manner that happens to favour their position."

Brigid steps in front of me and uses her body to conceal my hands from the stage.

"Don't waste any tears on Dawson. His fall from grace is long overdue."

I take out the folded piece of parchment. It reads:

I hereby compel Dawson Garvey not to speak for the duration of one hour, to commence immediately upon execution of this deed.

Signed and delivered as a deed by: Fiadh Whelan – the deer
In the presence of: Brigid Hughes – the sheep

I bring my matrice down and seal it with the image of a deer. Brigid does the same and witnesses it with the seal of a sheep. And we wait. Eying each other with anticipation as Dawson harps on.

And then it hits me.

It feels like someone punched me in the stomach. I slump forward, about to fall onto the dewy grass. Keefe catches me before I hit the ground.

"Are you all right?"

Brigid must have felt something similar because she grips my other elbow to hold herself steady. But the unpleasant sensation passes quickly and I'm left feeling a little drained of energy. Brigid also appears to have recovered.

"That could have been worse," she whispers in my ear. "It hurt less than I thought it would."

Meanwhile, it's clear to everyone else that something is wrong with Dawson. He opens his mouth to speak, but nothing comes out. Slowly the cheers die away and a woman nearby asks if he's having a stroke. Because Dawson just stands there, opening and closing his mouth like a fish out of water. It's mortifying for him and oh so satisfying to watch.

Brigid must feel the same schadenfreude because she can't stop herself from jeering at him.

"What goes around comes around, Dawson."

Both of us break down into cackles so loud they can be heard all the way from the stage.

I wipe a tear from my cheek just as Dawson's eyes land upon us. He knows what we've done. I can see it in the way his face twists with anger. A cruel contempt in his eyes. He drops his microphone and jumps down from the stage. Leaving an imprint in the soft, wet grass.

Bloody hell, I can't catch a break today.

Brigid tugs at my elbow and I look over to see Finley and Jaya separating from the rest of the Bebb Gwyn intake. They charge towards us, turnip lanterns swinging by their knees.

I take a step back, planning to run away, but Dawson is already upon us.

"Hey!"

Keefe shouts and shoves Dawson back.

Peadar and some of the other Heron Early apprentices hurry over as Keefe places himself between Dawson, Brigid, and me. And thank goodness, he does because Dawson's lost the plot. Nostrils flared, it's like he's gone to a dark place. He rips a turnip head from the hand of a nearby Ingram apprentice and flings it at Keefe, who manages to block the blow at the very last moment, by throwing an arm protectively over his head.

The turnip hits the ground, and the candle rolls out of its mouth where the flame dies on the wet grass.

The other Heron Early apprentices, already a few drinks to the wind, thanks to Keefe's cocktails, raise their turnips. And quicker than I would have thought possible, it's like the whole of Blackhall has split into factions. All facing off one another. A powder keg waiting to explode.

I take a deep breath and try to think of something to say. Anything to de-escalate the situation and cool things down. But then Brigid's voice rings through the tense silence.

"We know what you did, Dawson."

She raises her turnip and shouts, "May the punishment fit the crime," and swings it back in an arc a professional tennis player would be jealous of and smashes it against Dawson's shoulder. The hollow turnip explodes on impact. Bits of the root vegetable fly through the air.

And with the second shot fired across enemy lines, cries ring through the night as the other apprentices take the opportunity to settle scores and long-held grudges.

Retribution and retaliation are meted out in the form of turnips lobbed like grenades at members of competing law firms. One apprentice chases down another with a breathy threat.

"Watch me make a billable target out of you!"

While a separate apprentice swings her well ripened turnip like a baton at anyone unfortunate enough to cross her path.

"File this!"

Whack.

"Disclose this!"

Thunk.

"Read this!"

Wallop.

Jaya and Finley help Dawson up while Brigid heaves with excitement. Strands of her auburn hair fall loose from her bun and stream across her face. Her eyes burn with excitement. But that dies pretty quickly when an Ingram apprentice runs at us, full tilt. Full of righteous rage, she screams, "Heron Early, the pre-eminent Irish law firm, my ass!"

But thankfully, our would-be attacker is intercepted by another apprentice, who lobs a counter-attack turnip at her. The Ingram apprentice ends up tripping over her long skirt and lands in a heap in front of her attacker. And the other woman, in a voice so passive-aggressive I'll hear it in my nightmares says, "You told me you lost my book but, I saw it sitting in your office."

They've gone mad.

"We have to get out of here!" Keefe shouts.

I don't need to be told twice.

We stumble across the pitch alongside other apprentices attempting to flee.

Flap caps, bonnets, canes, shawls, and bowler hats lie lost and forgotten on the grass. And as we near the side-lines, we stumble upon another apprentice standing in the goal, a turnip held in each hand.

"Bill, bitch, bill," she shouts at anyone who tries to go home.

One apprentice breaks from the herd and charges ahead. Hoping to slip past without her noticing. She clips him on his ear and he goes down in a wildly dramatic tumble of limbs. His companion falls to his knees beside him.

"No, Jerry! You were going to bill three thousand hours. You were going to become a legend among lawyers," he sobs uncontrollably.

We give them a wide berth while someone else shouts, "Justice for Jerry!"

Screams ensue as more turnips are lobbed through the mist.

We rush under the arch. Turnips clutched close to our chests. Unwilling to part with our weapons until the battlefield is far behind us. We make it down the driveway and through the gates. Gardaí sirens wail in the night as we spill onto the street.

"Who called the police?" I gasp as we sprint over James Joyce bridge.

Peadar swings his turnip wide and throws it into the river Liffey. It disappears beneath the murky surface with a solemn splash.

"The residents must have heard our screams and presumed gangland warfare was to blame. We need to get out of here, now!"

We dump our turnips and, as they sink down into their watery grave, blue and red flashes light up the night sky as we seek refuge within south Dublin's maze of cobblestone side streets.

21

SEAL THE DEAL

We run like the hounds of hell are after us.

Peadar at the front of our group and Brigid by his side. Keefe grabs my hand when my high-heeled boots slow me down and together we dodge drinkers who ramble out of the pubs and onto the cobblestone side street.

"This way, quick!"

He shouts and I follow him. Content to be led for a change. Happy not to have to carry the burden of decision-making for one small moment. Because I am so weary; and tonight I did something very silly. And in doing so, I became a freer person than I've allowed myself to be in quite some time.

I wonder who this girl might be if I let her out for just one night. This version of myself I keep submerged beneath waves of heartbreak and loneliness that often overwhelm me. Who would she be if given the chance to emerge?

Brigid and Peadar race down a different street.

I pull on Keefe's hand and come to a halt.

"I need to catch my breath," I tell him breathlessly, as the others disappear around a bend.

Keefe walks back to me. A rumble of laughter spills from his lips and great, hearty laughter bubbles up from my own. The uncontrollable kind that has me bent over.

Tears stream down my face. My body releases the pent-up stress that has racked and ravaged it these past six months. That ate away at my soul from the moment Muriel went missing and I chose the path that led me past the gates of Blackhall and through the doors of Heron Early.

I stand up and Keefe is there in front of me.

Dark eyes stare deep into my own, right down to the ragged remains of my very soul. But I get the sense it's not the broken bits of me he sees, but something altogether more attractive and whole. Not the half-drowned girl within or the weathered, worn, and beaten woman on the surface; but rather, something that once was and possibly could be again. If I were to allow it. If I were to give up my vendetta and choose a happier life.

And, Muriel, forgive me, but in this moment, as Keefe moves closer to me and I sense the warmth of his skin, it's what I want most in the world. The promise of soft lips, whispered words, and something more.

He leans down.

"Ring, ring!"

Four bicycles whizz by. Their teenage riders dressed in tracksuits. Their faces concealed under pillowcases. Holes hacked out for their eyes and mouth. Eyebrows, moustaches, and other defining facial features have been sketched onto the pillowcases using thick markers.

A familiar wool hat, greener than the Irish flag, sits atop the head of the lead cyclist. While the second wears Peadar Ahern's black bowler hat. And as the bicycle boys speed down another side street, they're followed moments later by an annoyed Peadar.

"Give me back my hats, you hooligans!" He shouts and chases them into another cobblestone street.

"It's not every day you see fiddle faces."

Keefe turns to me, a perplexed expression on his face.

"The bed sheets those boys wore over their heads?"

I nod.

"Years ago, Irish children used to create those masks from discarded scraps of cloth they drew on. They called them fiddle faces. When I was a child, there wasn't much disposable income to buy Halloween costumes, so my aunt used to cut a few holes in a black plastic bag, stick it over my head, and tell me I was a witch."

Keefe walks with me to the end of the street, a concerned frown on his face.

"Was she not worried you'd choke?"

I shrug and pull my shawl closer against the chill October air.

"It was a simpler time."

"Well, I've had my fill of masks and concealed identities. Call me excessively suspicious but there's something inherently untrustworthy about an individual who needs to hide behind a mask."

I smile at him indulgently as we approach the Dublin bikes' stand. Two bicycles ready and waiting to be taken out.

"I don't know about you, but I can't remember the last time I rode a bike. Care to join me?" I reach out my hand to him.

He hesitates. "Don't we need helmets?"

"Absolutely. Do you have any to hand?"

"No?"

"Then we'll have to make do without them," I tell him as I back up the bike, put my foot to the pedal, and off I go.

I press down on the pedals and the streetlights speed past me. With a flick of the lever, I slip into a higher gear as I cycle across Wellington Quay and onto the Liffey boardwalk. The planks of wood clank beneath the wheels of my bicycle. While the brisk wind rips strands of hair from the tight bun at the back of my head.

Onwards I peddle until I pass the Ha'penny bridge on my right. Its railings a divine white under the light of the lanterns sat atop three magnificent arches. They banish the darkness that clings to the murky water. While a lone swan paddles into the soft glow before it disappears back into the night.

"Ring, ring!"

Keefe catches up to me. A devilish grin on his windswept face.

I laugh, feeling lighter than I have in a long time, and together we cycle past O'Connell Street. Where, despite the late hour, pedestrians lumber out of fast-food restaurants. Brown bags of savoury chips clutched in their hands. Salt stuck to the wrapping while vinegar drips enticingly from the edges.

Taxis zip past us.

We ride over water-logged potholes that reflect the glow of the overhead streetlights. Each jolt sends me forward in my saddle, but otherwise our progress is unimpeded. We soar through the misty road while the green traffic lights guide us home.

"Ring, ring!"

The bicycle boys fly by us with Peadar's hats still sitting atop two of them and disappear down the docks.

We turn onto Samuel Beckett Bridge and veer onto Pearse Street. The squeal of our rusty breaks echoes too loudly in the quiet space of Pearse Square. The shutters of the houses already drawn. The inhabitants tucked up in bed.

I park the rented bicycle outside of my flat and turn to Keefe who watches me from the saddle of his own. He looks handsome in his 1920s style suit. And still buoyed up from our night-time ride across Dublin, I ask, "Do you want to come in for a cup of tea?"

He smiles.

"Yes, I would."

I walk down the steps to the little red door of my basement apartment and leave the gate open for him to follow. I insert the keys with a well-practised twist of my fingers and the door swings open. Without looking back, I walk inside, fill the kettle with water, and place it on the stand to boil.

The front door closes with a soft click.

And as the faint hiss of boiling water reaches my ears, Keefe wraps his hands around my waist and turns me to him. Dark eyes envelop my own. They draw me to him with their intensity, a single brow quirked as he places a lone finger beneath my jaw. Tilting it upwards as he pauses. An unasked question brims in his eyes, in the arch of his eyebrow, quirked up just so. Little mannerisms I have grown to know so well in such a short space of time.

His face is like the open pages of a book. Both familiar and novel. I trail a soft finger down the ridge of his high cheekbone, marvelling at how his stiff exterior melts under my touch. His lips tilt at the edges and his spine bends towards me as we meet in a kiss that nourishes my tattered soul.

A soft sigh escapes me as we come together, and I luxuriate in the feel of him against me. And using the light from the streetlamp that flows through my front window, I slide the blazer from his shoulders and reach for the buttons of his shirt. One by one, I pop them open and walk him towards my bedroom.

His shirt flutters down and lies forgotten on the rug as he sits back and pulls me onto the bed. He lands on something hard, rolls over, and lets out a bark of laughter when he finds the pile of books I'd left scattered over the sheets. And with one hand on my back so I remain astride him, he deftly uses the other to grip the bedspread by its edges and pulls the books to the side. Treating them with the tender reverence they deserve.

When he's done, I push him down onto the bed that squeaks under our combined weight. My hands rove greedily over his bare chest while his fingers find the bottom of my dress and tug upwards. The lace garment brushes my skin as he lifts it over my head. My hair comes loose as I lower myself onto him and enjoy the warm feel of his skin against mine. My hands skirt lower until I find his belt and then I'm on my back. Keefe having arched his legs and unbalanced me. His form leaning over mine. Knees on either side of my hips. My hands free to do whatever I please, so I slide his briefs down his legs until he's forced to concede ground and roll onto his back once more. I tug the briefs free of his ankles.

He's up in a moment, unhooking my bra. His breath hot against my bare breast. The nipple hard from the cold night air and then he's there. Sucking, pulling, and teasing as I arch into him. I throw my head back in ecstasy and he grows hard beneath me. I writhe and rub against him. The feel of him against the light cotton of my underwear provides an unexpected and not at all unpleasant thrill.

And then I'm falling.

My head hits the pillow as he pulls my legs around his waist and tugs the underwear from my body. He leans down to kiss me. And we come together, harsher this time as I bite down on his lower lips. He groans, props himself up by his elbows, and the crackle of a wrapper being ripped open is amplified in my quiet, cosy, little bedroom. I use his distraction to bring his body closer to me. The soft weight of it, comforting and reassuring, while he lines his hips with mine.

One swift arch of my hips and then we are joined.

The sweet agony of the moment stretches out for as long as possible as I lean forwards and draw him to me. And then he's moving to a gentle rhythm that I do my best to interrupt. But after a few moments of this, I want more friction, more writhing, more pain. But he stays the course. He stills me with a well-placed hand upon my breast and bites. Not too hard, just the right amount of pressure, as I buck and my inner muscles seize joyfully.

He presses down on the bundle of nerves at my core and pleasure courses through my body. Keefe maintains the pace that has brought us to this point. A man who knows not to mess about when something beautiful is being created and we move together. My fingers grip the pillowcase as tension builds within me. And then he's there. Teeth lightly grazing the other breast until he pulls back and thrusts forwards. More forceful this time. The gentle tempo he had set gone. Replaced by something more urgent.

His muscles tremble from restraint and I give myself over to it. To the pleasure coursing through my body. I cry out as I'm overcome with it. Breaking around him as he arches his back and thrusts forward. Faster and faster. I turn to jelly beneath and then we're both falling. Him on top of me. A tangle of limbs with no beginning and no end.

Just us, the breath from our lungs, and the books by my bed.

Centuries pass and then he turns to me and says, "I wouldn't say no to that cup of tea, if it's still going?"

I laugh and roll out of bed. Searching for something to put on in the dark and stumble upon Keefe's shirt. I pull it on and roll up the sleeves. Stroll into the kitchen and turn on the kettle. I run my fingers through my hair as the kettle hisses. Sleep already tugging me back to bed.

Another long day of work awaits me tomorrow, but I shove that thought from my mind. I choose to focus on happier things while I carry two cups of decaffeinated tea into the bedroom. Steam rising from the large mugs.

Keefe has lit a candle on my desk and its flickering flame casts a long shadow over his face. He stares down at the picture of two little girls in their school uniforms who smile back at him.

"That's you," he says and points to me, "but who's that?"

He means Muriel.

My tongue becomes lead in my mouth. The thoughts I had so successfully submerged for the past couple of hours now bubble to the surface with vengeance. A hissing noise rings in my ears, louder than that of the kettle. I hand Keefe his tea and mumble, "It's my cousin. Careful, the tea's hot."

I walk over to the bed and place my mug on the bedside table. Carefully, I pick up the books and neatly stack them on the shelf. But Keefe is far too curious for his own good and plucks one out of my hand before I have a chance to put it away.

He places the candle on the bedside table so he can peruse its contents from the comfort of my bed. He props up a pillow and cracks the book open. His eyes wide when he realises the contraband I've been hiding at home.

"This is proving to be a night of many surprises. Why on earth do you have one of the precedent books from the Registry of Deeds in your room?" He asks me, chuckling as he leafs through the yellowed pages.

I shrug and try to pass it off as nothing as I slide in beside him and grab the book out of his hands.

"It makes for good bedtime reading. Puts me right to sleep."

He takes a sip of tea and watches me over the tip of his mug. Then, he plucks the book right out of my hand. My mouth agape at the audacity of the gesture done in the confines of my own apartment. He places his cup back down on the dresser and riffles through the book until he finds a suitable passage. He places his free arm around me and starts reading the mundane words aloud. I laugh at first and then lean closer to him as we peruse the arcane language until the candle burns low. The last thing I hear is the flame being blown out and I fall into the first nightmare free sleep I've had in six months.

Just us, the breath from our lungs, and the books by my bed.

22

OF GOOD STANDING

"What, in the name of all that is good and holy, did you think you were doing last night!?"

Joyce stares daggers at the first-year apprentices crammed into the Heron Early boardroom. Hungover heads on the lot of us. United in our collective misery, we face Joyce's wrath head-on. Black eyes and purple bruises bloom on some of the more unfortunate faces. While one particularly unlucky apprentice boasts a broken nose.

"The press got hold of the story!"

To emphasise her point she picks up a newspaper which reveals itself to be this morning's edition of The Irish Times. The heading on the front-page reads:

'The Turnip Turf War' — *'Competition amongst apprentice solicitors reaches terrifying new heights as turnips and fists fly on All Hallows' Eve'*.

Below the byline is a black-and-white photo.

It shows the back of a man's head that looks worryingly like Keefe. He wears a flat cap and holds a carved turnip in one hand while the other holds the hand of a young woman in a dark lace dress. A shawl is mercifully slung over my head, making it difficult to discern my features.

Still, I can't help but squirm lower in my seat while Peadar mutters darkly beside me about the bicycle boys and his stolen hats. Brigid sits on the other side of me. Her eyes glued to the table as Joyce continues her tirade.

"Each of you is a representative, not only of this firm, but of the legal profession as a whole. How you conduct yourself in public matters. You are supposed to be individuals of good standing in your community. Why is that necessary, you might ask? Because how the public perceives us matters. We are scholars who have dedicated our lives to study the laws that govern our country. Yet, as a result of your drunken and disorderly actions, you have brought the entire legal profession into disrepute."

She turns away from us to take a breath.

While she's preoccupied, Brigid whispers into my ear.

"Isn't anyone going to ask why it took only one wayward root vegetable to turn Blackhall into a turnip-fuelled fight club? Or care to wonder why we have so much repressed rage bottled up inside of us? Or ask what might be traumatising the future members of the legal profession they claim to care so much about?"

Or did we cause this, I ponder before turning to Brigid to voice my concerns.

"Is there any chance our dark deed backfired and somehow hexed everyone on that pitch?"

Brigid wrinkles her nose.

"I'm pretty stubborn but even I don't have the strength to strong-arm all of the apprentices into doing what I want. So no, I don't think we're to blame for this particular incident."

I shift uncomfortably in my seat as I look around the boardroom for Keefe. He's nowhere to be found.

A knot of apprehension forms in my stomach. Where is he?

Joyce pulls her shoulders back and continues her lecture.

"The firm is investigating the events that occurred last night. And when you leave this boardroom, know one thing for certain. Heron Early has a long, prolific past and a very bright future. One that cannot, and will not, be dimmed by a handful of bad eggs."

"More like rotten turnips," Brigid mutters under her breath.

Joyce stops by the door, her eyes fixed on Brigid who shrinks in her seat.

"Do you want to know the truth that no one else will bother to tell you? The Irish legal profession is a small one and all anyone of us really has in this world is our good name. You can spend your entire career building your reputation. And all it takes is one ill-conceived, reckless act to bring all of that good work crashing down around your ears."

I squirm uncomfortably in my seat. She's really laying it on thick.

Joyce storms off and the other apprentices filter out of the meeting room one by one. But I can barely move. The energy has been stripped from my bones and for a brief moment, I worry Dawson or Oscar may have executed another dark deed in my name.

But it's not magic that keeps me pinned to my chair. It's my own anxiety.

Since the first day I stepped foot in Heron Early, I've been out of my depth. Drowning under an insurmountable workload. Not able to see the shore with the ocean of documents standing between me and this deal closing. It's like I'm a broken piece of debris, lost at sea. Discarded and unwanted. I float wherever the tide takes me until the day comes when I finally dip beneath the surface. To lie forgotten and buried beneath the sands. The world above as lost to me as it is to Muriel.

Muriel.

I close my eyes. I'm here because of Muriel. I grasp onto that thought like a raft in stormy waters. And slowly, I drag myself back from the dark and resurface to find I'm alone in the boardroom.

Just as I was when I awoke this morning.

At some point, Keefe left in the night without a word. I woke with nothing more than two cold cups of tea by my bedside table. The only evidence, other than my discarded garments strewn across the floor, that he'd visited my apartment. That the night we'd spent together hadn't been some kind of fever dream conjured by my own overactive imagination.

With a world-weary sigh, I push my chair back from the desk and make my way down to Buach's office. I cross the M&A floor with sluggish footsteps. Una glances up from her computer long enough to glare at me. My eyes dart to the butchered structure charts cello-taped back together on the notice board and I lower them in shame. The sound of her typing follows me down the hallway to my office, where I find the door closed.

Buach is here. Wonderful.

I press down on the handle and force a smile on my face.

"Good morning," I whisper into the deafening silence of the room.

Buach's beady eyes track me to my desk while I do my best to still my thundering heart, take off my coat, and log in. Buach says nothing for a moment and looks down at the stack of documents piled on his desk. But I can tell he's not reading what's written in front of him. Because his eyes remain fixed firmly in place.

My breathing becomes shallow. The air I inhale not quite filling my lungs as despair overwhelms me. I glance at the door and wonder if I can escape the storm that's brewing on the horizon. If he'll call me back before I can get away. Before I can run to safer shores. Because he's the one in charge of this space, this office, and my career.

The negative voices in my head become louder as they whisper: he treats you badly because you don't deserve to be here. You're not good enough.

The man who commands this office like his personal fiefdom has been dismantling my confidence since the day they shoved me in here. An unsuspecting tribute to the altar of his particular kind of cruelty. For him to either whip into shape or flog to death.

From the moment I stepped foot in his office, he weighed my worth and found me lacking. An unwanted apprentice from the wrong family. A trainee without the right connections. Not exceptional enough to rise through the ranks. A body taking up space when there are so many others who would willingly step into this seat.

And now, I'm not sure I can find it in me anymore to prove him wrong.

"Fiadh, could you please send me the Share Purchase Agreement for Project Puzzle?"

I exhale a quiet sigh of relief.

It's a perfectly normal request and one I've prepared for. I spent the past week updating the warranties and indemnities within the SPA to reflect the findings from the latest due diligence review.

But there's something in the tone of Buach's voice that makes me pause. He's never spoken this politely to me before. As if I'm prey, he'd rather not spook before he's ready to pounce.

Why do I feel like I've stepped into a trap?

Pushing those thoughts aside, I scroll through the files until I come to the folder titled 'Transaction Documents.' But when I click into the relevant folder, I find it totally and utterly empty.

No.

A bolt of panic shoots through me. This can't be right. There must be some mistake. Clicking frantically, I exit that folder and search around the file space. Scrolling up and down, searching for another site containing the most important document in the entire deal. The SPA Hades Partners expect to receive today. But there's nothing there. As if the document I worked on never existed.

It's vanished.

My heart hammers against my chest and I pull up my inbox. I try to remember if I ever emailed the full version of the SPA to anyone and come up blank. No one had asked to see it before now. Fingers shaking over the keyboard, I scroll down and find messages from the other apprentices. Additional employment warranties from Brigid. Amendments to indemnities from Keefe. Permission to scale back the real estate protections from Peadar.

I stop. Take a deep breath. In through my nose and out through my mouth as cold sweat drips down my forehead. But my vision becomes narrower and darkness creeps in at the edges.

"You don't have the SPA ready, do you?"

I crack.

The tears I'd been holding back rush forward. Every shitty thing that has been said to me since I stepped into this office rises to the surface. A wave of grief that feels like an ache in my heart threatens to rip me in half. Yet, I just sit there and say nothing. Unable to save myself from drowning. Unwilling to reach for the shore.

Buach rises from his seat and I manage to mumble a few words in my defence.

"It was there. Drafted and ready to go. I swear it was there..." My voice trails off when he leaves.

I find myself alone and adrift. Utterly directionless except for an all-encompassing need to escape the confines of this building and catch my breath. Away from Buach, Una, Joyce, and the others.

The tears flow fast and freely down my face.

I rush past Una, push open the door, and hurry down the stairs. I'm about to high-tail it out the front door when the Paradise Lost picture hanging over the reception desk catches my eye. I come to a halt and stare up at Lucifer's fall from grace. Cast out of heaven to plummet all the way down to the pits of hell.

"Fiadh?"

Impeccable timing as always.

Keefe stands at the foot of the marble stairwell. Clad in his sea-weed-green wax jacket. His cheeks flushed from having just come in from the cold.

"Are you alright?"

There are so many responses I could give him. But I don't want to answer any more questions. Instead, I'd like some answers of my own. I point to the artwork adorning the wall.

"What do you think it means?" I ask him.

"The Paradise Lost illustration by Gustav Dore?" He asks with a confused glance at the drawing.

I nod. "Why did the partners choose to hang that particular piece of art in the reception area?"

He looks worried now.

"I'm not sure. Would you like to sit down, Fiadh?"

"I think they did it to send us a message."

That makes him pause.

"What... message do you think the partners are sending you through the picture?"

"That should we lose our good standing in this firm and fall from grace, may God have mercy on our souls. Because at any moment, anyone of us can be cast out those front doors."

Keefe says nothing. Deep frown lines mar his forehead.

"You think I'm crazy."

Not a question, but a statement.

He shakes his head and takes a step closer.

"No, but I disagree with your interpretation. I think Heaven is the outside world and this law firm is the bureaucratic Hell we can lose ourselves in, if we forget what's really important in life."

And that's all it takes for the tears to fall again.

"Why did you leave without saying anything?"

"I..." he starts and then stops. He runs a hand through his unusually messy hair. "Oscar messaged me earlier this morning. There was something important he needed to discuss in person. He drove by and collected me from your place. I didn't want to wake you."

"What did Oscar need to talk to you about?" I manage to choke out.

Keefe stays silent. He refuses to meet my eyes.

Fine then. It's clear where his loyalty lies and it's not with me. Let him keep his secrets.

"I don't want to see you again."

And without a backwards glance, I walk out the door and down the steps of Mornington House.

23

Up Or Out

I am adrift in a tide of misery.

I don't know where I'm going. My feet tread water until I find myself at Pearse Square, staring at my flat. Unwilling to go inside and be confined by the four walls of my bedroom. So, I sit outside. Fiddle with Muriel's bracelet and watch the local kids play in the small, grassy square. My backside numb from the cold, concrete steps.

The boys kick a ball aimlessly to each other as the landlady's black beast of a cat saunters down the stairs. It meows at me until I give in and stroke the top of its head. A content, purring noise rattles from its chest. Well, at least I've done something right today.

The sound of a door opening jars me from my thoughts.

"There you are," my elderly landlady says with a whirl of her cream cashmere shawl.

The cat mewls in delight and hightails it up the steps to her apartment. I rise shakily to my feet and nod to the landlady as I psyche myself up to enter the flat that reminds me too much of Keefe, heartbreak, and loneliness.

"Fiadh, would you like to come in for some tea and biscuits?"

I'm about to say no. The polite decline on the tip of my tongue but then think, why the hell not? I've got some time to kill before I go back to work and face the music.

"That would be lovely, thank you."

She gestures for me to come inside and, I close the door behind me. The aroma of old books lures me in and I wander into the living room while she busies herself in the kitchen. The hiss of a kettle and the clang of cutlery come from down the hallway while I find myself in a high-ceilinged room dominated by a crackling fireplace.

My attention wanders from the leather-bound books lining a gorgeous mahogany dresser, to a younger picture of my landlady alongside her red-headed grandchildren, to the diploma hanging on the wall. It's written in Latin but essentially translates as:

'Edna Morgan - Bachelor of Civil Law Degree - University College Dublin.'

"You have a law degree?" I ask my landlady when she shuffles into the room with biscuits balanced on a fine china plate.

"Oh, yes." She gestures for me to sit down on one of the comfortable lounge chairs set up beside the fire and looks for something on the mantelpiece. "Here," she says and passes a photo to me. It's a picture of Edna as a young woman with wild auburn hair. She wears black, ceremonial robes and holds a piece of parchment. She stands in front of the stained glass window at Blackhall. The words 'Veritas Vincet' written above an image of the lady of justice supported by two Irish wolfhounds.

"You're a solicitor?"

I'm amazed I never knew this.

"Well, I was," she says, taking a bite of her biscuit, as the cat jumps up onto the couch beside me. "I'm retired now."

I take a sip of my tea and let myself enjoy the warmth of the crackling fire. "Out of curiosity, which firm did you practise at?"

I take a bite of my biscuit. The chocolate melts pleasantly on my tongue.

"Heron Early, of course."

The biscuit turns to ashes in my mouth and I almost choke.

"How do you think you and your cousin got such a good deal on a flat in the centre of Dublin?"

"Am…" I start and then stop. "I thought Muriel was just lucky."

The landlady nods happily. "I like to rent out my basement flat to apprentices because you remind me of myself when I started out."

She places her teacup back down on the tray. "Tell me, are there any new developments concerning Muriel's disappearance?"

She asks the question as casually as if she's enquiring about a friend she hasn't seen in a few months. Completely unaware of the devastating effect it has on me. How my stomach churns at the mere mention of Muriel and the awful thoughts that whirl through my mind. Of whether or not she's even alive.

"No," I cough and put my cup back down on the delicate saucer. The cat inspects the contents with a wrinkle of its button nose.

"That's a shame," she tuts. "It's unfortunate her boyfriend wasn't able to shed more light on the situation."

Her what?

The world stops rotating on its axis as I stare at my landlady. "What boyfriend?"

She picks up a teaspoon and adds a sugar cube to her tea. Swirling it around, she replies, "I don't know what you young people call it these days. Let's say her 'fancy man' or 'buachaill'. You know, that MP's son. Oh, what's his name?"

"Oscar Pierce," I whisper, my voice raw sounding to my own ears.

"Yes, Pierce is the surname. I actually thought I saw him outside this morning with another young gentleman. The same one who dropped you off late last week. I hope you don't mind me saying this. I wasn't snooping you understand but, when I'm sitting here watching television, I can't help but notice who comes and goes from my own doorstep."

The rest of her words are lost to me. I thank her for the tea and stand. The cat hisses its annoyance when I jostle it out of the way, make my excuses, and leave.

I knew it.

I should have listened to my gut and not allowed myself to be swayed by Keefe O'Kelly. I'm such a fool. All clues point to Oscar. He was either responsible for Muriel's disappearance or, at the very least, he knows far more than he's told anyone.

And as God is my witness, I'm going to make him talk.

Half an hour later, I walk through Heron Early's front door. The person behind the desk picks up the phone the moment they see me. A startled expression on their face while Lucifer stares down forlornly at me from the canvas as I jog up the marble staircase. When I reach the M&A floor, I scan my card to open the door, but nothing happens. I scan it again and the little light that should turn green turns red instead.

That doesn't bode well for me.

One of the paralegals strolls out of the bathroom and scans their card. Without considering the ramifications, I walk in behind them. Scuttle down the hallway and keep my head down as I pass the practice assistants' desks. But nothing gets past Una. Her mouth opens in shock when she sees me, but I disappear into Buach's empty office and close the door before she can say anything.

There, shoved under the desk is my battered satchel and in it is my matrice. I snatch it up and, realising I don't have much time, I rush over to my computer, insert my username and password.

Login failed.

My heart sinks. Someone has cut off my access to the firm's system. They're trying to stop me from finding the work I've done to date. And without access, I can't prove someone set me up and deleted my files. I look around the room, desperate for anything that might help me, but Buach's room remains as cold and inhospitable as the day I arrived.

I get out of my chair and search for the only person that has the answers I need. The man responsible for all of this mess.

"Where is Buach?" I ask Una.

But Una's loyal. Even with me looming over her she says nothing while the others sip their afternoon tea and watch the drama unfold. But Una's eyes give her away. She glances at the meeting room. I stride down the hall and find Buach holed up in there with the Project Puzzle deal team. Brigid, Keefe, Peadar, and Joyce, all sat around listening to Buach.

He falls silent when I enter the room.

"Fiadh, you're not supposed to be here."

"Why?" I ask, surprised by how steady my voice sounds.

"You're suspended pending an investigation and review into your conduct."

And try as I might to steel myself, his words still land like a physical blow to the little girl who built her entire world around other people's expectations. Who believed her academic and professional achievements to be the sum total of her worth. And the woman who let a man as small and mean-spirited as Buach Scannell walk all over her in the hopes that one day, if she worked hard enough, she'd finally receive his gratitude and maybe even his respect.

"On what grounds?" I manage to choke out, while my gaze roves to Keefe who stares back at me sadly but offers no help.

"I would prefer not to do this here... but you failed to complete the tasks assigned to you and, in doing so, have jeopardised this deal and the firm's relationship with a key client."

I take a step back, trying to physically distance myself from his words, while Brigid and Peadar look everywhere but at me.

Joyce, of all people, is the person who comes to my defence.

"Fiadh, we're aware you've been under an immense amount of pressure lately."

And for the first time since entering the boardroom, I look over at her. What does she mean by that?

Joyce turns to Buach, tells him she can take it from here; and he strides from the room, refusing to make eye contact with me.

"Fiadh," she says quietly. "We know you hid things about your past from the firm."

The other apprentices don't know where Joyce is going with this. I can tell from the confused looks on their faces.

"Fiadh," she says in a concerned voice that's almost worse than Buach's accusatory tone. "Why didn't you tell us Muriel Hunt is your cousin?"

And there it is. My secret is finally out in the open.

"Hold on," Peadar says to Joyce, his face scrunched in confusion. "Muriel Hunt, the apprentice who torpedoed Project Puzzle and then ran away?"

Brigid interrupts him and sits forward in her chair.

"Isn't that the apprentice who had a breakdown and left the legal profession... sorry," she mumbles when I scowl at them both.

"The little girl from the picture," Keefe mutters and places his head in his hands.

And there it is. They all level accusatory looks at me in one way or another. Each wondering why I kept this secret from them. What else I might be hiding and what other ulterior motives may have driven me here.

"I'm being set up..." I try to tell them. "You have to believe me. We've been through too much for you not to. I may not have told you the entire truth, but you still trust me. Right?"

"You should have told me, Fiadh."

That's all Keefe says, before he walks out of the room.

Brigid marches after him while Peadar stares at the traffic trundling past the window and down Merrion Street. Refusing to meet my gaze.

I follow Keefe and Brigid into the hallway.

"Can't you see I'm being set up? Don't listen to Buach. There's more to this story than you realise."

They look at me like they don't know me. And it makes my heart hurt.

"Please say you believe me," I shout at Keefe as I'm led away.

But he says nothing. Brigid puts her hand on his shoulder and together they turn their backs on me and walk back into the meeting room to re-join Peadar.

I'm escorted down the stairs and out of the building. And as I stand across the street from Mornington House, car horns blaring all around me from furious drivers stuck in traffic, I suddenly realise what it's like to be roadkill. To be the unfortunate thing lying on the side of the street that no one wants to look at. Because it might make them feel uncomfortable for not stopping to help. For looking the other way. But why should they when there is no duty to rescue?

I don't know how long I stand there, staring forlornly at the cars that roll down Merrion Street while the cold November air nips at my fingers. Thinking about all the ways I let myself, my family, and Muriel down. Wondering how I could have been so stupid as to have fallen foul of the same malevolent forces that ruined Muriel's life. To have succumbed to the allure of the secret society that tore my family apart. To have offered them more of my soul than the part they'd already stolen.

And it's while I'm still standing on the side of the road, lost in my own morbid thoughts, that I see him. The man I followed to Dublin. The apprentice who knows more than he's willing to say.

Oscar Pierce pulls up in a Land Rover and parks outside of Mornington House. And when he darts up the cement stairs and disappears inside Heron Early, I stand there for a while. Weighing the pros and cons of what I'm about to do. But eventually, I realise all roads lead to Oscar and I may not get another opportunity like this one.

So, I cross the busy street, pop the boot of Oscar's car, and hop inside.

242

24

VARIATION DEED

This is fine.

Everything is totally fine. It makes perfect sense that I jumped into the trunk of Oscar's car. He's the hare. Quick as they come and hard to catch. But after all these months, I've finally outsmarted him. He can't slip away because I'm in the boot of his car. And wherever he goes, I go.

Although, as I lie in the dark, with nothing for company but my racing heart, I begin to second-guess my plan. And, as the rough fibres of the moulded carpet itch my cheek, I remember it's Thursday afternoon. Oscar probably stopped by Heron Early to join Buach's Project Puzzle deal debrief. So, why on earth did I lock myself in the trunk of a suspected murderer's car? And not just any run-of-the-mill murderer, but one who has mind-controlling abilities.

My breath comes in short, sharp bursts and there is no light. The cramped, empty space is as black as night. Impenetrable. The sounds of passing cars are muffled by the metal coffin I've locked myself inside of. I am utterly alone.

What have I done?

I reach into my satchel and pull out my phone. It's dead. Who was I going to call anyway? My erstwhile friends turned their backs on me, so I reach out my hands and skim my fingers along the sides of the boot. Looking for any telltale ridges or grooves. There has to be a lever I can use to pop the hood. Because I need to get out of here before I suffer a full-on panic attack.

There's a click, followed by a wobble and then a bang, as Oscar slams the car door shut.

I freeze.

Worried any sudden movement will warn Oscar he has an un-invited passenger in the back of his car. Nothing happens for a moment and then the engine purrs and the car rolls forward. Effectively putting an end to any last-ditch efforts to back out of this hare-brained plan. And with little else to do, I pull my knees to my chest and hope that today of all days, Oscar doesn't get rear-ended.

Time passes slowly.

Maybe an hour goes by while the car trundles through traffic. When it halts at, what I presume to be, traffic lights, I search for the emergency lever to open the boot only to have to abandon my escape attempt when the car picks up speed on longer stretches of road. Eventually, the journey from Hell comes to an end and the car slows to a smooth stop.

Click, wobble, bang.

Don't open the boot. Please God, don't open the boot. He has no reason to look inside the boot, I tell myself over the thundering beat of my heart. And as the silence stretches, I realise he must have left.

Relief floods my system and I lie flat on my stomach. My muscles cry out, sore and stiff from the journey. But I reach for the lever I'd found earlier and the hood of the boot pops open.

Late afternoon light spills over my fingers and, tentatively, I peer out. Oscar has parked the car on a deserted country road. Patches of grass grow in a straight line down the centre of the potholed lane. It's entirely devoid of other people or traffic. With Oscar nowhere in sight, I push the hood up, roll out of the boot, and crouch down on the other side of the car.

I can taste salt in the afternoon air. Waves break somewhere nearby. And as I peer around the wheel for any sign of Oscar, thorns from the adjacent hedgerow pull at my coat. There's a sandy beach in the distance. Devoid of any other people. The sea stretches as far as the eye can see. And at my back, a large red-brick Victorian building is set further up the hillside. A clock tower rises ominously from the centre of the complex. It dominates the skyline but is too far away for me to discern the time. Seagulls launch from its steeple into the morose sky. Their wings spread wide as they fly over alder trees, their boughs bent by the wind, and land on an indistinct gate set into a moss-encrusted wall. Stained from the sea's violent temper.

I scamper down the country road. Careful to keep my head well below the tip of the hedge and settle myself between the leaves of an overgrown bush. Crouched low and out of sight. From this vantage point, I can peer through the wrought iron gates into the green field beyond.

And there he is.

Oscar Pierce stands in the middle of an enclosed garden, oddly bereft of flowers or trees. The grass is freshly mown. Someone has even taken the time to lay a path of pebbles that lead to a stone sculpture at the centre of the lawn.

With his head bowed and his back to me, in the twilight, Oscar looks like a statue himself. Unmoved by the world around him. Utterly still and silent, until he shoves his hands deep into the pockets of his navy trench coat and turns around.

I remain deathly still, knowing the prickly leaves of the bush should be enough to hide me from his view but, still, I hold my breath when he walks along the gravel path. His attention focused on the beach mere metres beyond the wall. When he passes, I swear his gaze roves over the hedge and, for a heart-juddering moment, I think he sees me. Fortunately, his eyes move on, unfocused and unseeing. A few heartbeats later, the gate creaks open and his footsteps fade.

I'm alone once more.

I take a steadying breath and, slowly, I poke my head above the bush. Oscar's car remains parked up the country lane where he'd left it. Quickly, I check along the shoreline, until I find his footprints in the sand. Oscar walks with his back to me across the beach, towards the sea.

But why is he here?

Carefully, I disentangle myself from the bush and turn my attention back to the place he'd been standing only moments ago. And now, with my view unimpeded, I can finally see the stone cross that juts from the grass.

Tendrils of dread grip my heart, but I force myself to walk towards it. Even though I feel like I'm outside of my body, looking in at the stones plucked from the nearby beach that lie against the slab of granite. There's something written on the cross. It reads:

'*St. Ita's Hospital Cemetery. Grant eternal life to all who rest here.*'

This isn't a garden; it's a mass, unmarked grave.

I take a step back. Panic eats my insides, but I breathe through it. I'm being ridiculous. This means nothing. But then my eye catches on a flash of something silver and I reach for it before my mind can even register what my soul instantly recognises.

I hold a silver bracelet in one hand and trail my fingers over the claddagh heart I know almost as well as my own. Identical to the one I wear on my wrist. I bring Muriel's half of our friendship bracelet to my thundering chest. Oscar must have left it here. Which means he took it from her. And with that realisation, the sea breeze robs me of my breath, and I fall to my knees.

My cousin. My family. My friend. My tether to this life. The missing piece of my soul.

Dead and buried in the unmarked grave before me.

A chilling wail comes with the wind. The ocean sings its lament and aids me in my time of need. Lends its voice to mine as the seagulls soar overhead. Their cries match the guttural sounds that escape my lips as I plunge down. Drowning. Gasping for breath. I tear at my own clothes for purchase. Something to make me feel like I'm still alive. I grasp at my own skin and wonder how I can still be here while she is buried somewhere down there. Stolen from the land of the living and lost to the depths of hell.

My Muriel. My soul. My regret. My sorrow.

I failed to find her.

I fall to my knees and press my forehead to the ground. A supplicant at the altar of a cruel god and offer my tears to the land. To the soil that shelters her body while torturous images of her final moments shred what remains of the wasteland of my mind. The sea crashes against the rocks, an echo of my anger; it rises to engulf all in its raging waters. And as I lie prostrate before the cross, I hear the faint crunch of pebbles behind me.

Oscar Pierce has returned to the scene of his crime.

I place my dirt-encrusted hand into my coat pocket. My fingers curl around the cool handle of my matrice. While the other grips Muriel's bracelet for the courage to avenge her. Because if I cannot have restitution then I demand retribution for what was taken from me.

I draw myself from the ground and smile at the thought of the man who thinks to take me unawares. I think of the heinous tests he orchestrated and the hexes he executed against me. Little does he know that the lamb he has lined up for the slaughter will not go quietly. Cast out into the cold, I have become more wolf than sheep. And with that final thought, I take out the deed I'd drafted days ago and turn to face Muriel's murderer.

Oscar Pierce stares at me with eyes deader than those who lie in the graves beneath our feet. His gaze wanders from my tear-streaked face to Muriel's bracelet clasped in my hand. Damnation is etched into the lines of his face. And without a thought to the consequences, I bring my matrice down on the veracity deed.

I hereby compel Oscar Pierce to speak the truth and nothing but the truth, immediately upon execution of this deed.

Signed and delivered as a deed by: Fiadh Whelan – The Deer

"What happened to Muriel Hunt?"

The flare of Oscar's eyes is the last thing I see before the hex takes effect and we both hit the ground. I knew it was a risk to execute a deed without a witness. I expected it to hurt, to take more of my soul than usual, but this is something else. Something has gone wrong. I feel it in the marrow of my bones. It's like my very soul is being ripped from my body. I can't breathe. And something similar must be happening to Oscar because he gags and seizes violently on the pebble path. My vision goes dark around the edges as I reach for the cross. And too late, I realise I don't want to die. But my body gives out and my world goes black.

And then there's nothing but pain, suffering, and darkness.

Until I hear my name.

Air.

Beautiful, life-giving air fills my aching lungs. It burns my throat until I cough and turn on my side. I dig my fingernails into the dirt and crawl from the grave. The dark fogs lifts and, when my vision clears, I see a brown loafer I know far too well.

Keefe O'Kelly crouches beside me. His voice lost to the wind as I regain my bearings. The veracity deed clutched in his fingers. The word 'terminated' scribbled across the parchment followed by the seals of a swan and a sheep embossed upon its surface. Over his shoulder, Brigid and Peadar help Oscar to his feet.

I have been robbed of my answers. Of both the truth and my revenge. Why did the veracity deed backfire so badly when I hexed Oscar? I wonder in dismay. Still light-headed from the lack of oxygen but Brigid has questions of her own.

"What the hell is going on here?" Brigid shouts and plucks the veracity deed from Keefe's fingers.

"Ask the murderer!" I shout at Oscar, who takes one look at the bracelet still clutched in my dirty hand and bolts.

It takes my befuddled brain far longer than it should to register he's made a run for it. I've come too far to let the hare slip through my fingers. I sprint after him. Oscar is already out the gate. He bounds up the road with far more speed than I can muster, and I trail miserably behind him.

The faint shouts of my fellow apprentices indicate they're hot on our heels, but their voices are lost to the roar of the wind in my ears. Oscar turns off the road and bounds up the open field. His footsteps marking the wet grass as he legs it up the lawn. He's running towards the Victorian building at the crest of the hill. But if he thinks he's going to lose me inside, he's got another thing coming.

I'll uncover the truth, even if it kills me.

Through the dilapidated door he disappears and, when I come barrelling after him, I pass a uniformed man slumped over in his chair, half-asleep. He snaps to attention and picks up the phone while Oscar takes a left turn and vaults up a disused stairwell. I hear his footfalls amidst the sound of my own ragged breath. But I don't slow down. I can't. And when he makes a break for it down a deserted corridor, I follow him. Even though an alarm sounds in my mind, warning me Oscar could be about to spring a trap.

The offensive smell of mould hits me. Orange paint peels from the walls. My shoes batter the red-and-white tiled floor. Oscar looks over his shoulder to check if he's lost me. But I followed him all the way to Dublin. I'm not about to give up now. Even as my lungs burn and my muscles ache, onwards I run until he comes to a plain, unmarked magnolia door and disappears inside. He doesn't even bother to close it after him.

I barrel into the sparsely furnished room. My arms held in front of my face to block a blow that doesn't come. I halt in front of a single bed pressed up against a damp wall in the corner of a clinical bedroom. A warped wood cupboard open beside it. A few drab items of clothing hung up inside. The glow of a lone bulb casts a garish light over the miserable space. And as the heavy pants, curses, and thump of shoes indicate the other apprentices are not far behind, everything fades away the moment I see her.

Muriel.

My cousin sits on a plastic chair designed for a child. Her hair, long and lank about her face. She looks out the window at the sea beyond.

"Muriel!"

I fall to my knees and grab her cold hands. But when she looks at me, there is nothing. Eyes I know almost as well as my own gaze back at me. Seeing but not understanding. She's here but not really. She tugs her hands out of mine and leans back in her chair as if to get away from me. A distressing sound emanates from her lips as she curls in on herself. She rocks backwards and forwards. Looking everywhere but at me.

Keefe, Brigid, and Peadar crash through the bedroom door. I ignore them. My attention focused on the lost apprentice seated before me.

"Muriel?" It's both a question and a plea. "Please talk to me."

I try to brush a stray strand of limp, blonde hair, so similar to my own, from her face. But she shrinks from my touch as the chill November air seeps through the barely glazed windows. The seventies-style radiators doing little to add warmth to the room.

Peadar inspects the shabby room, a greyish tint to his face as he mutters, "I thought they shut St. Ita's Hospital years ago."

My gaze moves to Oscar, who just stands there. His eyes fixed mournfully on Muriel and, from the depths of his pocket, he hands a piece of parchment to Keefe. I jump to my feet and grab the deed out of his hands.

I hereby vary Muriel Hunt's memory so that she shall neither remember who she is nor where she came from. To come into effect immediately upon execution of this deed and to remain in place until such time as this deed is formally terminated.

Signed and delivered as a deed by: The Fox

In the presence of: The Badger

A gasp escapes me as I read the damning words.

The SoS did this. They altered Muriel's memories.

Without wasting any time, I reach for the fountain pen in my pocket, amend the wording, and take out my matrice. I look up at Keefe to see he already has his matrice in hand and together we terminate the variation deed.

I close my eyes as the dark deed takes its payment. Keefe's hand finds mine and together we breathe through the pain. And when it passes, I open my eyes to see Oscar on his knees before my cousin. His head pressed to her gloved hands. Begging her forgiveness.

But Muriel's eyes are fixed on mine.

"Fiadh, you found me."

And with four simple words, my tattered soul is made whole.

25

THE EGGSHELL SKULL RULE

"Get the hell away from her!"

I push Oscar aside and he goes to stand awkwardly beside Peadar while Brigid asks Oscar to explain what's going on. I ignore them all. My attention focused solely on Muriel.

Tentatively, I reach out my hand. She catches it in her own. Her grip firm and her eyes clear. The fog of confusion that had clouded them before gone now, as though it had never existed.

She glances from me to the sparse contents of her hospital room. From the chrysanthemum bedspread covered in flecks of magnolia paint over to her sparse furnishings. Muriel gets up from her dilapidated chair and goes to stand in front of the ceramic sink, stained blue by hard water. She looks into the square mirror bolted to the wall above. The surface treated with something to make it almost impossible for a patient to break the glass. She runs her hands over the grey tracksuit they dressed her in.

"How long have I been here?" She whispers, her voice hoarse.

A lump forms in my throat, but I force myself to swallow it and answer her truthfully.

"Six months."

Muriel leans over the basin, her face deathly pale as she lets that sink in.

"Where am I?"

"Good question," I say to Oscar, accusation dripping from my tone. But he ignores me and continues to watch Muriel in a manner that makes me distinctly uncomfortable.

It's Peadar who eventually answers her question.

"We're at St. Ita's Hospital. It's a mental health facility outside of Dublin City."

He walks around the room with a distinctly uncomfortable look on his face every time he spots the mildew that grows on the windowsill or the damp contents of the lone cupboard that houses a mixture of shabby tracksuits and hospital gowns.

"The Irish government was supposed to have closed this place years ago."

Brigid crosses her arms and eyes Muriel warily.

"Well, I didn't see any other patients on my way up here."

I ignore them both and ask the question I've wanted an answer to for six long months.

"Muriel, what happened to you?"

She blinks and turns to me. Her sea-blue eyes catch on the oak matrice still clutched in my hand and she reaches for the dark deed that put her here. With a slender finger, she traces my seal and smiles at me.

"A deer suits you, Fiadh." But as she reads the rest of the variation deed that stripped her of everything she was and knew, her smile fades. "Someone at Heron Early did this to me."

"Was it him?" I point an accusing finger at Oscar, ready to hex him, guilty as he is. But Muriel merely shakes her head and goes to stand beside him. Making me question if she's still a bit befuddled from the effects of the variation deed.

He stares forlornly at her.

"Fiadh and the others," Oscar says with a nod towards Keefe, Brigid, and Peadar, "started their apprenticeship at Heron Early two weeks ago."

Muriel stills. "Which team?"

"Buach's," he says quietly and reaches for Muriel's hand. She takes a deep breath, clearly rattled by this information.

"I don't understand," I start and then stop when Muriel rests the back of her head against the windowpane. She closes her eyes, and I can't help but notice she's still holding onto Oscar's hand, like it's her lifeline.

"She did this. She hexed and sent me here. Safely out of the way, where no one would find me." Muriel opens her eyes and with a start I realise there are tears in them. "And even if they did, no one would believe me." This last part she whispers to Oscar, who hangs his head in shame.

"Who, the fox or the badger?" Keefe asks, his gaze fixed on the deed Muriel holds in her hand.

"The fox," she replies and brings the parchment closer to her face. Tears flowing freely down her cheeks.

"Who is the fox, Muriel?"

Muriel locks her eyes on mine.

"Joyce Larkin."

Keefe breathes out a curse that doesn't bear repeating while Peadar looks like he's actually going to throw up. He runs a hand through his loose curls and walks out the door mumbling he needs some fresh air.

Brigid raises her hand and waves to Muriel.

"Hi. We haven't been formally introduced, but my name is Brigid Hughes, this is Keefe O'Kelly and the dramatic lad who wandered out the door like his entire world is crumbling around him was Peadar Ahern."

Muriel blinks at Brigid and then seems to remember her manners. "Am, hello…"

Brigid lowers her hand and cuts to the chase.

"Could you explain why Joyce Larkin, the Heron Early apprentice mentor, would want to hex you; and also, if it wouldn't be too much trouble, could you please tell us who the badger is?"

Brigid nods to the deed still clutched in Muriel's hand and judging by the way her voice wavers at the end, I can tell she's more concerned by this debacle than she's letting on.

Muriel glances at Oscar, who squeezes her hand, as if to give her reassurance.

I don't like that one bit.

"Why don't I start from the beginning. Four Heron Early apprentices, including Oscar and I, were tapped to join the SoS shortly after we entered Blackhall. We passed the initiation trials and signed our indentures. But then I started to notice some odd things were happening around the office.

"Documents were disappearing or reverting to earlier drafts; and I thought nothing of it for a while until, one day, someone hexed me to hear an Irish reel over and over again. I couldn't sleep for nights on end. I thought I was unwell for a while until I confided in Oscar who had experienced the exact same thing. Together, we searched the Registry of Deeds for whatever deed was driving us up the wall and it was there, late one night, that I stumbled upon Joyce.

"She was in one of the older, less used sections of the Registry, so I bided my time until she left and found the dark deed she'd tried to hide there. It was some sort of an ear worm hex, executed by a fox and witnessed by a badger. I confronted Joyce outside of Blackhall, but she wasn't alone. A man in a badger mask appeared and, before I could get away, they hexed me. And that's the last thing I can remember clearly."

Keefe comes to stand beside me. Concern lining his face. "I don't understand. Why would Joyce do that?"

Muriel lowers her eyes. "To make sure I couldn't tell anyone she was the one sabotaging the Project Puzzle publishing acquisition so that Buach would lose his prized client, Hades Partners."

I give a frosty glare to Brigid and Keefe.

"There, you hear that. It must have been Joyce who deleted my work from the system. She made people think I was losing it, just like she did to you, Muriel."

"Hold on," Brigid says, still not convinced even though Muriel literally holds the proof of Joyce's treachery in her hands. "What would Joyce have to gain from doing something like that? Isn't her job at risk if Buach loses his biggest client?"

Muriel sighs and her shoulders slump. "Actually, Joyce stands to benefit the most. If Buach is booted from the firm, in all likelihood, Joyce will be invited to take his place in the Heron Early partnership."

Keefe shakes his head. "But would she really do all of this just to make partner?"

Muriel shakes her head, tired of trying to make them believe her. But I do. I believe her.

"How did Joyce manage to get away with this?" I gesture at the hospital room.

Muriel taps the badger seal.

"Someone high up in the SoS is helping her."

"Yes," I say and point at Oscar who has remained eerily silent this entire time. "And he's standing right there. Keefe, Peadar, and I found a dark deed filed in the Registry which Oscar executed with the fox. He smudged the writing to cover up whatever dark deed he'd executed. It proves he's working with Joyce."

Oscar lowers his eyes to the ground in guilt but still he doesn't utter a word in his defence.

"Fiadh," Keefe starts, but I cut him off.

"You coward!" I shout at Oscar. "Admit you mistreated my cousin and tell us who the badger is!"

Oscar opens his mouth and, for a split second, I think he's going to give us a name, but instead he drops to the ground. Brigid and I jump back in alarm as Oscar convulses on the red-and-white tiled floor. Strangled noises come from his throat. Angry veins protrude from his neck and his face turns a violent shade of red.

Just as it had when I'd hexed him at the graveyard.

But instead of disowning him, Muriel falls to her knees and tries to help him.

"Breathe, Oscar. Don't think about the question or the answer. Put the words from your mind and think of something else. Look at me. Focus on my face and nothing more."

Brigid catches my hand, a shocked expression on her face, while Keefe and Muriel help Oscar to his feet. Eventually, oxygen passes through his lips and down into his lungs in painful, ragged gasps. Muriel holds his face in her hands.

I open my mouth to ask what's going on but Muriel raises her hand, halting the words before they pour from my lips.

"Don't ask him any more questions. Joyce must have placed a heavy gag order on him. He can't speak about her involvement in my disappearance or the identity of the badger without choking."

He stills. His eyes focused solely on Muriel's and within them is a hope I've never seen burn so brightly in Oscar Pierce.

"I suspect Joyce was worried I'd confided in you and, rather than make a second apprentice disappear, and the son of a high-profile politician no less, she and the badger must have hexed you and used me as leverage to make you execute whatever dark deed Fiadh found in the Registry. Thus, implicating you in their crime."

Oscar presses his forehead to Muriel's while a sudden realisation dawns on me.

"That's why you couldn't answer my question in the graveyard. Because you're already subject to a gag order."

"The eggshell skull rule," Muriel breathes. "You have to take your victim however you find them."

Oscar looks at me with tired eyes as Keefe thinks aloud.

"That's why we found you both half-dead in the graveyard. The veracity deed was going to drain Fiadh of her soul until Oscar answered her questions truthfully. But Oscar couldn't comply with its terms because of the gag order he was already under."

Keefe runs a hand through his hair. "That dark deed would have killed you both if we hadn't terminated it in time."

Muriel places her gloved hand tenderly on Oscar's cheek.

"You helped Fiadh find me."

I scoff; he did nothing of the sort.

"He did not. I hid in the boot of his car and followed him here."

Muriel actually laughs at this and looks at Oscar as if to say, what did I tell you? She's really something.

"Wait a minute," I say and turn to Oscar. "If you've had the variation deed that altered Muriel's memories this entire time, why didn't you show it to someone so they could see what was going on and help? Someone could have rescued her months ago."

Keefe steps forwards and saves Oscar from attempting to answer and thus gagging again.

"Because your cousin's variation deed was locked in Joyce's office. Oscar asked me to spy on Joyce and give him the code to the safe, but he wouldn't tell me why he wanted it, so I obviously refused," he says with a beseeching look at Oscar before he turns back to me. His eyes solemn. "But when Buach and Joyce suspended you earlier today, I realised something strange was going on. So, while Joyce was preoccupied having you thrown out of Heron Early, I called Oscar and told him I'd help."

Realisation rushes over me in waves.

"That's why you ran into Heron Early this afternoon and left your car unlocked outside..." I say to Oscar and then stop and really look at him. "You left the SoS note in Muriel's bedroom on the night of her vigil, hoping I'd find it and follow you back to Dublin." My eyes meet

Oscar's and I swear they twinkle with mischief in response. "You did lead me to Muriel."

I'm not sure how I feel about this and I turn to Keefe, my mind racing.

"But how did you three," I say with a vague gesture at the corridor that Peadar still hasn't returned from, "know where to find us?"

Keefe and Brigid share a loaded look.

"After you left, the three of us went back into the boardroom. We watched you jump into the boot of Oscar's car. It was parked on Merrion Street, in full view of the window. But luckily for you, Buach and Joyce hadn't returned yet."

Brigid shakes her head. "Fiadh, you are many things, but stealthy is not one of them."

Keefe nods and I have to try very hard not to be offended by that comment.

"After he'd already left, I rang Oscar and told him he had an unexpected passenger in his car. He told me to get to St. Ita's graveyard as quick as possible, so we hailed a taxi and when we got here, we found you both at death's door. We saw the deed Fiadh had executed, pieced together what must have happened, and terminated it."

Muriel glances around the spartan room. "I can't begin to imagine the amount of energy Joyce had to expend in order to suppress my memories for months on end."

Brigid shakes her head and goes to stand by the door. "That explains the thick layer of cosmetics she wore to work every day. We thought she had dark circles under her eyes because she worked too hard. Who would have guessed she got them by tormenting and undermining her junior staff members. I mean, at this point, does that woman even have a shred of soul left in her body?"

Brigid raises a good point.

Oscar stands up and attempts to speak, looking like he's putting great thought into every word he utters.

"We don't have much time. There's a tribunal of enquiry meeting at seven p.m. tonight. Joyce has accused Fiadh of executing unsanctioned dark deeds and has petitioned the Council of Hons to have her struck from the SoS register. She's going to ask them to execute a gag order to stop Fiadh from discussing any SoS-related matters ever again."

"Of course, she has," Keefe replies and throws a worried look in my direction. "Joyce will ensure the terms of the gag order are drafted broadly enough so as to encapsulate any knowledge Fiadh may have of Joyce's nefarious activities or her involvement in Muriel's disappearance."

Oscar says nothing in response which is answer enough.

"Great." I throw my hands in the air. "So much for all that talk about checks and balances on the power of the SoS and it's reverence for the truth."

"We're wasting time," Oscar says and looks down at his watch. A deep frown on his face. "We have just under two hours to get to the Tribunal and expose Joyce before she has Fiadh gagged, kicked out of the SoS, and ostracised from the legal profession entirely."

He turns to Keefe, but whatever he was going to say is interrupted by the sound of footsteps pelting up the corridor. Peadar rushes through the door, catches Brigid by the arm, and pulls her into the hallway.

"Dawson, Jaya, and Finley are coming! We need to hide, now!" He shouts over his shoulder.

"What the hell?" I start, but Oscar has already grabbed Muriel and I race after them. Not willing to let my cousin out of my sight. Keefe close on my heels.

"In here!" Peadar shouts and disappears behind a door that turns out to be a supply closet. It barely manages to fit six fully grown apprentices inside of it. And I find myself pressed uncomfortably close to Oscar while Keefe is inches from my face. Thank God, it's too dark inside the broom cupboard for him to see the flush that rises to my cheeks from his proximity. Brigid meanwhile pushes what feels like a mop into my face and hisses, "That snake must be working with Joyce."

"Be quiet," Peadar whispers. "If they can't see us, they can't hex us."

I'm about to ask how exactly he knew that Dawson and the other Bebb Gwyn apprentices had arrived and why he thought it would be a good idea to trap us in a closet, when I hear a door creak open down the hallway.

"Here, Peadar, Peadar, Peadar!"

Dawson's disembodied voice echoes off the tiles and down the silent corridor. He says the name in quick, rapid-fire succession. It reminds me of how a farmer calls the cattle in from the field.

Boom.

It sounds like someone kicked a door in.

"Here, Peadar, Peadar, Peadar!"

Boom. Goes another door.

"Word on the legal street is that a group of Heron Early apprentices have gone rogue. Executing dark deeds and putting some very high-up noses out of joint."

Boom.

I jolt and Keefe grips my hand to steady me. That one sounded like it was close.

"The SoS are coming for you!"

I flinch, certain Dawson's about to uncover us. But the boom before we're busted never comes and, instead, we hear a new voice.

"Hurt your foot smashing the doors in, did you Dawson? Why don't you check out the rooms at the end of the corridor in case they're hiding there and I'll open the ones up here using my hands. Like a normal human being," Jaya gripes at Dawson from somewhere in the corridor.

"Peadar, Peadar, Peadar!" Dawson shouts, but this time his voice comes from further down the hall.

I sigh in relief and feel the tension drain from the others only for the closet door to be wrenched open. We blink in the harsh light while Jaya's eyes dart from Peadar to the rest of us, packed into the janitor's closet. She opens her mouth as if to shout for Dawson and then stops when Muriel silently places her hands together and begs for her not to turn us in.

Jaya frowns at my cousin. She assesses her lank hair, food-stained grey tracksuit and, then without a word of warning, Jaya yanks the variation deed out of Muriel's hand.

I'm about to grab it back but Muriel stops me.

Jaya's eyes dart across the dark deed and then her eyes go wide when she beholds the images of the fox and the badger that sealed Muriel's fate.

Boom.

Jaya looks at Muriel, indecision written across her face. Boom. Goes another door, closer this time and she makes up her mind. Jaya opens the closet door wider and whispers, "Run."

We don't need to be told twice. We barrel down the corridor. Passing old toys and clothes strewn across the floor of the abandoned hospital ward. Under flickering lights, we descend an old staircase, splash through puddles formed from leaky ceilings and, when Oscar presses his weight against the emergency exit at the end of the stairwell, we're free.

The sun has already set and the dark is cleaved apart by the light of a lone streetlamp on the country road up ahead. The chill sea breeze pulls strands of my hair loose while we run for Oscar's car. We jam ourselves into the tight space as Oscar takes the wheel and shoves his key into the ignition.

"Have you checked the news?" Keefe gestures to his phone as Oscar speeds down the deserted road. "The Gardaí have set up check points all around the Four Courts on the basis of some anonymous tip they received. The roads are closed. How are we going to make it there on time?"

Feck.

"I may have a solution," Brigid shouts from where she's squished between Keefe and Peadar. "If you can get us to Grand Canal Dock, I can take it from there."

26

LET THE FLOODGATES OPEN

"It's time to open the floodgates!" Brigid shouts at me from the steering wheel of the canary-yellow, amphibious vehicle she drives down the slip into Grand Canal Dock.

"The what!?" I scream back at her over the roar of the propellers of the Viking Tour Boat as the amphibious vehicle morphs from a bus into a boat and plonks itself ungraciously into the canal's murky water.

"The Camden sea lock," she says and points at the old pier up ahead.

Buildings hem us in on all sides save for the limestone lock that's so old, we're not sure if it will actually open.

"This is the key," she says, shoving a rusted iron bar into my hands. "Climb onto the pier, find the lock chamber, and use it to open the wooden part of the gate." She increases the speed and I have to close my mouth before I swallow some of the foul-smelling water that laps against the Viking Tour boat. "I'm not going to lie to you. It'll be difficult. The gates are in a derelict state, but the winches of the lock chamber should still open if you put enough elbow grease into it."

Brigid turns her attention away from me and focuses on steering the craft as I shuffle to the top of the boat, holding tight to the steel rail that runs the length of the vehicle. Peadar hands out Viking helmets from the storage trunk and I gratefully accept the scarlet life jacket he offers me.

"It's smart really," Muriel says as she plonks the horned helmet on her head. "If anyone sees us, they'll think we're nothing more than aimless tourists."

She's still wearing the red gloves I suspect Oscar stole from my cousin's wardrobe on the night of her vigil. It feels like it happened a lifetime ago and I give my cousin a sly look from where I grip the railing. The frigid winter wind whipping at my hair. Because under the Irish Celtic calendar, winter begins on November 1st.

"As opposed to members of a secret society of solicitors off on a quest to restore our good standing within the legal community?"

"That's still better than the ill-fated fellowship we formed on Croagh Patrick," Brigid shouts as more floatation devices on the side of the bus expand the deeper into the water we get.

"Brigid!" Oscar shouts over the noise of the engine. "Are you sure you know how to operate this thing?"

"Absolutely," she replies with a sly grin as she sails the boat one-handed up to the gate. "I did this every Summer for a bit of extra cash. Plus, the plan is simple. We're going to open the sea lock, sail down the River Liffey, and pull up outside of the Four Courts."

Oscar still doesn't look convinced, but Brigid throws a Viking helmet at him and I'm about to make a quip about needing to respect the captain's orders when the boat jerks and I nearly tumble into the canal.

"You okay?" Keefe asks as he places a steadying hand on my elbow.

I nod at him gratefully just as Brigid curses from behind the steering wheel. "I thought he wouldn't be here this late!"

I follow the direction of Brigid's gaze and see a man running across the docks.

"He's attracting too much attention!" Oscar shouts as other pedestrians stop to watch our great escape.

"Fiadh, you have very little time to get that gate open," she shouts as the owner of the boat comes barrelling around the corner towards us. And even from this distance, I can tell he's raging.

I waste no time and scramble up the ladder, slam the key into the lock, and pull with everything I have.

It doesn't budge.

The mechanism is ancient, rusted, and more stubborn than I am.

I can hear the man over the sound of the wind. He bellows, "Stop, thieves!"

"Oh, great," Peadar grumbles from his place beside Brigid. "In a misguided attempt to clear our names, we are now breaking the law."

The gate still won't budge but a moment later I feel another set of arms around mine and together Keefe and I pull. The gate moves a couple of inches but nothing more. And it's not until Oscar and Muriel clamber up and lend a hand that floodgates open with a rush of water.

"Come on!" Brigid screams as we jump back down into the boat and land with a jarring thud that reverberates deep in my bones.

Brigid doesn't waste any time and seizes her opening. "Hold on to something," she shouts and floors the gas. The back of the boat sinks into the water and the front rises as we pass under the Samuel Beckett

Bridge and make our way down the River Liffey that is mercifully at high tide.

Keefe has been unusually silent for some time and, with a slight prod from me, he turns to face the rest of us, concern etched across his face.

"What if the Costelloe, Ingram, and Nettleford apprentices haven't been ignoring us because they failed to make it into the SoS. What if they were made to forget the SoS even exists?"

Everyone looks at Oscar who manages to bite out a pained confirmation. "Variation deeds are allowed in select circumstances when approved by the Council of Hons."

I let this worrying revelation sink in but something else has been bothering me since the hospital and I have to know the answer.

So, I turn to Peadar, who is whispering directions to an irritated Brigid and ask the question I've been afraid to find the answer to.

"How did you know Dawson was working with Joyce?"

The colour leaches from Peadar's face.

"What do you mean?"

"When you saw Dawson outside the hospital, you knew he was going to try and hex us... but how could you have known that's what he'd do?"

Brigid looks back at me from her position by the steering wheel.

"What kind of question is that? Dawson sabotaged us when we faced the mountain and then showed up out of the blue at the hospital. Of course, he was going to try to hex us again."

"Sure," I say, not taking my eyes off Peadar who hasn't said a word in his own defence. "And we assumed Dawson was the one who hexed us at work yesterday, but he would have needed a witness. Tell us the truth Peadar, did you help Dawson hex us?"

No one speaks over the hum of the engine. Even Brigid is quiet, her hand steady on the wheel as she waits for Peadar to explain himself, but he doesn't. Even Oscar looks surprised. So, Joyce didn't inform him of all her accomplices. Interesting.

Muriel is the first to break the silence. "When did Joyce get to you?" She whispers. And it's Muriel's quiet but strong voice, raspy from months of disuse, that cracks Peadar Ahern's affable facade.

He scrubs his hands over his face as if he can wash away the dark deeds of his past.

"I didn't know what Joyce was really doing, you have to believe me!" He hangs his head in shame. "She asked me if I would like to form an alliance."

Keefe scoffs disbelievingly.

"And that didn't seem suspicious to you?"

Peadar's eyes dart around the boat, searching for sympathetic ears or, perhaps, a way out.

"I thought she wanted to help me. To mentor me. How in the world could I have guessed she was tormenting and incapacitating apprentices to further her own ambitions? No reasonable person would think that!"

"When did she get to you?" Oscar asks, his tone tinged with deadly menace.

Peadar sighs and rubs his eyes as we sail down the Liffey.

"It was the morning after we faced the mountain. Joyce asked us to come to her office. I was the first to arrive. She said I'd impressed her.

That she'd heard about how I hid the last boat and said she could use a man like me on her team. Someone who thinks two steps ahead."

"And that, in and of itself, didn't sound like a massive red flag to you?" Keefe shouts at him.

Peadar flinches from his accusatory tone. And even I'm a little taken aback. I don't think I've ever seen the swan man this angry. But Peadar regains his nerve.

"When a senior associate taps you on the shoulder and asks you to do a favour for them, of course, you accept. She told me that Bebb Gwyn wants to merge with Heron Early and, if it happens, there'll be layoffs. She said I wouldn't have to worry though because there's always work for diligent people who are willing to go above and beyond to get the job done."

He's breaking my heart. "What did she ask you to do, Peadar?"

This takes the wind out of his sails. "She had Dawson and me execute two dark deeds. The first was the dysmenorrhea deed that I also hexed myself with, thank you very much."

"And what was the second?" I press.

Peadar sighs, clearly uncomfortable with the question.

"She gave specific instructions to have you and Brigid act on your worst impulses and dampen your inhibitions. But in my defence, those hexes were supposed to be far worse than they ended up being."

I have to snort at that. "Oh, ya? And please tell me, how did you lessen the side effects of the deed that almost cost me my career?"

And with an utterly earnest face, Peadar responds, "By drafting them really badly. With the vaguest wording you will ever read. I'm genuinely surprised the hex even worked. And when I agreed to remove your inhibitions, I thought that, at worst, we'd find you and

Keefe kissing in the boardroom. Never in my wildest dreams did I think you and Brigid would go on a rampage that would be whispered about around the firm. A story that becomes more dramatic with each retelling."

There's a moment of stunned silence to this as Brigid fumes behind the wheel.

"Did Joyce ask you to do anything else?" She hisses.

He hesitates and then closes his eyes. Too ashamed to even look at me.

"She asked me to let her know if I ever heard or saw anything of interest."

"And did you?" I push, even though I can already guess the answer.

He nods forlornly. "I told her you were looking for deeds linked to Muriel Hunt."

Oscar steps closer. Putting himself between Peadar and Muriel and he looks positively apoplectic.

"I'm sorry," Peadar raises his hands in contrition. "But if Fiadh had been honest from the start and had informed me the Muriel she was searching for was her missing cousin or that she suspected someone in the SoS was responsible for her disappearance, I never would have told Joyce what I'd seen. Or gotten caught up in her dark deeds. You have to believe me!"

He looks at each of us, his eyes pleading.

"Ask yourself, what you would have done in my situation. Can you really blame me for doing whatever I had to in order to survive?"

"Yes, I absolutely can, you traitor!" Keefe huffs and, with Oscar's help, the two of them haul Peadar to the back of the boat and shove him against the starboard side. Looking for all intents and purposes as if they're going to throw Peadar overboard and be done with him once and for all.

"I didn't know what she was really up to. You have to believe me!" Peadar shouts.

And I do believe him, or at least I want to. But there's something else that's been niggling at me.

"On Croagh Patrick, when we were all under the influence of a dread deed, what did you think was happening, Peadar? What did it make you believe?"

There's silence for a moment as he continues to wrangle against his assailants.

"That everyone else was conspiring against me. It's what prompted me to run away from the other apprentices and hide the last currach. But in all fairness to myself," he shouts as the River Liffey strips the wax from his hair, "it turns out that Dawson really was trying to sabotage us. And because of that, I unwittingly attracted the attention of what I now realise is a very unhinged solicitor who is willing to sacrifice everyone in order to further her own ambitions."

And as the lads get ready to push Peadar overboard, I look at him and wonder if, without truth, there can be trust. Or if I have to trust in order to deserve the truth. In any event, Peadar doesn't deserve this. None of us do. Because I believe Joyce convinced Peadar that she'd seen something worthwhile in him. That so long as he did whatever she asked, regardless of the toll it took, she'd look after him. That it would all be worthwhile in the end.

Joyce had played on his insecurities just as Buach had tried to play on mine.

"Leave him go."

Keefe gives me a startled look but wrenches Peadar back up.

"Why, so he can betray us again?"

I ignore him and face Peadar.

"You saw what Joyce did to me, to Muriel, to Oscar. Are you going to help us clear our names and show the SoS what's been going on under their noses?"

Peadar shouts, "Yes! I'm on your side. I always have been, even if recent events may have led you to believe otherwise."

"That's good enough for me," I say to the others with a shrug. "I'm willing to trust Peadar will do the right thing."

"Quiet!" Brigid hisses from the front of the boat. "There's a Gardaí checkpoint up ahead. Sit down, put your life vests on, and try to pretend you are tourists enjoying a lovely jaunt down the River Liffey."

Peadar looks sceptical but, after Keefe throws a life jacket at him, he sits back down and whips out his mobile. Looking for all of the world like he's taking a selfie in his Viking costume.

Muriel and Oscar follow suit as Brigid picks up a microphone.

"Coming up on our right is the Four Courts of Ireland. And why is it called that you might ask? Because the building itself houses four courts. The Supreme Court, the Court of Appeal, the High Court, and the Dublin Circuit Court."

Keefe looks positively bewildered by this and it takes everything in me to grit my teeth and not laugh at the thick north Dublin accent Brigid has suddenly adopted.

"In 1922," Brigid continues, "a section of the Irish Republican Army in staunch opposition to the Anglo-Irish Treaty occupied the building in what became known as 'The battle of the Four Courts'. And when the forces of the Provisional Government attacked, the shelling led to an explosion that destroyed the Irish State's records dating all the way back to the twelfth century."

Peadar is clearly annoyed and mutters darkly from the back seat. "That's a rather vague summary of an incredibly complex moment in Irish history."

"Quiet, Peadar!" Brigid hisses as we float past the checkpoint where two uniformed Gardaí gape at us as we sail by.

After a few tense minutes, Brigid pulls up in front of the Four Courts. Our presence concealed by the trees that line the river. The road outside is utterly deserted as a result of the Gardaí diversions.

Brigid turns off the engine, tension leaking from her shoulders; and as the boat judders to a halt, she says, "I got us here. Now I sincerely hope someone has a plan to get us inside."

27

EQUITY WILL NOT SUFFER A WRONG WITHOUT REMEDY

The salmon and the sow guard the entrance to the Four Courts.

Two loyal foot soldiers stood amidst rows of Corinthian columns. Their black robes stark against the sandstone wall while four more masks watch the river from the top of the domed roof. Their attention fixed on the Viking tour boat drifting lazily down the River Liffey. Our helmets placed strategically throughout to make it look like a group of tourists are still aboard.

Oscar wandered away as we disembarked from the boat and, for a few gut-wrenching minutes, I wondered whether he'd sold us out. I even readied myself to break the news to Muriel but, instead, Oscar reappeared with our SoS robes in his arms. He shoved a brass mask into our hands. And as I run my finger over the exquisite markings of my deer mask, a lone fleeting thought runs through my mind.

It fits me perfectly.

But once again, the salmon and the sow stand between me and my freedom.

"She shouldn't be here," the sow hisses at Oscar when she spots the deer mask on my face and makes to sound the alarm.

"Please don't, Lucile."

The sow stops in the doorway and turns to watch my cousin walk up the concrete steps.

Alby takes off his mask, surprise etched across his face. "Muriel! Where have you been?" But before he can ask anything else, Lucile shoves him aside and hugs my cousin like a long-lost friend. And after a moment's hesitation, Alby does the same.

"I'll explain everything," Muriel says and pulls her own owl mask over her face, "but please, if we were ever friends, let us pass. We have information the Tribunal needs to hear."

The sow and the salmon exchange a loaded look and stand aside.

"Hurry," the sow says. "The session is about to start."

We spill through the mahogany door and into the cavernous round hall. Our footsteps too loud against the brown-and-white marble tiles. Magnificent stone pillars bear the colossal weight of the domed roof above our heads.

"Where do we go?" I ask and flinch when my voice reverberates around the draughty chamber all the way up to the panelled roof. And I swear, it feels like the windows themselves stare down at us disapprovingly. Like they know we don't belong.

Oscar leads the way, the long ears of his mask tilted towards me in silent mockery.

"If you were an elite, secret society, in which court would you choose to hold your mock tribunal of inquiry?"

"Well, it's obvious when you put it like that," I mumble, and we hustle towards the Supreme Court.

"There you are!"

Dawson appears at the top of a stone staircase dressed as the snake he is. But he's not alone and a wave of SoS members flow down the steps like a dark tidal wave that has the power to wash us from the face of the earth.

"Run!" Oscar shouts and we sprint down the hallway.

The flurry of footsteps adds speed to my charge and, when a gloved hand reaches out for my robes, I jump forwards and hurl my body against the door. The following thuds thrum through my body as each of the others throw themselves upon the mercy of the lady of justice and seek sanctuary within the walls of the Supreme Court.

Keefe is the last to reach the entrance and, with one final push, the door bursts open and we land not upon the doorstep of the Supreme Court but into the judge's chambers, where a sly fox watches us fall into her trap.

"Be a dear and tell Dawson to come in, would you Peadar?" Joyce says as she pulls the fox mask from her face.

With a click, Peadar closes the door behind him and before any of us can make a run for it, the telltale sound of a key locks us inside.

"This is where blind faith gets us," Keefe mutters with a world-weary sigh, while Brigid, Muriel, and Oscar choose a few more colourful descriptions for the rat who sold us out.

"Muriel," Joyce interrupts. "How nice of you to join us. Fiadh must be delighted to have found her long-lost cousin." She picks up a pair of dark, leather gloves from the table. "Your vigil was lovely, by the way. Really moving."

"How could you do that to me?" Muriel hisses at Joyce. Angrier than I've ever seen her.

Joyce holds up a leather gloved finger just as Peadar and Dawson open the door and step into the room.

"All will be revealed in good time," Joyce purrs and snaps her fingers.

Too late, I spin around only to watch Dawson and Peadar bring their matrices down on the piece of parchment.

I open my mouth to beg Peadar to stop and reconsider, but nothing comes out. Alarmed, I turn to the others but they gape back at me. Eyes wide with fear.

"For the duration of the Tribunal, you may only speak when spoken to and may utter nothing but the truth, or so help you."

Joyce winks at me, like we're in for a real treat if we attempt to lie.

"Thank you, Peadar. Helpful as always, unlike others I could mention," she says with a mock incline of her head to Oscar who looks fit to explode. That poor lad has so many gag orders on him it's a wonder he can still breathe.

The main chamber opens and Una Bewley, of all people, pops her head around the door.

"They're ready for you."

Her eyes widen a fraction when she sees us but, before I can attempt to cry for help, she's gone again. Having ducked back inside the Supreme Court.

Joyce strides self-assuredly to the door. "Do hurry up. It never ends well if you make the Council of Hons wait."

My gaze wanders to Peadar but he turns away. The coward can't even face me. I throw a contemptuous look in his direction and assess our options. But with Dawson and Joyce's people guarding the hallway, there isn't much we can do other than follow Joyce into the courtroom filled to the brim with masked members of the SoS.

Joyce motions for us to stop in front of a raised wooden platform where seven masked individuals are seated. And at the centre of the judges' bench, sits the badger. A powerfully built man with a stocky frame. And if it wasn't obvious to me before, I now realise with deadly certainty that this tribunal will not be impartial.

"Fiadh Whelan, you stand accused of executing a dark deed without the express authorisation of senior members of the SoS. How do you plead?"

Keefe flinches beside me while Brigid takes a step back. She's worried they'll interrogate her next, considering she was the one who witnessed that particular deed on All Hallows' Eve.

"Chief Hon," Joyce interjects, "I have already taken the liberty of executing a gag order that stipulates the defendants may only speak when asked a direct question. If I may approach the bench, here is the aforementioned deed, for the Hons to review at your pleasure."

The badger motions for her to step forwards and flicks a lazy eye over the deed that has so casually stripped me of my constitutional right to freedom of speech.

"This appears to be in order. Registrar, please file this deed," the Chief Hon hands the parchment to Una who sits directly below him. She doesn't even bother to look up as she transcribes every word uttered in her courtroom.

The badger gazes down at me once more.

"Fiadh Whelan, the first named defendant, you stand accused of executing dark deeds against a fellow apprentice. How do you plead?"

I open my mouth, ready to defend myself and elaborate on the extenuating circumstances that led to my actions but, as soon as the thought crosses my mind, a wrenching, burning pain flares across my palms. Horrified, I look down to find ugly red welts marring the centre of my hands.

It feels like I've just been whipped.

"Ms. Whelan, do not waste any more of this Council's time," the Chief Hon groans, his mind clearly already made up.

I clench my hands and attempt to ignore the searing pain. I want to scream in frustration.

"Yes," I manage to croak. "I executed a dark deed but only because I had to." But I needn't have bothered trying to explain myself. The moment I said yes, the badger leaned back in his chair and crossed his arms.

Muriel steps forwards and waves her arms wildly, trying to flag the attention of anyone who might be willing to listen, but not a sound comes out of her mouth.

My heart batters against my ribcage as Joyce approaches the bench with a second piece of parchment.

"On the basis of her confession of misconduct, I move that the Council proceed to immediately strike Fiadh Whelan's name from the SoS register, bind her with a gag order, and execute a variation deed that shall alter her memories, so as to protect the knowledge our society has safeguarded for over a millennium."

My heart sinks as each of the Hons nod their heads in approval. The Chief Hon reaches for his matrice to seal my fate.

"Stop!" Peadar roars from the back of the courtroom and, while all eyes are on him, Dawson slips a piece of parchment into Brigid's hand. She frowns at him, wary of whatever he's given her and what his ulterior motives might be.

"Fiadh and the others are innocent. Joyce is to blame for all of this."

A collective gasp runs through the rows of seated SoS members at Peadar's dramatic outburst.

"What is the meaning of this?" The Chief Hon sputters while some of the other masks attempt to tackle Peadar to the ground. "Order, order, I will have order in this courtroom!" The Chief Hon shouts. "Remove him from this courtroom at once."

"No!" Peadar shouts as he struggles. "Listen to her, just hear what..." and the words die on his lips as he's dragged towards the exit.

A woman in the front pew who wears the brass mask of a hound rises to her feet.

"I motion that we hear what the apprentices have to say and, in particular, I would very much like to hear from Muriel Hunt, who has been missing these past six months."

I know that voice.

"This is most unusual," the Chief Hon starts but is interrupted by Una Bewley, of all people.

"Actually, as an honorary life member of the SoS, the hound is well within her rights to request this of the Council."

The Chief Hon begins to disagree but is cut off by the hound herself. And I can do nothing but stare in disbelief as my landlady, Edna Morgan, lifts her mask and stares down the Chief Hon with the kind of defiance I can only hope to emulate someday. While Brigid takes a step back in shock and mouths something I can't quite make out.

Not waiting for him to respond, Edna, the hound, turns to my cousin.

"Muriel, please tell us where you have been these past months."

Muriel stares at her in disbelief, clearly as surprised as I am to realise her old landlady is a member of the SoS, but she doesn't waste the opportunity she's been afforded and, with a jerk of her arm, she shrugs off the hands of the masked SoS members who attempt to hold her back.

"Six months ago, Joyce Larkin executed a variation deed with such onerous terms that not only did she alter my memories but made me forget who I was entirely. She left me a mere shadow of my former self and locked me in St. Ita's hospital, where I was kept under constant supervision. She falsely led the SoS, Heron Early, and my own family to believe I'd been negligent in the performance of my duties and concealed her own involvement in my disappearance."

The badger has the gall to snort in derision at her claim.

"Preposterous. First, St. Ita's Hospital is not currently in operation; and, second, what possible motive would a solicitor of good standing in the legal community, such as Joyce Larkin, have for orchestrating such an alleged crime?"

Too late, with a jerk of his head, he realises his mistake. He asked Muriel a direct question and she can speak nothing but the truth.

"Because I figured out Joyce was sabotaging a project so as to undermine Buach Scannell. And in doing so, she set Buach up to lose his position at Heron Early so that she could pave her own path to partnership. But I made the mistake of confronting Joyce, and she altered my memories so that I could tell no one what I'd discovered. She used me as a means by which to control Oscar Pierce, the only other person I'd informed of her treachery. She subjected Oscar to a gag order that rendered him unable to tell anyone what had happened to me, what Joyce was planning, or the identity of those she was working with."

Murmurs break out amongst the Council of Hons. I look over at Joyce who remains cool and collected. Why isn't she worried?

Joyce thrums her fingers against the desk.

"The Council should be made aware that Muriel Hunt is in fact a close relative of Fiadh Whelan and is merely trying to deflect blame from a family member who is facing punishment for her transgressions. I call on Dawson Garvey, the subject of Fiadh's dark deed, to shed further light on these matters."

Dawson steps away from Brigid and saunters up to the bench like he owns the place.

"Dawson, please tell the court how Fiadh Whelan and the other named defendants acted in concert to hex you on the night of All Hallows' Eve."

Dawson lifts the snake mask from his face and, with a sinking heart, I realise we're going to lose. They don't care what we have to say. This inquiry was decided before we ever stepped foot in this courtroom. And yet, Dawson says nothing. His gaze fixed solely on Brigid as whispers break out amongst the spectators.

"Silence!" The Chief Hon shouts over the ruckus. "Is there any basis to these claims; yes or no?"

"Yes," Dawson replies.

My heart sinks while Keefe hangs his head beside me in despair.

"But to the best of my knowledge, it was in retaliation for the dark deeds with which Joyce forced Peadar Ahern and me to hex Fiadh and her fellow apprentices."

Gasps ring out around the room, but Dawson's not done.

"Today, my fellow apprentice, Jaya, informed me about Muriel Hunt's incarceration in St. Ita's hospital and upon further investigation, I have come to suspect that Oscar Pierce is under the influence of a separate gag order executed by the same Joyce Larkin. Before this trial commenced, I searched Joyce's possessions and found the aforementioned gag order in her handbag. I hold it here in my hand and motion that the Council of Hons terminate Oscar Pierce's gag order and hear what he has to say."

Oh, my God.

"Now wait just one moment," the Chief Hon shouts. "You are merely an apprentice and as such, you are quite unable to motion the Council to do anything of the sort."

My landlady rises to her feet. "But I am entitled to motion the Council and on the basis of what we've heard here today, I think it's in the society's best interests that we invite Oscar Pierce to address the bench."

Dawson steps forwards and hands the piece of parchment to the Hon wearing an elk mask. The elk surveys the parchment, reaches for a fountain pen, and amends the wording.

"Council, if you please," Joyce starts and then stops as a different council member places their seal upon a separate piece of parchment and she's rendered mute.

"Now, now Joyce," Buach's voice rings out from behind the elk mask. "You must only speak when spoken to."

Of course, Buach Scannell is a senior member of the SoS.

I just can't catch a break.

Buach passes the parchment to another one of the Hons. The badger tries to object, but Buach doesn't give him the chance. He and the other Hons bring their seals down upon the parchment and Oscar Pierce falls to his knees.

"Everything they said is true," he gasps – and the courtroom erupts into mayhem.

28

THE TRUTH WILL WIN

"Quiet!" The badger roars as he attempts to regain control of the situation.

But Oscar Pierce has had to hold his tongue for too long and he refuses to be silenced again. He rises to his feet and shouts so that even the blind lady of justice atop the Four Courts will hear him.

"Phelim O'Kelly, the Chief Hon and the badger, was not only aware of Joyce's dark deeds, he was also her witness and used his position as managing partner of Bebb Gwyn to coerce Dawson Garvey to hex the Heron Early apprentices!"

All eyes fall upon the Chief Hon for his rebuttal.

"This is absolutely untrue. These apprentices want to fling mud to cover up the stench of their own misdeeds. Members of the Council, we cannot allow ourselves to entertain such accusations, or we risk the floodgates opening to further, spurious claims."

Buach lifts the elk mask from his face and bloody murder written across it.

"Joyce, are these accusations true?"

Quiet descends on the courtroom as everyone leans forward to hear what Joyce has to say. And instead of the usual air of indifference I've come to expect from her, for once, Joyce's eyes are suddenly full of sorrow as her gaze wanders from Oscar to Muriel and then me before hardening once again as she focuses on Buach.

"What was her name?" Joyce's voice comes out as a mere whisper, but it travels around the court room, nonetheless.

"Who?" Buach asks, a little too carefully.

That was clearly the wrong thing to say because Joyce throws her head back and cackles in response. It's a hard, dry laugh that escapes her lungs until she's forced to bend over her documents to catch her breath. Her hands clasp the sides of the teak desk, white knuckles straining under the force of her grip, like it's her last tether to this world.

Phelim, the badger, takes advantage of the situation and fills the awkward silence with a further command.

"We shall adjourn until order has been restored to this courtroom."

He motions for the masked members to take us away.

"No." Joyce raises her hand to stop their approach. "They've been through enough, Phelim." She turns her flinty eyes on Buach.

"My daughter's name was Lucy. Don't you remember her?"

Buach leans back from the bench as though he can distance himself from what Joyce is about to say.

Joyce laughs again but whereas the last one was tainted with anger, this one is tinged with a sour note of sadness.

"I can't bring myself to claim my daughter was the light of my life, or my reason for existing or any of the usual expressions a devoted mother is expected to parrot. Because she wasn't. I am my own person.

Someone who existed long before my daughter came into this world. I had a life, a career, and ambitions before she arrived. Ones I make no apology for. But that didn't mean I loved her any less for it.

"Lucy crashed into my life like a storm and washed away everything but my most firmly rooted beliefs and dreams. And my career that had been so important to me now flowed concurrently to the little tributary of her life. Maternity leave, toddlerhood, nursery, and then school. Days dedicated to fitting client and partner requests around her schedule. Neither done to perfection but, nonetheless, the demands of my legal career always took priority.

"Because how could they not, Buach? When you made it clear that a top law firm is a competitive environment in which to work. We're told from our first day that the client must come first. Where praise and flattery is heaped upon those of us who succeed, even as our personal lives unravel in the background and our health falls by the wayside.

"From the moment I walked into your office as a newly minted apprentice. Green as they come, you groomed me to become the insecure overachiever you needed. And in order to avail of the opportunities that came so easily to the apprentices who entered this profession with the right connections, I was eager to do anything to prove my worth."

Buach throws his elk mask on the table. His face purple as a turnip.

"What in the world are you talking about? You asked for everything I gave you. Opportunities that many would have given anything for. And let me remind you, Joyce, in case you have conveniently forgotten, you pushed aside other associates as you climbed that ladder. While the knowledge I shared with you, the experience you gained, and the exposure I gave you to the best clients and the biggest deals was more than you could have gotten elsewhere. And not once did I put a gun to your forehead and force you to do any of it. You chose this life and this career for yourself."

Joyce laughs again and this time a single tear rolls down her cheek.

"You're a user, Buach. You used and manipulated me for your own personal gain. And yes, it was made very clear to me that I could get off the ladder at any point and walk away. But the drop looked fatal from where I was standing and that's the thing about the types of people law firms like Heron Early hire. We find it awfully difficult to put our health and happiness first. Because it's so easy to declare what you should be willing to put up with in order to earn a high salary when you're not the one in the trenches fighting for your life. Buried under a mountain of expectations and drowning in a sea of misery you may never rise from.

"But through all of that, I had a little light that guided me home every night. That is, until my world went dark. You remember how it happened, don't you, Buach?"

Buach says nothing. His mouth set in a grim line. No one has gagged him. He chooses to remain silent.

"No?" Joyce grimaces. "Then let me remind you of the deal that brought us to New York. The all-nighter you had me and the other associates pull in order to finalise the transaction documents."

"False," Buach blusters. "I never asked you to do any such thing."

Joyce snorts. "No, of course not. But you did tell us the client expected to have the documents finalised by the time we got off the flight and that, if we didn't, not only would the client be unhappy but the entire deal would be jeopardised. And what would a bunch of well-paid solicitors like us be expected to do? Go to bed and leave both you and the client down?"

She shakes her head. "Of course not. We're trained to exceed expectations. And when you asked us to set aside our phones so we could do a final read through the transaction documents, I did so without question."

"Joyce," Buach pleads, "what happened to Lucy wasn't my fault."

Joyce's face hardens. "No, Buach. You weren't the one behind the wheel of the car that hit her, but you were the reason my phone was turned off when the call came to tell me my daughter was in critical condition in hospital.

"Corporate culture, big law's obsession with excellence, and chronic burn-out is what stopped me from checking my phone before the flight took off. And it cost me everything! I lost my chance to be there when she passed away. Before her little light was snuffed out. And the darkness I waded through in the aftermath of her death led to the dissolution of my marriage."

She coughs out a bitter laugh. "And do you remember what you said to me when I eventually came back to work? You called me into your office, sat me down on that wretched leather chair, and told me a solicitor can always find solace in their work. That keeping busy had kept you sane through some of the worst moments of your life and that I too would get through this.

"And I clung to work like a drowning person does to a piece of debris in stormy waters. I tried to find comfort between the pages of books, binders and boxes upon boxes of bloody documents. I billed record numbers of hours for the firm. Doing the work of many to distract myself from a loss so bone-deep that, if I were to fall into that sea of despair, I'd disappear."

She stops and gazes at the other six Hons before addressing the masked SoS members who watch silently from their pews.

"And is it any wonder I wanted revenge?"

Keefe gestures at the Hons to terminate our gag orders and two of them helpfully comply.

"But why me?" Muriel's voice rings out, loud and clear. "Why make me suffer the way you did? Why do those terrible things to Fiadh, to Oscar and God only knows who else got caught in your vendetta?"

"Ah," Joyce says with a sad smile. "You see, revenge is addictive. It lures you into its sweet embrace until you find yourself committing dark deeds in its name. And you, my dear, reminded me far too much of myself. Brilliant, ambitious but so naive and vulnerable to the machinations of a man like Buach. I watched you and then Fiadh lose precious parts of yourselves as you sat in that cold, inhospitable office. Just as I once did. I saw how you grasped for any scrap of validation he was willing to throw your way.

"He was going leave you a soulless husk of your former self unless I did something about it."

My hands shake but my voice remains mercifully steady.

"Are you actually trying to argue that you were helping us!?"

At this, a truly menacing smile spreads across her face.

"Not in the least. I became what I needed to be in order to survive. And in doing so, I became the villain of your story while trying to become the saviour of my own. But make no mistake; when Muriel became suspicious, I had to remove her from the playing field. Because a game was afoot. One that had been years in the making. One that

I was going to win. And although you may not believe me, to have let you carry on working for someone like Buach would have been a worse fate than what I did to you both. Because if I hadn't removed you from Buach's grasp, well, you would have become like me. And that was something I refused to let happen."

"How does the Chief Hon fit into all of this?" My landlady asks, staring between Joyce and Phelim.

"Phelim, as the managing partner of Bebb Gwyn, wants to merge our two firms. And if Buach lost his top fee-paying client to Bebb Gwyn, the Heron Early partnership would have little choice but to accept Phelim's offer. And when the merger took place, Phelim was going to promote me to the partnership; that is, if I hadn't already been invited to join based on my years of dedicated work and stellar billable hours. Because you were going to back me for promotion to the Heron Early partnership, weren't you, Buach?"

Buach's silence is damning.

"No, I thought not. I was too useful to keep stringing along as your top associate. So, from my perspective, it was a win-win situation. I wanted to strip Buach of what he loves most in the world, his career. Just as I had lost what I held most dear to me. While Phelim would become one of the most powerful legal practitioners in the entire country."

"This woman is unwell," the Chief Hon blusters. "I will no longer let my good name be called into question. These are lies, all of it; and I hereby order that Joyce Larkin be removed from the courtroom."

"But this isn't the first time you've used dark deeds to get what you want, is it Phelim?"

I blink in surprise as Keefe addresses the Chief Hon.

He holds up his hands in mock supplication.

"That's why you wanted me and the other Heron Early apprentices to fail the initiation tests. It's why you used your position as the managing partner of Bebb Gwyn to lean on Dawson, an ambitious first-year apprentice, to sabotage our boat. It was all so that I wouldn't figure out you have the ability to make people do exactly what you want. Because that's what you did to your ex-wife, right, Phelim? You abused your power to have my mother sign a separation agreement that left her with nothing. To this day, she doesn't understand why she signed it. So, your little agreement with Joyce is really just the tip of the iceberg of what you've been getting up to. Isn't it, Dad?"

The Chief Hon who wears the mask of a badger, is Keefe's father.

My head is spinning.

"Be quiet, you ungrateful brat!" The Chief Hon sneers at him. "Or you'll find yourself the subject of another misconduct investigation."

"I don't think so," I say and hold up the piece of parchment Dawson slipped into Brigid's hand earlier. "We took the liberty of executing a veracity deed. Everything Joyce said was true."

Joyce blinks in surprise at the dark deed.

How wretched must her soul be not to have even noticed she was under the influence of a hex?

The Chief Hon stares at the parchment in my hand but he regains his composure faster than Joyce.

"This is outrageous. By her own admission, Fiadh Whelan has executed yet another dark deed that she, as an apprentice, has no right to dabble in. It goes against the fundamental rules this society is based upon and as a result, this evidence is inadmissible."

Joyce guffaws and takes in great heaving lungfuls of air to which Buach seems to take personal offence.

"And what may I ask, do you think you have to laugh about, having confessed to crimes that will see you struck from the roll?" He asks as his calculating eyes drift between his senior associate and the Chief Hon.

Joyce wipes a tear from her eye. She looks happier than I've ever seen her.

"Because the truth always wins and your time is coming to an end, even if you're too stubborn to realise it. You might not see the cracks, but the foundations you built your career upon are crumbling, Buach."

29

— · —

THE SWAN EFFECT

Edna Morgan takes the stand.

"Gran?" Brigid says, her mouth wide open in shock.

Is everyone in Dublin related to each other?

Edna smiles dotingly at her granddaughter and then trains her flinty eyes back on the bench.

"Council members, I motion on the basis of the information shared here tonight that Phelim O'Kelly be immediately suspended from his position as Chief Hon and that he and Joyce Larkin be held in temporary custody while a full and thorough investigation is carried out into their clandestine activities."

Buach speaks over Phelim who pleads for his colleagues to hear him out.

"All those in favour?"

Buach lifts his right hand, followed by three other council members. "Four in favour and three dissenting. The motion passes. Take them to the holding cell," he instructs the masks who stand by the door. "And as vice-chair, in the interim, I shall take on the mantle of Chief Hon as per the rules of our society."

And with an astonishing degree of nerve, Buach Scannell sits in the Chief Hon's seat.

I can't keep quiet. Not after everything that's happened.

"On the basis of the information shared here tonight, I beseech the Council to obstruct Buach Scannell from assuming the role of Chief Hon pending an investigation into the accusations levelled against him by Joyce Larkin."

"Denied," Buach shouts. "An apprentice who is under investigation does not have the right to motion the Hons."

"No, but I do," my landlady says in a haughty tone. "And I motion that the position of Chief Hon remain vacant until such time as a proper vote can be held to fill the role."

The hands of each of the other five Council members shoot into the air.

Joyce's cackle echoes down the hallway.

Other masked members of the SoS raise their voices as questions are asked and accusations are lobbed around the courtroom. But it all falls on deaf ears as I hold out my hand to Muriel and together we walk out of the courtroom. The noise of the other SoS members fade as we leave them to face the mess they created and stroll arm in arm past the spiral staircase and back into the Round Hall.

I make a break for the entrance, eager to be rid of the place but Muriel comes to an abrupt halt. Oscar has followed us from the courtroom. He stares down at the hare mask clutched in his hand and back at my cousin.

"They let us go. The Council have bigger fish to fry than some over zealous apprentices who've read too many precedents for their own good."

Brigid strolls past them both, a mischievous look in her eyes, and comes to stand beside me.

"It's chaos in there. I swear, it's like their worst nightmare has finally come true and the floodgates have been opened to let in a torrent of what both Phelim and Buach are referring to as 'dubious claims devoid of merit'."

While Muriel and Oscar continue to make moon eyes at each other, I wonder aloud.

"What will the SoS do now that they've been forced to face their own misdeeds?"

Brigid chuckles in response. "I'd give them a day before they've forgotten all about this and are back at their desks, focused on meeting their billable targets."

Muriel frowns at me, having heard the tail end of our conversation.

"But you heard Joyce. They're not going to allow Buach to go on torturing apprentices. Are they?"

I sigh. "If you'd asked me that question the other day, I'd have said yes. But who knows. Maybe Joyce will have the last laugh, even though I'll never forgive her for what she did to us."

Oscar nods his head. "Well, Buach's in for a nasty surprise when he learns it's pens down on Project Puzzle. Hades Partners lost the auction. Persephone Capital swooped in at the last moment with a higher bid and the deal closed earlier today."

Brigid can barely stifle her smile. "Oh no, that's terrible news."

Oscar, far chattier than I've ever known him to be, shrugs. "I don't think there are any heroes in this particular story. Just varying shades of grey and the crappy choices we each faced. Speaking of which..."

he trails off as Keefe walks out of the courtroom followed by an oddly elated Peadar Ahern.

"Rat!" Brigid hisses at him as he approaches. "Why did you help Joyce place a gag order over us? If Dawson hadn't switched sides at the last possible moment, we'd all be royally fecked right now."

"Hey," Peadar says and raises his hands to halt the verbal abuse. "It all went exactly according to plan. We found the missing apprentice and saved Fiadh's career in the process. The truth really did win in the end."

Keefe snorts. "Explain?"

"When I saw Joyce had us cornered in the judges' chamber, I convinced Dawson to turn against her. I told him that, if he could draft a veracity deed and slip it to Brigid, we'd handle the rest."

Brigid blinks in surprise at this turn of events. "And how exactly did you convince someone as self-interested as Dawson to do that?"

Peadar shrugs and walks towards the front door.

"It didn't take much convincing. He was already on the fence since Jaya told him what Joyce had done to Muriel. Plus, he's still infatuated with you, so that helped."

And speak of the devil, Dawson saunters out of the courtroom alongside Jaya and Finley. And just before he exits the Four Courts, he has the audacity to wink at Brigid.

"You're welcome!" He shouts at her.

Brigid scowls at him. "Keep walking, Dawson. The road to redemption is longer than that."

And as Dawson shakes his head and walks away, the rest of us consider what we would have done in Peadar's situation and come up short.

"Well, I don't know about each of you, but I'm exhausted," Peadar says and stretches his arms. "It's hard to believe we're only two weeks into our apprenticeship. Like, how are we supposed to survive two years of this?"

"I'd like to say it gets easier," Oscar replies as he places an arm over Muriel's shoulders. "But I'd be lying."

It's Muriel who surprises me by saying the most sensible thing I've heard since starting this apprenticeship.

"Go home to your family, Peadar. Spend time with the people who'd prefer to see you happy rather than worked to death in order to achieve an optimal utilisation rate."

And as Peadar is about to argue, Oscar puts a hand on his shoulder and shushes him.

"Don't worry. The work will still be waiting for you when you come back on Monday."

And with that, Oscar and my cousin walk out of the Four Courts and down the quay. Completely content in each other's company. And not wanting to be a third wheel or get in the way of Muriel's well-deserved happiness, I let them off.

"When you're ready, let's catch a bus down to Ardmore," I shout after her. "I know some people who are dying to see you."

I can't help but smile at the thought.

"Sounds like a plan," Muriel says, with a cheeky grin.

"Oh, to be young and in love," Brigid says with a mischievous glint in her eyes.

Even Keefe smiles at that. "So, we found out who some of the other members of the SoS are. No surprises the ultimate villain turned out to be my sorry excuse for a father. And then of course, there's Buach. Any ideas who the rest of the SoS members are?"

"My grandmother," Brigid shakes her head looking back at the courtroom as my landlady's voice can be heard from inside, bringing order to the courtroom.

"I guess that's the point of the masks, right?" I ponder out loud as we make our way outside. "We never really know the person concealed beneath them. They could be the apprentice sitting in the office next to us, the associate on the other team or the litigator standing across from us in court."

Keefe nods. "And therein lies the power of the SoS. It's a Society of Solicitors that was here long before we were born and will exist well after we're gone. We are them and they are us. Tied together by our training and shared experiences in ways that will bind us for life. Whether we like it or not," he adds with a sigh.

Peadar bobs his head sagely and then loudly whispers to Brigid as they walk away, "Is that good or bad? I can't tell in my sleep deprived state."

We all burst out laughing and, after a couple of moments of this, I'm forced to shake some sense into myself.

What on earth is wrong with me? The SoS has brought me so much hardship. So, why in the world do I still want to be a part of it? And as I gaze at the apprentices before me, the answer becomes clear.

It's because of them.

And then it's just me and Keefe as we stand at the foot of the Four Courts.

The chill November breeze rustles the stubborn leaves that cling to the trees lining the banks of the River Liffey. Their dried, yellow husks crackle as they billow past us down the road. Up ahead, the Gardaí dismantle their checkpoints and the traffic begins to flow once more down Inns Quay.

And as I stare into Keefe's dark eyes, it suddenly feels like there's an ocean between us. Countless half-truths and lies to wade through. I lower my eyes and look anywhere but at him. Suddenly unsure how to bridge the divide.

"Have you heard of the swan effect?" He says out of nowhere.

And I laugh. Unable to help myself as he takes my hand in his and pulls me across the road. He stops in front of the water and points to a pair of swans that glide gracefully down the River Liffey. I turn from the swans to look up at him and we come together. My lips pressed against his. Enveloped in the arms that keep me warm against the brisk November evening.

"Look at that, ladies and gentlemen. Love is not dead in Dublin!"

Startled, I pull away from Keefe just in time to see a Viking tour bus speed by. Passengers with horned helmets take pictures of us as the tour guide tells them about the famous battle for the Four Courts that took place here years ago.

I take Keefe's hand in mine and we walk along the River Liffey towards the Ha'penny Bridge, until eventually, Keefe asks the question even I don't know the answer to.

"So, what next?"

For the first time in a long time, as seagulls soar overhead, I think about what it is that I might want.

"Did you know Waterford is beautiful this time of year?"

He smiles at me.

"Oh, I know. A lost-looking apprentice once told me it has over fifty beaches. And that's something I have to see for myself."

30

Epilogue

A couple of days later...

I'm back in a room that isn't really mine, sat on a bed more familiar to me than my own, while I stare out at the sea. The square top window cracked open to let the fresh sea breeze into the house. The sounds of the waves as they crash against the beach are a balm to my soul. While Muriel can be heard downstairs laughing with her mother.

My cousin's absence over the past few months was explained away by her having been admitted to hospital as an incapacitated 'Jane Doe'. The St. Ita's records confirmed her story and our family eagerly lapped up the explanation, not wanting to look a gift horse too closely in the mouth.

My phone buzzes.

Save Our Souls Group Chat

Peadar has added Keefe

Brigid - Stop what you're doing right now and come see what's happening in Buach's office!

Keefe - I'm down in the canteen. What's going on?

Brigid - Buach finally came back to work today and, when he opened his window, a hoard of angry seagulls invaded his office.

Peadar - I genuinely can't tell who's louder. Buach or the screeching seagulls.

Brigid - I think this might be the best thing I've ever witnessed in my entire life.

Peadar - Fiadh, I can't believe you're missing this. When are you coming back?

Fiadh is typing

Brigid - Ya, Fiadh. When will you grace us with your presence?

Peadar –...Are you coming back?

Fiadh - ;)

WANT MORE?

Sign-up to Tara's Newsletter

Subscribe to Tara's newsletter to be in with a chance to receive advance reader copies of future books www.taraotoole.com/newsletter

Socials

If you liked *The Lost Apprentice*, consider supporting the author by leaving a review wherever you discuss fine books or follow Tara on TikTok or Instagram @thetaraotoole

Other Books by Tara O'Toole

If you're in the mood for more, ***check out The Rite of Radnick*** – an edge-of-your-seat, epic fantasy romance at *https://www.tarao-toole.com/books*

ABOUT THE AUTHOR

Tara O'Toole is a teller of tales and writer of stories involving romance, edge-of-your-seat suspense and generous doses of the fantastical. Suspend your disbelief, all ye who enter — but no need to abandon all hope because her books are actually rather entertaining.

Tara's debut fantasy novel, *The Rite of Radnick*, won the Fictionary Book of the Year Award in the adult category. While her other titles include a deliciously quirky, rivals to lovers fantasy book called *The Lost Apprentice* — which can basically be summed-up as dark academia does a graduate recruitment scheme.

Tara grew up in the Irish countryside. And when she wasn't *occasionally* helping on her family farm, she could be found with her head stuck in a book or wondering when her letter from Hogwarts would finally arrive. These days, she spreads her time between the bookshops of Cork and London.

To be in with a chance to receive free advance reader copies of future books, subscribe to Tara's newsletter at https://www.taraotoole.com/newsletter

Or follow Tara on TikTok or Instagram @thetaraotoole

Also By Tara O'Toole

The Rite of Radnick Duology

The Rite of Radnick

The Act of Ascension

***

The Lost Apprentice

All books can be ordered from *https://www.taraotoole.com/books*

ACKNOWLEDGEMENTS

To you, the reader who finished a book about a bunch of apprentice solicitors darting around Dublin and hexing each other with dark deeds. Thank you for reading Fiadh's story.

To Taras, thank you for many things, including that day, years ago, when a Viking Splash Tour guide saw us holding hands and shouted, "Ladies and Gentlemen, love is not dead in Dublin!"

To Aileen, thank you for being the first person to read Fiadh's story.

To Mam, thank you for encouraging me to shoot for the stars.

To Dad, thank you for never doubting I could do it.

To all of my family, thank you for helping me come as far as I have.

Thank you to Linda O'Donnell for your sage advice and passion for all things romance.

Thank you to Lilly Bartsch for cheering on Keefe and for helping me see turnips can be both a haunting and hilarious motif.

Thank you to Streeper Clyne and Rodney McWilliams for reading earlier drafts of this book and reacting with enthusiasm, rather than horror, to the idea of a magic system based upon the strict legal formalities required to execute Irish deeds.

Thank you to A.N. Deeb and Whitney Dobek for sharing your fondness for this world and its characters with me.

Thank you to the Fictionary community of writers, where I first read the opening sentence of *The Lost Apprentice* and received the encouragement I needed to finish this book.

Thank you to the Miblart team and their talented artists for creating this beautiful book cover.

And a final thanks to Gwyneth Marjorie Bebb, Maud Ingram, Karin Costelloe, and Lucy Nettlefold, who, in 1913, took a case against the Law Society of England and Wales to allow women to sit the Law Society's entrance examination. Thank you for opening a door the rest of us could walk through.